THE LONELY STRANGERS

By Charity Blackstock

WOMAN IN THE WOODS
FOGGY, FOGGY DEW
THE SHADOW OF MURDER
THE BITTER CONQUEST
THE BRIAR PATCH
A HOUSE POSSESSED
THE GALLANT
MR. CHRISTOPOULOS
THE ENGLISH WIFE
MONKEY ON A CHAIN
THE KNOCK AT MIDNIGHT
THE WIDOW
THE LEMMINGS
THE DAUGHTER
THE ENCOUNTER
THE JUNGLE
THE LONELY STRANGERS

The Lonely Strangers

Charity Blackstock

Coward, McCann & Geoghegan, Inc.
New York

First American Edition 1972

Copyright © 1972 by Charity Blackstock
All rights reserved. This book, or parts thereof, may not be reproduced in any form without permission in writing from the publisher.

SBN: 698-10478-1
Library of Congress Catalog Card Number: 72-87575

Printed in the United States of America

THE LONELY STRANGERS

Chapter 1

WHEN COLL WAS a small boy, his father took him to Edinburgh. It was there at the Cross that he heard the three blasts of the horn.

"What is that for?" he asked his father. This was twenty-six years ago, and he was then nine. He had never heard such a thing in his life.

"That," returned his father, whisking him away, for there was a large crowd round the Cross and many angry people, "is for a proscribed man—"

"What is a proscribed man?"

"You ask too many questions. An outlaw, son. The three blasts of the horn signify the sentence and the disgrace. I do not know what the man has done, but it must be something serious, for this means he is forever on the run, he can never come home again."

"He must be a very wicked man," said Coll, with the portentous self-righteousness of his age, and his father looked at him, half-laughed, then spoke of something else.

That was twenty-six years ago.

"We are all of us put to the horn," said Coll at thirty-five. He was now six foot and a married man, with a wife and two children still in the Highlands. He shook his shaggy red hair as he spoke, as if to cast the sentence off his shoulders. He looked at his three companions and grinned at them. But they paid him no attention, only Davy shot a spiteful glance at Aeneas, saying, "Except you perhaps, my lord," which was his fashion of addressing him and did not signify that he had a title.

Aeneas received this silently, with a bland look of distaste. But then he and Davy had never got on from the very beginning, which was natural enough, for Davy at the best could only be called a Highland reiver, and Aeneas was a gentleman whose cattle might have suffered at Davy's hands, a few years back. However, there was little point in quarreling, even for someone as aggressive as Davy, who added, "We're worth nothing but a wee tin whistle," then played three reedy toots on it, which was his habit whenever members of the Skulkers' Club met.

And so the Club, which was set in a small alleyway off the Place Maubert, the poorest quarter of Paris, was once more declared open.

Originally, when the Club had been started, in 1746, after Culloden, with the Rising shattered, the Old Pretender mourning in Rome, and the Prince safely away in France, there were fifteen members. All of them were Scots, all were attainted or condemned to perpetual banishment. Only Tom Ryder was the exception, being English, but he was no more fortunate than the rest of them; if he so much as set a toe on his native shore, he would be instantly hanged as a traitor and deserter.

But now, two years later, there were only five regular members left, for some of them, despite the attainder, had slipped back to Scotland, others had gone to the Stuart court in Rome, and one gentleman, bored to death by inaction, had joined the French army.

There was Coll himself, Coll Macdonell. There was wee Davy, five foot two; it was unlikely that he had any family, and certainly not a wife. If this had been so, he would certainly have boasted about it, for he boasted about everything else. There was Dr. Tullideph, a Lowlander who had come to live in Aberdeen, the English Tom, and Aeneas, who called himself Smith, which was plainly not his name, who was as tall as Coll, a great deal more handsome, and who owned a strange, dangerous presence that was not lovable but which automatically made him the Club's president. There was also Grizel Ryder, Tom's Scottish wife and the cause of his defection, but the Club was no place for a woman, at least not of Mistress Ryder's gentle sort, so she never came there, and indeed, only Coll and Aeneas had ever met her. In any case the poor lass was breeding, and as if this were not enough, had Tom's health to deal with; he had developed weak lungs after lying out for two nights on Culloden Moor, and his coughing must have kept her awake at nights.

The five gentlemen tended to spend a great deal of their time sprawled about the vast, bare, straw-strewn room which was the Club premises. It was set over a wineshop and was furnished with nothing but barrels, all empty as Davy had discovered in a thirsty moment. The shopkeeper, who was called Jean-Pierre, permitted them to use the room as they pleased, for they invariably bought two or three bottles every time they came, wine being the one thing in Paris that was cheap. He once remarked that it was better having Scots for tenants than thieves—a malicious customer suggested that the two were synonymous—and at least they paid for their drinking on the nail. But it was not much of a place. At all times the rats scurried about, chirruping in the wainscoting; in the winter the room was fiercely cold; and now in the summer it stank like a fox's den. Yet the five of them almost invariably drifted there in the evenings, for they had nowhere else to go and no money to spend.

They had not even anything in common, except their situation. In more ordinary circumstances they would hardly have exchanged the time of day. They were not drawn together so much as kicked, by extraordinary events over which they had no control, thus creating for themselves a kind of desperate acquaintance. Coll was wary with Aeneas, with whom he should, by birth and background, have had most in common, found Davy entertaining and untrustworthy, thought Dr. Tullideph a dead bore, and only with Tom, the Englishman, could occasionally unburden himself, knowing that at least he would not be grossly misunderstood. It was as if they were all bound by a hangman's noose, and Davy, who could barely write his name, had fixed a piece of rope above the window, tying it into a slipknot so, as he said, "to remind us all of our latter end." It was the only decoration, apart from the barrels and a mountain of empty bottles that no one ever removed.

The five of them sat on the barrels or aimlessly paced up and down. Sometimes they talked of the possibility of another Rising, but this was hope rather than fact. Otherwise there was an endless amount of *tracasseries*, scandal and gossip. Here the Prince, who might be said to have brought them together, provided most of the entertainment, in his violent affair with Madame de Talmond, who was not only no beauty but years older than himself.

"I saw her once," Aeneas said. He was the only one of them to penetrate court circles. He lived a life quite remote from the rest of them. Coll often wondered why he came to the Club at all. Perhaps, despite his cold, composed exterior, he too was homesick for the Highlands, compelled to seek the company of compatriots. "Her mouth is fallen in," he said, "her nose is crooked, and her glance wild and bold. Her bosom and arms are enormous, but her talk is witty, which I suppose suffices."

Madame de Talmond and Charles made each other's life insupportable. The whole business was like a play that was all *spectacle*. Not a day passed without their throwing the furniture at each other, in her room full of cats, embroidered stools and pictures of long-dead Sobieskis, and the drunken abuse screaming out of the windows made passersby turn up their eyes.

"He should not let her talk," said Davy solemnly. "I never do. It's a pure waste of time. After all, what are the lassies for? Not for talk, that's certain."

He was a little cock sparrow of a man, as skinny as he was small, with a delicately colored nutcracker face, and impudent, darting eyes. To a stranger it might seem ridiculous that he should brag so of his conquests, but his companions knew perfectly well that wee Davy had enormous success with women, from the whores who sheltered in the alleyway below, to fine ladies who seemed enchanted to take him home with them. It was impossible to imagine why. He was not young, he had had no education, and he would have lambasted the wind for disarranging his thick, graying hair. But one glance from those wicked, appraising eyes, and the ladies fell flat on their backs like submissive dogs, accepting mockery, insults and shameless flattery from this ugly little devil as if he were a reincarnation of Don Juan.

Coll said once, in one of his pontifical moods, "We always think of Don Juan as handsome. I don't believe it. I am sure he was nothing of the kind. If he'd been so bonnie he'd never have troubled himself with the ladies at all. No. I'm sure he was a little spunky man with no looks whatsoever. Like wee Davy. It's always the ugly little runts who can't leave the women alone."

Whether or not this was true, Davy was probably better off than any of them. He was by nature a roamer, he had never lived soft, and it seemed to matter little to him if he straddled his native Ross-shire moors or the dirty streets of Paris. There seemed nothing to tether him to home, and he apparently came out in the '45 because it was a grand brawl and he had to be in the middle of it. The only marked thing about him that did not quite fit in was his bitter personal hatred of Aeneas, whom he could hardly speak to civilly, and whom he was always threatening to dirk. However, Aeneas received his hostility with contemptuous amusement, and as they were all, by reason of their predicament, emotionally quick on the draw, Coll chose to remain silent, and Davy never offered any explanation.

He was in addition a Catholic, passionate but only devout when it suited him. On cold winter days he went regularly to mass, making this an excuse for leaving his ladies when he had done with them. "I must away to the kirk," he would say, to the astonishment of his partner, and he would leap out of bed, his eyes shining with lechery and mischief, then scuttle down the stairs, never to appear again.

THE LONELY STRANGERS ⁄§ 13

He never spoke of the Prince. Sometimes Coll almost believed he had never heard of him until he came to France.

But his confessor must have an interesting time. And they all smiled at the thought of Davy confessing, for he had a great gift of the gab and would certainly make each shabby encounter sound like the rape of Helen of Troy. Any priest, after a session with Davy, would probably take to his bed, and be thankful that it was a celibate one.

The five of them seldom talked of home. They had all shared in the scrape, there was nothing new to say about it, and there was no point in ceaselessly lamenting their misfortunes. As for their skulking adventures, these had already been recounted at the beginning, it would be boring to repeat them, and they were best forgotten. Only when a letter arrived were the subjects of home and family mentioned. This occasion was a rare and remarkable one, but they themselves, with the exception of Davy, wrote vast and frequent letters, for there was nothing else to do, in this strange, cutoff world where they were always alone and always strangers.

And so they passed their lives in a twilight, gossiping, joking, brawling, encircled by scandal makers, by the alien Parisians, and by the innumerable spies from every possible quarter, who scuttled round the city, eyeing each other sideways and spreading rumors like jam on bread. The King was dead, the King was alive, the King was going out of his mind. The Prince was planning once more to invade England, the Loch Arkaig treasure had at last been recovered in its entirety, a French fleet was at Brest, ready to set sail. The Prince was going to marry a dozen different royal ladies, the Prince had snubbed the Pompadour who had slapped his face, the Prince was flirting with the duchesse d'Aiguillon. There was always something new to recount, there was no one to be trusted, and they all existed on charity from the French court, at the rate of seven hundred livres a year for table and lodging, with a bare three hundred for clothes, washing, fire, candles and tobacco.

Only the rumor of the Loch Arkaig treasure, with its corrupting French gold that had already set clan against clan, all shuffling and peeping and grabbing and lying and spying—this had a solid foundation of truth, and so was barely mentioned. Coll, about to write to his Jean, felt his blood prick at the thought of it, the growing belief that one day soon, despite everything, he might once more set foot on the heather-covered moors that seemed to him more beautiful than anything else in the world.

But this must never be set down on paper, even to Jean, and never mentioned in speech to anyone, though it was true that most of the spies were so palpably what they were that they might as well have had the word *espion* painted across their faces. Davy had once suggested to an emissary from the English government, notorious among the Scottish émigrés, that he should wear a false mustache and always walk with his cloak cast across the lower part of his face; the gentleman had been furious but continued to spy as much as ever.

However, to commit anything secret and vital to a letter would be sheer lunacy. Coll only wished he could write it, for it burned in his mind, and he had so little other news. He sat in the far corner of the room, his long legs astride a barrel, so that he could rest the paper between them. He was for that moment almost a child again in his longing, and his face, as he thought of Jean and Amy and Donald, and the house on the edge of Loch Maree, was young and vulnerable, with the soft mouth that suggested weakness, and the square chin that implied obstinacy. His red hair, the color of an autumn leaf, was unwigged; he had been accustomed to wear it so at home, and now he could not afford the services of a wigmaker. His one peruke was tidied away for the grand social occasion that had never so far arisen; in due course, unless he was very careful, the rats would have it, the voracious Paris rats, and then he would no longer be fit to appear in high society. It was not a matter that kept him awake at nights. He felt that his social days were done, he could not see himself being invited to Versailles, and the fine ladies dressed as bejeweled whores, with enough bosom showing to send the minister at home into a dead palsy, had no appeal for him. He preferred the company of Jean-Pierre, his landlady and even Paulette, though the last was firmly pushed out of his mind as he started the letter to his wife.

He had once, in the endless spare time available to him, calculated that he spent enough on ink and paper to keep himself in candles for the whole year. He wrote sometimes two or three times a week. She did not always answer, but certainly the letters were lost. Everyone knew the post was unreliable; it was no fault of hers. As he wrote the first few lines, he paused to gaze ahead. He saw her so clearly, and the house. Because he had been pardoned on condition of perpetual banishment, his belongings had not been taken from him; there would, thank God, always be a roof over their heads, sufficient money for Jean, for ten-year-old Amy, and for little Donald who was only one when the prince landed at Moidart. But the vision of them all, the fact that Amy must have changed beyond recognition, that he would in all probability not even know his own son, hurt damnably, it always hurt. This was something that time could never heal, only aggravate. Coll closed his eyes tightly for a moment, so that the room with its dirty straw, the barrels and that *memento mori* dangling by the window was shut off from him. He no longer saw Aeneas talking desultorily with Dr. Tullideph, or Davy swigging his *pinard* from the bottle. It was at such moments that he refused to take in that, whether there was another Rising or not, he might never see his home again.

And all for a moment's impulse, all for the ambition of a young man he did not know, all for a few romantic months of victory that might now be sunk at the bottom of the loch for all the good they had done anyone.

He was convulsed with a sick, physical longing for the white peak of Ben Eay, the islands in the loch, Eilean Suthainn with its three small lakes, and the ancient chapel on Isle Maree. He could smell it all, the mixture of peat and heather and water, the smell that was like no other smell on earth, certainly not like the stink of dirt and sweat and urine that rose up from the alleyway, through the window. For one sight of the loch, just one, dear God, just one, he felt that he would gladly surrender everything, his life included.

The pain was such that he believed he could not endure it. Then he shook his shoulders as if to drop the memories from him, and set grimly to writing, his pen scurrying over the paper.

"My dear Life," he wrote, "how do you and how does my infantry? Donald must be growing fast, and Amy almost a young lady. But you, my lass, I think you must be dreaming or rather fallen into a lethargy, for I have not heard one word of you this past month. This surprises me, for you cannot believe me unfaithful. I have wrote once every week since we parted, and sometime more. But I believe that perhaps your letters are lost, for I hear from my spies that all letters are kept up at the post office three or four weeks or they be delivered. As they can't read all the letters they only open the ones to the most suspected persons, and in case there should be any information in the others, they don't deliver them until it can't be of no use. . . . As for me I live mostly on credit, being as always necessitous for want of money. Fortunately I have a gold watch and some other movables which I'll sell or pledge, and happily too it is summer, so I need only buy enough wood to boil my pot and need not yet think awhile of the winter fire."

He broke off, then scrawled out the sentence about needing money. This sounded too much like a cry for help, and he could not endure that his proud Jean should read it. And the word "unfaithful" made him pause again. But then Jean would never know about Paulette, and indeed the two of them were such worlds apart in every possible way that the similarity between them was less than that between the street below and the beautiful loch that flowed beside his home. He continued more lightly, asking for news of the children, sending them foolish messages that would make them laugh, then at the end, "And so, my dearest dear Body, farewell."

Yet the thought of Paulette stuck in his brain. He assured himself repeatedly that if he fell in love with a woman of his own sort, that would be unfaithfulness indeed, that would be unpardonable, something Jean could never be expected to condone. Paulette was simply a necessity, involving neither feeling nor emotion. It was, however, as he had to admit to himself, unlikely that Jean would view the matter in such a light; in these things men and women felt differently. Perhaps if she knew, or someone told her—there were so many spies and tattlers these days—it would be farewell indeed.

Farewell.

Occasionally, looking into the bitter truth of his heart, he believed it really was farewell, *adieu* as the French said, had been so a long time ago. Jean had always disapproved violently of his coming out, and in August, back in that year of 1745, they had quarreled day in, day out, with her accusing him of caring nothing for his children and less for her, to go on this harebrained expedition for the sake of a young man he had never ever seen.

"I'll not be waiting for you," she told him in her temper. "I mean that, Coll. This will end badly, and you need no spaewife to tell you so. It will end in disaster for all of us, and I cannot endure that my children—our children—should be sacrificed for your folly."

"Do you call it folly?" he asked. Then as she made a gesture of fury and wretchedness, "Well, if the worst comes to the worst, you can always bring them on a little outing, to see me hanging on the gibbet."

Then she went white as if she would faint, the smooth, sun-browned skin drained of color so that the tan stood out yellow on her cheeks. He tried at once to put his arms round her, but she pushed him away almost frantically as if she could not endure his touch.

She said again, "I mean what I say, every word of it. My father was in the '15, and so sore wounded that he died of it. And for what? For a silly man who now, they say, holds court in Rome, a court without a king, with all his courtiers hangers-on, begging him for money he cannot give them. I mind how my mother suffered. I will not have my children undergo what I did, watching her. Oh, I cannot prevent you, I know that, you was always an obstinate, thrawn devil, but how can you be so foolish? You are proposing to give up your life and mine for a boy who means nothing to any of us. But of course there is a reason. Shall I tell you what it is?"

He smiled at her. The smile was painted on his angry lips. "I cannot stop you," he said, "but you talk too much, Jeanie, and I should have beaten it out of you a long time ago."

She said defiantly, choosing to ignore the last remark, "You are doing this simply because all your so-called friends are pulling at you. You are shamed not to be with them. You make me sick. Do you believe Glengarry cares a rap? He is a foolish old man, entirely given over to the drink. He would sell the prince for a mutchkin of whisky any day, and you know it, your face tells me you know it. What call have you to follow him? He has never done anything for you; he'd see us all hanged to save his skin. This is no longer the old world, Coll. The chieftains cannot press men like you into action." Then she met his smile with her own, a miserable, trembling affair, but still a smile. "You'll hang us all for a dream and a dram."

He slapped her across the cheek, and was instantly filled with penitence, for he was not a brutal man, and did not believe that a husband had such a right. But there was too much truth in what she said for him to keep his temper, and she was right; lately he had taken to drinking too much, following perhaps old Glengarry's tottering footsteps. And because he was ashamed, he roared at her, calling her a stupid bitch, a Hanoverian whore, she had best go live in England, for that was where she belonged. He shouted this, and a great deal more, while she stormed back at him through her tears; then they both became suddenly aware of Amy, seven-year-old Amy, standing in the doorway, round-eyed, appalled. And Coll was wildly ashamed of himself, and they at once made it up, gathering Amy into the reconciliation.

Three weeks later, he left, to join Glengarry's regiment. The explanation was not entirely Jean's, though her words had some truth in them. It was as if he were driven on by something he himself could not fully understand. Jean was right: It was not as if he were a tenant to be pressed. He was a tacksman, a landowner, he was free to do as he pleased. But it seemed as if history assembled together its traditions and kicked him forth, whether he wished it or not; the past had become a driving force that he no longer had the moral courage to withstand.

Jean said good-bye to him very civilly. She made no further reproaches. She looked pale, and there were shadows under her eyes. She embraced him, then watched as he hugged the children, clasping them so tightly that Donald protested, kicking at the compelling arms. Then he left. He looked back once. But they were gone, they were already inside the house, and the closed door somehow made him feel a stranger, already almost an exile, as if he no longer belonged there. And the loch looked gray and cold in the dying August sun; there were purple and black shadows across the moors. The beauty and desolation of it smote him like a hand; for that one brief moment he could almost have abandoned his purpose and returned home.

But he did not. And there was the victory of Prestonpans and the triumphal entry into Edinburgh. There was the march across the border into England; there was the arrival at Derby. And then there was the march back.

He was to see Jean and the children once more. It was before Culloden, when he contrived to take a few days' leave. He turned up at the house, exhausted, dispirited, aware that the golden cause was now irretrievably tarnished, though he did not yet foresee complete defeat.

He told Jean, who greeted him with a kind of wild despair, "It will last a long time yet. But I doubt there'll be a real victory. When we turned back at Derby, something died in the men's spirit, even Falkirk could not restore it. We marched out but we slunk back. It's hard to explain. But sometimes I believe there will never again be a Stuart on the English throne."

She asked, beginning to cry, "What will the ending be? What can it be?"

It was bitterly cold, with threatening snow. It was the month of February. Coll could not have any vision of a moor with bodies lying thick upon it, and Cumberland's soldiery stumbling through them with their bayonets, but he smelled the snow and he smelled disaster too. "I do not know," he said curtly. "Before God, I do not know." Then he looked at her as if he would devour every inch of her, and pulled her into his arms, holding her tight against his chest. He said in a desperate voice, "Are you going to wait for me, Jeanie? You said you would not, and it may be a long, long time. Do you still say the same?"

She only said, "Don't go back. Please don't go back."

"I must," he said.

Then she made no more protest, only laced her arms about him and kissed him over and over again, the tears pouring down her cheeks. It was as if she were indeed saying adieu.

Perhaps she was trying to say it, and could not put it into words.

She had been a handsome girl, and she was now a handsome woman, with a great dignity to her, and a character far stronger than Coll's, as he very well knew. He was too much the prey of his emotions, too easily raised to the heights, then knocked down spinning, but Jean, until now, had always remained calm, a rock for him to lean on. Her black hair was now streaked with gray, her eyes were big and dark. She came from the islands, and still held a trace of their lilting speech. Coll, up to the age of twenty, had laughed at the thought of love at first sight; he met Jean at a dull dinner party, and never really considered another woman again. Their marriage had been secure, loving and happy, until the summer of 1745 when a young man and his companions landed at Moidart, and raised the standard at Glenfinnan.

He had two days at home. During those two days they neither of them discussed wars or politics; only just before he left, he said to her, "Why? I don't understand. You are a Highlander, your own clan is out. This is surely a grand moment in our history, whether we win or lose. I'd not have expected this of you, Jeanie, to put the children before everything else, even me. Why are you so angry with me? You must tell me why. Well?"

She answered with a flash of the dark eyes, "You should see that the answer is obvious. Of course I put the children first. Why should I sacrifice Amy and Donald to some silly princeling who quarrels with all his best friends and leaves the country he has come to save in ruins? It is you who should tell me why. I still don't understand. I think I never will."

He shrugged this off, not wishing to waste the last few precious moments in a quarrel. But then to his distress and dismay she sank down beside him on her knees, caught his hands in hers and pleaded.

She said, her voice hoarse with emotion, "You must surely put the children first too. I know how you love them. And myself too. But that don't matter, and the children do, they have all their lives before them. If you lose—"

"We'll not lose, for God's sake!"

"Are you so sure? If you do lose—if—what will happen to Amy and Donald? You'll be attainted. You know that as well as I do. Maybe you'll be—oh, I cannot speak the words. To me it is simply daft, from beginning to end. We are well off here.

The English king don't harm us. And the army is already breaking up, and no one but a fool could think that the English Jacobites will ever join us. Why, they're too busy drinking toasts to risk their lives in battle."

Coll gave her a wry smile, for this was true enough: If the drinking of toasts could have done it, the Stuarts would have been back long ago, on a wave of enthusiasm and claret. But Jean went on passionately, "You may lose your home, your lands and your money. You seem to expect us to starve for your romantic heroism."

He did not remember how he replied. Perhaps he had not replied at all. There was so little time left. But they did not have to starve, after all, though there was a bad time when Hawley's men descended on the house and took everything they could lay their thieving hands on.

"My bedding," Jean wrote to Coll, "my table linen, every book, my repeating clock. Even Donald's shirts, which would hardly fit the fat general, and also that japanned board you gave me, for the chocolate and coffee cups. Why, they even went through my kitchen stores, grabbing spices and a stock of salt beef I had laid by...."

But General Hawley at last departed, and so did his men; Jean managed to find fresh stores, and life went on, almost—as Coll once thought bitterly—as if he had never existed. She was always a good housekeeper, with a flair for finding what she wanted, even in difficult times. And always, when he wrote to her, he spoke of her joining him in a little while, a few months at most, when he had a little more money and was able to find decent accommodation for them all.

"We will be happy again," he wrote then, the words spilling out like the ink that formed them. "Oh, how I miss you, how I miss you!"

She answered politely, sometimes lovingly, but never referred to the possibility of coming over to France. Several times she offered to send him money, but he always refused, though often he had so little that if it had not been for Paulette and Jean-Pierre, he might have nearly starved. The only things he asked for were books and copies of the *Caledonian Mercury*, and sometimes these arrived, though often they did not; that, as he knew, was no fault of Jean's. Once he begged her to try to send him some salted fish and a few bannocks, as if the familiar food could solace his frantic homesickness. She complied immediately, and the package arrived. Only the fish, for all it was cured, stank so that he could not eat it, and the bannocks so carefully wrapped were as hard as stones. But these he ate, nearly breaking his teeth as he did so, and the dry, floury taste brought back the longing and deprivation so that he could not bear it, and after that he stayed in his room for three days.

He might not have emerged even then; he might have turned into one of those crazed eccentrics who were to be found among the exiles: people who no longer cared, who did not wash or dress decently or comb their hair, who wandered about the streets filthy, bearded and alive with lice, talking to themselves, drunk from morning to night. But Paulette came looking for him, bringing with her a bowl of soup and some wine. He shouted furiously at her, but she paid no attention, only mumbled at him in the odd way she had, heated up the soup and insisted on his drinking it. He wondered afterward why she had taken so much trouble, for she never displayed the least affection; she was not a warm or lovable person.

And he wondered again in a confusion of fear and self-mockery what Jean would possibly say if she knew that her respectable husband—he had always been a conventional man

—was almost one of the ponce boys who kept their whores like a herd of cows, sending them out to grass, and milking them for the proceeds. It was not something he could bear to think of for more than an appalled second. He pushed the thought instantly away from him, and set down to finishing his letter.

There was not much that he could say, for letters were constantly opened, and he dreaded getting her into trouble with the authorities; also, somewhere deep inside him, was a mistrust that he was ashamed of but could not entirely ignore. So, having written about nothing for three pages, he sealed the letter, enclosing with it a small piece of dried basil. In his courting days he had always enclosed sweet herbs with his letters and sometimes a sliver of southernwood. Now he always persuaded Paulette or his landlady to hand over some of the herbs she used in her cooking, and it was one of these that he slid into the folded pages. Later he would find one of the little Savoyards to take it to a friend who would then pass it on to the carrier.

He put the letter in his pocket, then lay back on the barrel, his head against the wall, his arms folded across his chest. He watched from beneath half-closed lashes Dr. Tullideph who seemed as usual to prefer his own company and who, after the few words with Aeneas, sat on his barrel, with as much dignity as was possible in the circumstances, reading his book. Coll was always a little envious, for the doctor seemed to have an endless supply of literature; the volumes must have been very precious to him, for he always refused point-blank to lend them.

They called him Tully, when they remembered. He was the kind of man who was easy to forget, his appearance did not invite a nickname, and his first name was Alexander, which somehow was absurd. He was tall and corpulent, with a round, white, heavy face, and very pale-blue eyes. He had no teeth at all, which was odd in a physician, and which made his eating unpleasant to see. He had a way of speaking into his chest so that it was difficult to understand what he was saying; as however he usually remained silent, this did not matter. He came from somewhere in Aberdeen, but was a Lowlander by birth. They could none of them understand the reason for his coming out. On the rare occasions when he referred to the scrape, it was always with the utmost contempt and disapproval. He never spoke of his own home; no one knew if there were wife, children or family. Coll thought sometimes that his exile must be a voluntary one. He longed to know why it had ever happened, for there was a portentous respectability to Dr. Tullideph; if he had ever misguidedly thrown his cap over a windmill, he would have rushed to collect it on the other side. Moreover, he never touched a drop of alcohol, which was remarkable to his companions who most of the time drank enough to float a seventy-four-gun ship. And certainly he never joined in the wild horseplay that they all fell into, which sometimes verged dangerously on a brawl. But he was of course a much older man. Davy called him "glumpy," a word of his own fabrication that summed up the doctor very well. Nobody liked him, but nobody disliked him either; he gave out nothing to provoke any kind of emotion, never smiled and tended to eye them all as if they were outlandish animals, especially Davy with his boasting and wild ways.

But then Davy was a real Highland cateran, and if he had come across some wandering cattle in Paris, would have stolen them without hesitation.

As for Aeneas, who was occupied in reading a letter—a mighty long one too, it seemed to be about a dozen pages—

Coll wondered again why he did not like him more. He was on the whole an amiable, rather lazy person, who liked rather than disliked—it was much less trouble. But Aeneas in some strange way made his hackles rise, which was unreasonable nonsense, for not only was he good-looking, with a sardonic sense of humor, but was also better off than the rest of them and could be very generous in moments of necessity. Coll had never once asked him for help. He borrowed the odd franc from Davy and sometimes from Tom, who was deplorably open-handed and would have given a thirsty passerby his last drop of wine. But Aeneas he could never bring himself to approach. Yet, like all of them, he was puzzled by the mystery that surrounded him, and once he said, "Why the devil do you come here? There must be much better places for you to go to."

"What could be better than here?" asked Aeneas.

Coll looked at him once and briefly, up and down. The wig was freshly powdered and curled, the suit was of fine cloth, the shirt silk, and the cuffs neither frayed nor torn. This was every inch a gentleman, unlike the rest of them who, in their darned, shabby clothes, were more like a band of robbers. He shrugged. He said, "You could hardly call it paradise."

"It's the company I prefer," said Aeneas. The words were warm and friendly; it was odd that the look in his eyes was neither.

Coll did not pursue the matter, except in his own mind which, being barren of almost everything except longing and unhappiness, was quick to seize on something to occupy it. Certainly Smith was not the name, none of them believed that, and even Aeneas, when he mentioned it, would smile fleetingly as if the absurdity of it amused him. But who he was they could not find out, though Coll believed he had a title;

once his sharp eyes had seen on a letter—Aeneas had an enormous correspondence—the phrase, "Your Lop's humble servant." He nearly asked outright, then restrained himself. It was after all none of his business.

And they all had their mysteries. Their companionship was based solely on the present. Davy never now spoke of his Highland days, nor did he mention the hulks where he had been lodged for six weeks before his escape. There were four hundred died in the three ships off Tilbury, but Davy was not one of them; neither starvation, disease nor brutality could keep Davy down. But how he managed to escape, he would not say. As for poor old Tully, he spoke of nothing, and even Coll himself, though he sometimes read out small sentences from Jean's letters, never mentioned what lay cold within his heart, that dreadful possibility that Jean would never cross the Channel, that he might never see her or the children again.

Tom of course held forth at length. He hardly ever stopped talking, except when the illness clutched at him; then he could only speak in whispers, if at all, for fear of the blood that might suddenly pour forth. Sometimes he had to stay in bed, and they did not see him at all. But on his better days he talked and flailed his arms while doing so; sometimes, perhaps when the fear of death was in him, he grew abusive, and once fell into a violent brawl with Davy that started as a jest and nearly ended in a coffin.

"Haggis!" he declaimed, God knows why; they had none of them touched such a thing for years, and there was little reason for Tom to start shouting about it.

But Davy, at once the affronted Scot, leapt to his feet and planted himself menacingly before him, the top of his chauvinist head just touching Tom's breastbone.

"Haggis," said Tom again, grinning down at the little man, now swelling like a turkey cock. "Why, I vow it's nothing but a bad French *hachis* boiled in a stinking sheep's bag that always tastes of wool and often of something worse."

That was enough. Davy could not have cared if haggis had been proscribed like the tartan, indeed had probably never eaten it, but that an Englishman should speak so of a Scottish dish was sufficient to fire his always inflammatory temper. And this in a way was so with all of them; when a man is exhausted and lonely and depressed, any joke can turn sour. Mostly they checked themselves before it became too dangerous, but this time Tom chose to pursue the matter, and suddenly Davy was upon him, both fists flailing. It was Aeneas who saw his hand reaching into his stocking for the dirk.

He separated them. He was tall and very strong. He seized Davy round the waist, pinioning his hands as if he were a naughty child, while Coll flung himself upon Tom who, already exhausted after the brief struggle, weakly protested, then collapsed against him.

Five minutes later they both apologized, Tom wildly, theatrically—"You have always been my friend. How could I treat you like that? I must be out of my mind"—while Davy, wholehearted in apology as in temper, assured Tom that he looked upon him as a brother, there would never again be words between them, Tom must have a dram of good Scots blood in him, it was not possible he was all English, and everyone knew that haggis was the filthiest food imaginable, only fit for pigs—

Aeneas, cutting across the melodrama, remarked dryly, "You nearly let that dram out, Davy." He had not missed the glint of steel.

And Davy actually blushed, extraordinary in one so shameless, but then he had the fine, delicate skin of the Highlander, and the color came to it easily. He at once turned his back, his face tight with sulks, but Tom, recovering, would have none of this, pulled him round, clapped him on the shoulder, then pushed into his hand a bottle of wine.

They ended dead-drunk. They both fell to the floor and were left there, lying in the straw, while Aeneas called on Mrs. Grizel to report that her Tom would not be home till much later. He did not mention what she said to this, but everyone knew she was deeply in love; she probably laughed and turned down the bed for him.

They all liked Tom. He could not after all help being English, and he at least had had the decency to change to the right side. He was as frail as he was truculent, the height of him made the thinness almost grotesque, but they said that one word from Mrs. Grizel was enough to calm him, even when the fever burned in his bones and the coughing doubled him up.

Dr. Tullideph remarked unexpectedly, "And where is Tom tonight? I've not set eyes on him for three days."

It was so unusual for the doctor to vouchsafe a comment on any of them that they all turned to stare at him. The legend ran that if they were all swinging from the ceiling, Tully would after one glance find himself a barrel, and settle down to reading his book.

Coll said, "Maybe the poor fellow's sick again. Perhaps one of us should call on Mrs. Grizel. She is a good wife to him, she may need our help."

Aeneas said quietly, "No, Coll. Not a wife."

"What the devil are you talking about?"

"She's a wife no longer. She is now the Widow Ryder. Tom

died last night. I have been trying to find the right moment to tell you."

They all fell silent.

They hardly knew Grizel Ryder at all. Coll, who had met her once sometime back, remembered vaguely a quiet young woman with an odd, gruff voice, tall and plain, now carrying her first child. He thought with a sudden pang how damnably alone she must feel. She was a Scots girl, a Mackenzie, whose family had cut her off when she married an Englishman. She had escaped with Tom to France, after two months' lurking in the hills, which could hardly have helped his consumption. Then the two of them found an attic room in Paris, not far from the Club. Even then it must have been a lonely life. There were other Scotswomen in Paris with their husbands, but they were mostly highborn ladies, who would have no time for Grizel Ryder, a farmer's daughter married to an Englishman. The only other Scots girls were not of a kind she would wish to meet. As for the Parisians, they adored the Prince who paraded himself before them in such magnificent costumes—the latest was a deep-rose velvet—and were highly amused by his amatory scandals, but in the rest of the bedraggled exiles who had no money to spend, they had no interest, they shrugged their shoulders and ignored them. Grizel Ryder must sometimes have felt entirely isolated, and now she was isolated indeed, with a fatherless child on the way, and no one to help or support her.

Coll, always overemotional, was engulfed in a pity that brought the tears to his eyes; then Aeneas' next words brought his head round sharply, both pity and tears knocked away.

"One of us," said Aeneas, "must go round to her. She will presumably still get Tom's money, but even that is not certain. I think we'll have to see that she is provided for. Besides, we must offer our condolences. We cannot leave her there without so much as a word. I know Tom would have wished us to go."

The sentiments were unexceptionable, but the voice was at its most pompous; Aeneas' handsome face was grave with death, the voice sunk the appropriate semitone.

At that moment they all disliked him cordially. Then they all burst out speaking at once. It was not that they were hardhearted; it was simply that the thought of a weeping widow was unendurable, someone and something more to tap their already overburdened emotional resources.

Their indignant, self-defensive voices crashed out in canon.

"Is the loon clean daft?" Davy, of course. "There's the poor lassie half dead with shock and sorrow, and a common Highlander like myself arriving on her doorstep. Why, man, it'd be terrible, terrible. She needs a woman to look after her."

Aeneas did not like being crossed. He snapped, "Can you not provide one?" at the same time as Dr. Tullideph who, looking colder and more remote than ever, said, "I have an appointment tonight. I cannot break it."

"Liar!" snapped Davy, with some justification, for Tully, as far as they knew, did not have a friend in the world, and went home every night as soon as the clock struck eight.

Coll spoke in a more restrained manner. His conscience was biting into him. He said quickly, "I hardly know the girl. I've only seen her once. I doubt we'd recognize each other if we met in the street. You're the one to go, Aeneas. After all, she knows you best, and she'd trust you. A woman who has just lost her husband would not like a comparative stranger interfering in her affairs."

Aeneas surveyed them, his face a little blown. He seldom permitted himself to be provoked into a quarrel, even by

Davy, who would provoke anyone, but there were moments when he appeared to despise them all. He looked as if he despised them now. So vast was his personality that they almost forgot that he was indeed the proper person to go, as their president and as the one who knew Mrs. Grizel best, and they began reluctantly to despise themselves.

They were not wishing to be unkind. They had all loved Tom, with his Englishy humor, his wild ways and moods that flickered up and down as the fever took him. It was almost impossible to realize that never again would they hear the dry, brittle, painful cough preluding his arrival, and his savage gaiety about his own illness. "There's bloody Jack again," he would say, dabbing at his lips. Then he would wave the red-stained handkerchief at them, and they would all laugh, not because they lacked compassion, but from sheer relief that an unbearable tragedy had somehow become a joke. But now they were all consumed with the selfishness of people preoccupied with their personal disasters. Each felt that he had enough on his plate. It was simply not reasonable to be expected to dole out sympathy to someone else, a comparative stranger.

They were all on their feet now, prepared to say like Tully —a doctor, after all, surely he was the one to go—that they had an urgent appointment, they were very sorry for poor Mrs. Grizel, but unfortunately....

Aeneas spoke again. He had, as Coll observed, offered no comment on the suggestion that he should go, himself. He said coolly, "Obviously the best thing is to draw lots for it."

To this they all rather sullenly agreed. It was one of the unwritten rules of the Club, and it was something they had done many times before. Only usually it was not for something so serious. It was perhaps for someone to buy an extra bottle of wine, interview a difficult landlord, compose some letter of application. This was different. Coll was again possessed of a horrified compassion, warring with a determination not to get involved. He looked with sudden anger at Aeneas, who was gathering up straws from the floor, and he had to remember that whoever lost a draw, it was never Aeneas himself. He longed to say this, but managed to bite it back; they were already on the verge of quarreling, and a brawl would hardly help poor Tom's young widow.

He met Aeneas' eye, that cold gray eye that so seldom matched his smile. The lips were smiling now as if Aeneas somehow read his thoughts and was amused by them. But he now had three straws for each of them, and he was carefully measuring them on his knee so that they were all the same length, except for the one long one that would determine the draw. Then, having done this, he threw them all into his hat, and each, with dutifully averted head, selected his three.

Coll heard Davy exclaim, "Ha!" in a delighted voice, then saw Dr. Tullideph almost smile, if one could so term that brief convulsion of his cheek muscles. He looked up at Aeneas, then down at the long straw that dangled between his fingers. He swore beneath his breath, then in sudden rage, said, "You should be the one to go, sir. You know her, after all." Then he added in a thick voice, "How strange it is that you never lose. In the whole of our acquaintance I believe you have never drawn the long straw."

"Are you accusing me of cheating?" asked Aeneas.

"I am accusing you of nothing," said Coll. "I am only remarking on a certain strangeness. I trust you have no objection to that." And as he spoke, he knew instinctively that Aeneas, with his gentlemanly ways and bland manner, did indeed manipulate the straws, perhaps picked up three extra and produced them at the right moment. It would be inadvisable to play cards with someone so deft-fingered; perhaps that was how he earned his money. But Coll did not say this, only turned away with a shrug of the shoulders. Unlike Davy, he was not a fighting man. He said, "Very well. I accept. Where does she live? I've forgot the address."

Aeneas told him, looking for some reason slightly discomposed. Perhaps Coll's words had hit home, perhaps he resented having his bluff called. He said stiffly, "Do you really mind?" Then he said, "The errand after all has to be done. And it will be a great kindness to this poor young woman."

"I'm going, am I not?" said Coll fiercely, staring at him. He mistrusted such meekness. Then he grew aware of the silence of everyone in the room. He saw that Davy was gazing at him hopefully. Nothing delighted Davy so much as a fight, and that between Coll and Aeneas would be something extraordinary. Even Tully had looked up. Coll bestowed on them a grim smile. Bored they might be, but he was not prepared to solace their boredom in such a manner.

He said, "Not this time, friends. Not this time!"

Then, without another word, he turned on his heel and made his way down the stairs to the wineshop.

Chapter 2

THE SHOP was full, as it always was in the evenings. Jean-Pierre came forward to shake Coll's hand, offered him a glass of wine which Coll refused, saying he had an appointment.

In the doorway he paused to look back. He liked Jean-Pierre, a handsome man enormously stout but with a fine profile, who talked violent revolution, who prophesied that in a few years' time the heads would roll. "Yours will roll before if you don't hold your tongue," Coll said, but he laughed as he spoke, for he did not take Jean-Pierre very seriously. Paris spoke a great deal of revolution these days, then fell into ecstasies over dear papa Louis, whom five minutes back they had wanted to decapitate. The honest citizens had toasted Louis XIV's corpse with curses, yet turned out in thousands for the next coronation. It reminded Coll of the weeping woman running to see the execution of a highwayman, crying her eyes out in pity for him, and determined not to miss a minute of the drama. So he listened to Jean-Pierre's outbursts, nodded his head gravely at the recounting of the king's extravagance and innumerable mistresses, and he was glad of the warmth and company, for even on a summer's day his room was bleak and cold.

Now, looking back, he wondered for a second if Jean-Pierre were a true prophet, whether his noisy, amiable customers, who always seemed to speak in a roar, might in truth turn into a revolutionary army. He found it difficult to believe. They were kindly in their rough way, and because Coll did not, as they said, put on any side with them, made quite a fuss of him, treated him to wine, even sometimes asked him home to supper. Then for some odd reason the lively scene made him remember Tom, who was lively no longer, and he set out for his widow's room, filled with pity and astonishment that he would never see him again, who must now lie in a pauper's grave, far from his own land.

Once—oh, God, not so long ago, only last week—once they had all fallen into the kind of conversation they sometimes indulged in, prompted by a drizzle outside and self-pity within.

"They'll all have forgotten us by now," Coll said.

They were drunk. They were greetin'-fou, except of course for Tully who eyed them with the smug contempt of the abstainer, Tully who lived on another plane, who was always inward on himself.

Davy exclaimed in dramatic gloom, "Why, even Death has forgotten us."

And Tom said in his dry whisper, for this was one of his bad days, and bloody Jack was thumping at him, "Sh! He might hear us."

Death had heard. The old bastard with his grinning mouth and rattling bones—Death had heard. He had not forgotten Tom Ryder, who must have swum out of life in his own blood, leaving nothing behind him but an emaciated body, and the curled-up thing inside Grizel Ryder's belly.

So Tom was dead, at thirty-four years of age, which was not very much, but he, Coll, was thirty-five and alive and, as if to repel the thoughts of death that moved within him, he stared around him, almost grabbing at the familiar scene, as if to prove to himself that he was not yet done.

It was seven o'clock. The streets were almost empty now, for the workers had gone home, and the *ton* were entertaining themselves at the Opéra. It was a dangerous hour. The watch had not yet come, and the thieves and pickpockets were creeping softly about their business, ready to brush against anyone who looked as if he were worth the robbing, perhaps to hit him over the head, then run for their lives. Coll did not trouble himself about them. He had nothing to steal. What money he did have jingled in the pocket of his sadly worn coat, and he guarded this so that any thieving hand must meet his own. Marauders must have shrugged at the sight of him; the shirt he wore was frayed at the wrists, and his breeches had a patch, badly put on, in one knee. There was even a button dangling on the coat; Coll half-moved his hand to break it off, then forgot about it.

This was no place for the fine ladies and gentlemen, though occasionally they traversed it in their sedan chairs, and sometimes a coach sped through as fast as possible, to be away from the dirt and stench of the ugly poor. But here the rich were not in possession, and the pretty ladies in their perfumed silks, with their escorts finely bewigged and pomaded, ran the risk of filth being thrown into the carriage, of obscene taunts yelled at them by the *harengères*; sometimes the carriage was overturned by a herd of oxen, or blocked for hours by a water cart, so that the travelers were forced to descend, to pick their dainty way through the garbage and sewage that the dustmen never managed to remove.

Coll was too used to this to pay it much attention. He bought himself a cup of coffee at a street corner, though he could ill-afford the two sous; after that he walked on again, passing, with a reluctant, sideways glance, the street where he himself lived, the Rue Saintonge, where he lodged in a tiny, dark, bug-infested hole that looked out onto a yard, a urinal and a blank wall.

At home the sweet air blew in from the moors. The loch gleamed silver in the starlight. Only the sound of wind and water broke the silence, and everywhere was space and soft colors, the purple of the heather in autumn, the gold of the whin in spring, everything so fresh and clean, so spacious and wild.

The homesickness clamped down on him again like a physical pain. Always he believed himself rid of it, always it returned. He felt that he would give up twenty years of his life, even join Tom Ryder in his wretched grave, for the sight once more, just once more, of the hills and the moors and the trees that grew at the loch side. On this harsh summer evening he could feel again the rain against his cheek, the soft Highland rain, see the purple, gray and green shadows on the mountainside. To deprive a man of his life was bitter, but to give him his life and take from him everything that meant home, was a cruelty not to be borne.

Coll stopped for a moment, looking with sick revulsion at

the street around him with its open drains; everything was tawny with dust as if water had never touched it. As he stood there, blind to the people walking past him, one of the town whores, thinking he was a prospective client, came softly up to him, to whisper invitation. He was startled back into reality. He looked down into the weary, painted little face. She was, he saw, quite young, a country girl perhaps who had come hopefully to the big city where the streets were paved with gold. But the freshness and innocence had departed long ago, there was an ugly open sore on her lower lip, and the thought of that poor, poxed mouth pressing against his sickened him so that he pushed roughly past her.

He heard her swear after him in gutter words. The milkmaid days were long since done. He did not even turn his head. He understood well enough what she was shouting at him. He, like all of them, spoke fluent French now, even Davy, though he never troubled himself about grammar, and simply slung the words together as they pleased him. For the others the French accent came easily enough to the Scots tongue, but the language they spoke was the coarse colloquial argot of the citizens, and sometimes Coll, on the rare occasions when he met people of his own kind, tended to become tongue-tied, for fear of tutoying a stranger, or of some inappropriate phrase popping out of his mouth, like the toad in the fairy tale.

He saw now that he had arrived at the street where the Widow Ryder lived. It was the kind of street they all knew. Seven hundred livres did not procure a mansion in the Faubourg Saint-Germain. It could well have been his own lodging, except that here was a filthy, stinking, narrow tenement set in a vast cobblestoned courtyard, hemmed in by wretched blackened houses. The street was crowded with beggars, carters, harlots and sellers of nostrums, the latter probably being cabbage water or worse.

Coll pushed his way past them into the courtyard, and then into the tenement where the concierge popped out of her room, in the inquisitive way of her kind, and eyed him as if she were sure he was there for some sinister purpose. She looked as if she proposed to interrogate him, but Coll, disliking her bad-tempered face, brushed past her and began to climb the stone steps.

He had only visited Tom once before, but he remembered that the room was at the very top. This at least was farther away from the sounds and smells of the street below, but the stairs were dangerous, being worn and slippery, and on the second floor the banister was broken away so that there was a sheer drop to the hallway below.

When he reached the door, he found that his mouth was dry with apprehension. He had no idea what would greet him, but almost certainly there would be an exhausted, hysterical woman who would collapse weeping onto his shoulder. He nearly turned back and ran down the stairs, then he grew ashamed of himself, pushed the weakness away, and knocked on the door.

She opened it immediately. She must have heard his footsteps which resounded hollowly on the stone floor. She was not crying. She seemed in no way hysterical. She stood there in silence, looking at him.

He thought he would not have recognized her. He saw a young girl, tallish—perhaps five foot six or seven—and very thin, except for her belly, across which she had clasped her hands, as if protecting the inmate from his gaze. She wore an apron over a plain gray gown, and her thick brown hair was neatly pinned back. It is only in the storybooks that suffering beautifies, and whatever looks she had once had were gone; the face was gaunt with suffering, grief and perhaps lack of proper food, the eyes were still fine, but otherwise there was nothing to notice or remember. Only the voice was strange, and Coll did remember that voice; it was deep and a little harsh.

"Is it myself you are wishing to see?" she asked.

Coll said awkwardly, "Mistress Ryder?"

"Yes."

"I have come—" He stumbled, paused, then went on again. "I am Coll. Coll Macdonell. I think we met once a year ago. I daresay you have forgot. I am—was—a friend of your husband's. I—we are all so very sorry, and we wondered if we could help in any way, that is, all of us at the Club." Then because this was clumsy and absurd, no way to speak to a girl who had suffered such a terrible loss, and who looked as if she were not much more than in her early twenties, he said abruptly in a different voice, "Your Tom was a fine man, one of the finest. I cannot even now believe he's gone. You must let me do everything I possibly can to help."

She looked at him gravely. Then she stepped aside, saying, "Thank you. I mind you very well. Tom always spoke of you as his friend. Will you please come in?"

Coll stepped inside the room, closing the door behind him. He was aware immediately of a strange smell, almost indefinable yet which somehow permeated everything. He looked around him with a faint curiosity, for his former visit had been brief, and he and Tom had gone out again almost at once. It was plain at first glance that this was a woman's room. There was little in it, and certainly no luxury, but there was nonetheless a brightness, an air of being swept and garnished, unlike his own place which was always thick with dust and usually littered with the remnants of last night's supper. There were a few cheap flowers in a jar on the mantelpiece, the floorboards were scrubbed clean, there were curtains at the window, and the oil cruisie that provided the only illumination was polished so that it shone.

There was only one chair, and she motioned him toward it, but he could not sit while she stood, so he made his way toward the bed, which was in the darkest corner, proposing to seat himself on the coverlet which was humped over the blankets.

She raised desperate eyes to him, then glanced at the bed, her breath catching. He heard the gasping sound. She said in a dragging voice, "I daresay you wish to take a last look at him." She did not seem to notice his horrified gaze. "He was so fond of you. He often told me about you. He said you were the only one of them he could really talk to. I am sure you would like to say good-bye."

He realized then what the smell was. It was the smell of death. The hump under the coverlet, where he had been about to sit down, was not blankets. It was all that remained of Tom Ryder. He was so shocked that for a moment he could not speak. This girl who was so young, who was carrying her first child, had not only endured her husband's death, but had been forced to remain shut up in the room with his dead body, and not one soul to speak a kindly word to her, only that damned old limmer downstairs who did not look as if she would raise a hand to help a starving child.

He came up silently to stand beside Grizel as she lifted back the coverlet.

Tom's face looked up at him, yet it was no longer Tom. Someone—was it this girl, had she had to lay him out in addition to everything else?—had tied a cloth under the chin and closed the eyes. The face was all structure, sunken, tallow white, mindless with innocence. It was no longer human; it had in the strange way of death gone back to its beginning. It could almost have been the stone effigy of a saint, though, God knows, Tom was no saint, swearing wildly at the blood that burst from him, then drowning his fear and anger and pain in wine. The blood was drained now. There was no more pain. This gray bony thing would soon be hidden forever beneath the earth.

Coll had seen a great deal of death. In his flight from Culloden Moor, he had passed a hundred or more lying sightless there, with the snow falling on their aghast faces. He had heard the groans and shrieks of the wounded and dying; he still heard them in his dreams. His nostrils had been filled with the smell of pain and fear and dissolution, and he had seen, as it seemed to him, the end of his own race; it was as if they were all dead, there could not be any living bodies in the world. Scotland had become a graveyard; only he was somehow left alive.

But this was different. Tom Ryder had not died on the battlefield, but away from his own land and people, with only this girl who loved him beside him at the end. Coll could bear it no longer. He turned away a little blindly, to find that Grizel, for the first time since he had seen her, was crying. She had turned her back to him. She made little sound, but her shoulders heaved and shuddered with sobbing.

He forgot everything but pity. He put his arms around her tenderly, turned her and pressed her against his chest as if she were one of the bairns at home.

"My poor lass," he said. "My poor, dear lass."

Then she cried in good earnest, and he was thankful, for it

was not right for her or for the baby to push this dreadful grief down inside her. He continued to hold her without speaking, while a tear or two of his own was forced from him, blending with hers. When at last she raised her head, her face red and swollen with weeping, he said gently, "I would offer you a handkerchief, mistress, but faith, I no longer have such a thing. My last was so torn that I threw it away."

She shook her head, released herself and once more turned her back on him. She began to dry her eyes with the hem of her apron.

He watched her. He found the droop of her shoulders intolerably pathetic. Then he exclaimed as if the words were pumped out of him, "How long have you been here, all alone like this? It is not right. It is not human. Why didn't someone from the house—"

She interrupted him in so hard and matter-of-fact a voice that it was difficult to believe she had been crying. "Oh," she said, "what is right or not right scarce matters. What do you think I could do? We are not princes, are we? We have only the one room. The concierge, Madame Thierry, hates us. I think she hates everyone, unless they pay her lots of money. You cannot imagine her helping me. And—and it was in the middle of the night that my dear died, and now they will not take him away until the dark comes. Madame says it would frighten the other tenants and death doesn't give the house a good name. Sometimes I think she would throw me out into the gutter, if she could. Perhaps she will, now Tom is dead."

He exclaimed, shocked, "Are you telling me you have been alone with—with *him* since last night? Was there nobody at all for you to turn to? I do not mean in this house, but you must have friends."

"Who could there be?" said Grizel. "We are strangers here.

We know no one." She looked at him, almost with pity. Despite her swollen eyes, her face was perfectly composed. "And after all, this is the last time I shall ever see him." Then she burst out, "Do you think I could be afraid of him dead when I loved him so much alive? It happened this morning. It was two o'clock. He had a terrible fit of coughing and—and—" She made a helpless gesture with her hands, and her face momentarily puckered up. "What was I to do? Oh, what was I to do? There was no one to call. There wasn't even time to find a doctor. I could only hold him in my arms, and then it was so quick. I suppose I must be grateful it was so quick. They will be coming for him presently." She stretched out her hand, a hand rough and chapped with work, and laid it on Coll's. "He will have a pauper's grave. We have no money. But it don't matter, I keep telling myself it don't matter. And it's stupid to greet because he'll lie so far from his home, that don't matter either, nothing matters to him now. I only wish I could be with him."

Coll said with unhappy awkwardness, "You must not say that. Why—"

"I have the bairn to think of," she said, and gave him a bitter smile. "Is that not what you were going to say? I know. It's what they'll all say. You must think of the bairn, it's Tom's bairn. It's what he would want." Then she cried out in a ringing voice, "I don't care about the bairn. It's Tom I want. Oh, Tom, Tom—"

"My dear," he began, then stopped, for he did not know what to say.

"Oh," she said more calmly, as if somehow he were the one to be comforted, "you must pay no attention to me." Then, a little mockingly, "You poor fellow. You come here to do a good deed, and all you get is me railing at you like a fishwife.

Never mind. I daresay you'll go to heaven because of it." She paused and went on in a different voice, "Will you do a further good deed for me?"

"Anything—"

"Ah, don't say that. You don't know what I might be asking of you. But this is not so much. Don't be angry with me for asking. It's just that when they take him away, will you come with me, please? I think he would like to feel a friend is with him. Will you?"

He had to notice that it was Tom who would like it, not herself. He said, "Of course," then as if this were a stage cue, heard the footsteps coming heavily up the stairs. He saw Grizel go white, and was afraid she would faint, but the next instant she had recovered herself and opened the door to two men outside, who were carrying between them a coffin made of the plainest, roughest wood. She asked them to come in, her voice dull and calm.

Tom Ryder had known what he was about, when he chose this Scottish girl for his wife.

The men looked red and embarrassed. They were not after all unkind, and they plainly wished that Grizel were elsewhere, but this was their business, they had done it a thousand times before, and they handled Tom's body with efficiency and without ceremony, stuffing it into the coffin where, so small and shrivelled had it become, it lay there like a doll. But then, instead of instantly closing the lid, they paused, and one of them, crimsoning to the eyebrows, turned toward Grizel, who was standing there motionless, hands clenched and held to her breast.

He said in a thick, awkward voice, "If madame would care to look for the last time, perhaps to say adieu—"

But she shook her head. She was unable to speak. And Coll

felt within his own bowels her horror and desolation, knew that for her this was the most dreadful day of her life, that it was almost more than she could endure and still stay alive. He could not think of one word to say, but laid his arm about her shoulders; the bones were so rigid that he might almost have touched the coffin itself.

Perhaps death for the rich was a more elegant affair. But not always, even for a king. When James II died, they distributed his remains so widely that his very soul must have disintegrated: his brain to the Scots College, his heart to the Convent of the Visitation at Chaillot, and his bowels fairly divided between the English College at Saint-Omer and the parish church of Saint-Germain. There would surely be something of a hiatus on the day of resurrection. His son was nicknamed Jamie the Rover, but it was to be hoped that his dissected parts would not rove so indiscriminately.

At least Tom Ryder would be buried in one piece. The cortege stumbled down the steep steps, the men cursing as one or the other nearly dropped the coffin, then looked guiltily at Grizel who followed them. But she only gazed ahead, her face blank and pale. It seemed to Coll, who had clasped her hand in his, that death surrounded them, stinking in his nostrils, clammily enfolding his eyes, so that he could have cried out with the poet: *Timor mortis conturbat me.* He believed then that death in an alien land was the final insult. Tom would lie and rot, away from the Kentish orchards that bred him; the very soil that lay upon him would be foreign. His hand gripped Grizel's so hard that it must have hurt her, pressing the plain gold band of her wedding ring into her flesh, but she made no protest, indeed was not perhaps aware of it. Only when at last they came down into the courtyard, with the concierge crossing herself behind them, did she emit a little sobbing sigh, and he thought she was about to weep again. But she did not, only watched, her chin uptilted, as the coffin was shouldered onto a cart in the street outside, then came after it, walking as she must once have done on the Scottish moors, moving proudly as if in defiance.

They both climbed into the cart, with the coffin lying between them. Coll would have lifted Grizel up, but she refused his help with a violent shake of her head, and clambered up on her own, to sit there, both hands flat on the box, the fingers moving a little as if she were seeking the body within.

And presently they stood side by side in the small, uncared-for cemetery, where Parisian paupers lay in the uncut grass. There was no priest to say a prayer. There was no one there but the two men and themselves, standing in the dark, as the grave, illuminated greenly by a lantern, received the remains of Tom Ryder, English deserter, Scots patriot, in his cheap, wooden box. And throughout Grizel watched, motionless and tearless, not even uttering a sound as the last shovelful of earth was thrown into the pit.

Then she said, her voice clear in the cemetery silence, "Will you say a prayer for him, sir?"

He was appalled. He was not a praying man. He struggled to think of something, and his mind was barren of words; there was not even a sentence in him that he could mumble. But Grizel was looking at him, and the two men, assuming that it was their duty to wait until the words had been uttered, leaned on their shovels in a dull kind of patience.

And Coll, stumbling among emotions and memories that beat upon him, could only think of a song he had once sung, and he spoke awkwardly a verse of it that Jean had once translated from the Gaelic, which ran:

> O where shall I gae hide my head?
> For here I'll bide nae langer,
> The seas may row, the winds may blow,
> And swathe me round in danger,
> My native land I must forego
> And roam a lonely stranger.

Then he said, "God rest his soul," and it seemed that he was nearer tears than she, for she still stood there, dry-eyed, only murmured after him, "God rest his soul." She appeared to be unaware of everything around her; it was as if she would stand there forever, and it was Coll who, seeing that this was expected, even from the poor, handed a few coins to the men.

Then they were alone.

He waited for a while, not wishing to disturb this last moment with Tom, but suddenly he could stand it no longer. He said, almost desperately, "Come, madam. Come. You will be better at home. Let me take you back." He wanted to add, "You must think of the child"—but did not dare.

But the words reached her, perhaps even the words he dared not say. She gave a great, shuddering sigh, passed one hand briefly across her eyes, then permitted him to take her arm and lead her out of the cemetery.

They walked back to her room, close to each other like lovers. But Grizel was away in her lonely sorrow, she seemed unaware of her companion. When he spoke to her, she did not answer, yet he continued to speak, for he could not bear the silence.

The strange, elemental platitudes of death— "At least," Coll said, who was not normally so platitudinous a man, "at least he died quickly, with you beside him to the end. It is surely better than going to the Hôtel-Dieu. They say they lie six in a bed there, feet to shoulder. I hope I am dead before it comes to that."

And, "You must not think you are alone. We will all look after you." He added, his voice trailing, "And the child, of course. I'm sure Tully—"

He broke off, defeated. It made no difference. He could see that she had not listened to one word that he had uttered. He began, in a kind of self-defense, to consider if he could persuade Dr. Tullideph to do his duty by Tom's widow. The doctor was fully qualified, they all knew that, for once, in a rare moment of—what? pride, self-vindication, defiance? —God knows, but he had shown them the certificate entitling him to be a physician. But he never seemed to practice nowadays, though in a poor neighborhood he would have been welcomed and could have earned himself small sums of money. Only once, when Davy in some brawl or other arrived at the Club with a great gash across his wrist, did Tully perform according to his profession. He had made a good job of it too, cleansing the wound, then binding it firmly and neatly. But Coll could not see him turning out to deliver a child, even if that child were that of a friend and a compatriot.

What the doctor did with himself throughout his days, Coll could never imagine. The rest of them managed somehow to occupy themselves in their own way. Davy roamed the city, and in so doing contrived to gather to himself a suspiciously large amount of goods and small change; they all knew he was light-fingered, and that his whores paid him, not he them, but why not? The world presumably owed him something for the dunts it had given him. Aeneas lived his own private, very private, life in circles that the others did not touch; he dined out frequently, and sometimes appeared at the Club for only an hour or so, before he went elsewhere to places and people he never mentioned. As for Coll himself, he read voraciously, wrote endless letters and, when he was not so occupied, wandered into small cafés where he now had a number of friends, chatted with Jean-Pierre and his landlady, or simply roamed the streets; he was a gregarious man and had an inquisitive eye.

But Tully seemed to do none of these things, indeed he seemed to do nothing whatsoever. In the evenings he always went back to the room they had none of them seen, presumably read, then went to bed without even the consolation of a bottle of cheap wine.

Coll said now, seeing that they were nearly back, "I think you should eat something." And as, still in her unhappy daze, she did not answer, he repeated, giving her arm a squeeze, "You should eat something."

She silently shook her head.

He insisted, "But you must. You look half-starved. When did you last eat?"

Then she cried out in so hysterical a fury that he backed from her, and passersby turned to stare, "Oh, why can't you leave me alone?"

They were now at the entrance to the courtyard. Coll, who was after all in an emotional turmoil himself, said stiffly, "I apologize, mistress. I wish you good evening." And he swung round on his heel, and began to walk away.

But despite his affront he was compelled to turn. She was still standing where he had left her. She looked so unutterably forlorn that he was overcome with instant remorse. He came back to her at once. He saw that she was crying again. For God's sake, she was a young girl, she had just lost an adored husband, she was alone and friendless, she was pregnant and, from the look of her, near her time—and he had to take offense, simply because she shouted at him in a hysteria of grief. He deserved to be shot—

He said gently, "I'll leave you alone, if that is what you really wish, but I do think you'd better let me come in with you. I couldn't bear to think of you all alone in that room. Don't you think you'd feel better if someone else were there? May I not come? If you don't want to talk, I promise to be silent."

She sobbed, "Please don't leave me." Then, as if to herself, "I don't know what to do, I don't know what to do."

"Well," he said, relieved that he was allowed to stay with her, "that's something we can discuss later."

He crossed the courtyard beside her. Madame Thierry was standing in the doorway as they came in. She was an old woman and fully as disagreeable as Grizel had described; her face was seamed with temper and grievance. Coll had often thought that these women were a race apart, overinquisitive, suspicious, mischief-making, always ready to report to the police. If a revolution really came, these harridans would be in their element.

She took one look at Grizel, then snapped in a shrill, vicious voice, "So you're bringing men in now, are you, madame? With your poor husband not yet cold in his grave—if he was your husband. This is a respectable house, let me tell you." Then, as Grizel remained pale and silent, she began to screech at her, calling her names that Coll could only pray she did not understand.

Coll urged Grizel up the stairs, then turned on the concierge in a black fury, calling her an old bitch, and telling her if she didn't shut her mouth, he'd shut it for her, the house was about as respectable as the brothels in the Parc-aux-Cerfs, and if there were any more of this nonsense, he'd call the watch. His rage was heartfelt enough to frighten her, and she fell silent, her eyes murdering him, while he followed Grizel up, saying angrily as they turned the corner on the first landing, "Do you get very much of this?"

She replied wearily, as she trudged up the stairs, "Oh, yes. And there will be plenty more of it. There are some people who will always take advantage of a woman on her own." She added, "I have already found that out while Tom was away. Men especially grow so insolent. It's as if they know there's no one to defend you. I expect it will be much worse now."

"You are not on your own!"

"Am I not?" Her shoulders heaved up once in a great sigh. Then she said in a calmer voice, "In any case she has some right, for we owe her three weeks' rent. Of course Tom—Tom just laughed at her when she scolded. He used to fling his arms round her and tell her she was so beautiful she couldn't possibly need money as well. She never knew what to make of him. She called him *'ce fol Anglais.'* I think in her own way she liked him, though he spoke such terrible French. But then everyone liked Tom. Now it's different. I expect she will turn me out. It don't really matter anymore."

They were now at the top. They could hear the sounds of the house around them. A man and a woman were quarreling on the landing below. From another room came screams of laughter and the strains of a drunken song. Coll was thankful that he had accompanied Grizel, and even more so when they entered the room, for what with the dim light from the cruisie and the crumpled, unmade bed, there was a chill, wretched air to it that, now that even Tom's wasted body had gone, would have reduced this poor girl to a state of despair.

He stood there for a moment without speaking. Then he demanded in a peremptory voice, "Do you have any wine?"

"Yes," she said. She turned an astonished face on him, as if this were the last thing she had expected. "There's always wine. Tom used to say that. There's always wine, he said."

It was what they all said. Wine was cheap. Wine kept the pangs of hunger at bay, it raised the spirits and dulled the memory. They always had wine, all of them (with of course the exception of Tully); they always managed to buy a bottle even if there were nothing to eat.

"I believe we would drink wine on our way to the gallows," said Coll, as he tilted the bottle into the chipped cups that she held out to him, "and I would never decry its value. But I would be happier, Mrs. Grizel, if you could manage to eat something, even if the idea sickens you." He stooped a little to peer into her drawn face, now gray in the dim light. "You must be as angry with me as you please, but I'd be willing to swear you've touched nothing since yesterday."

And as he spoke these words, he wished with passion that they were back home and not in this appalling room, back in a house where there was warmth and peace and friendliness, where Jean would run to make hot drinks for this lost and lonely girl, cozy her, be kind to her, tuck her up in bed with clean sheets and warm blankets, and stay by her side.

"It's a fine life we lead," he said irrelevantly, then, in the same brisk tone, "What about this food, girl? I suppose you have none here."

She said faintly, "There is some bread."

"That's better than nothing."

"And a couple of eggs. I think there might be a bit of cheese. I don't know. I haven't had time to think of such things."

"Well, you've time now," he said. "Get it all out, and I'll show you what a fine cook I am."

But her eye had suddenly caught the dangling button, now hanging by a thread. She said in a more normal voice than he had yet heard from her, "Why, you're quite undressed. Give me your coat. It looks terrible."

He opened his mouth to protest, then understood that she would be happier if she had something to do, someone to care for. This, as he was beginning to see, was Grizel's way. He took off his coat, smiling, and handed it to her. It was strange to have a woman caring for him again. It brought an unexpected glow of happiness to his heart. Paulette would not have noticed if he were in rags, for she was not that kind of woman, and the thought of this made him realize that he too was beginning not to notice; his linen was not always as clean as it should be, and at this very moment there was a day's stubble on his chin. He passed a self-conscious hand across the bristle, and vowed to shave as soon as he got home. Then he wandered over to the cupboard at the far end of the room, presuming that such food as there was would be there.

There was very little. There was one egg that he would leave for Grizel, the heel of a loaf, a piece of cheese, and some potatoes, that last resource of the starving; only the poorest ate them, and he had in his time passed days with nothing else. He cut the bread and cheese into two portions, and came back to where Grizel, now kneeling on the floor, was busily sewing on the button.

He stood there, the plate in his hand, looking down at her. She had beautiful hair. Grief had dowsed her looks, but the bowed head gleamed in the light of the cruisie, the brown hair was soft and thick. He had a desire to pass his hand across it. He thought that when she met Tom she must have been a comely lass, not exactly pretty, but gay and lively and quick of speech. And Tom . . . they had none of them known Tom as he used to be, but it was not hard to imagine how he was, violent, ribald, hot-tempered, as prone to tears as laughter, who had fallen with a crash for this farmer's girl from the enemy side.

"That'll happen to you, Davy," Coll said once, irritated by the little man's boasting, exhausted too by the eternal recounting of new conquests, none of which seemed to last more than a night or two, for Davy, once he had conquered, lost interest and charged forth in search of a new battlefield.

Davy replied cheerfully, "Never. Never! Why, I'd be as dead as a herring before I'd think of such a thing. For one thing I could not stand her clapper. Besides, the lassies are fine for the night, but now, Coll laddie, can you see me coming ben to the wife and bairns? Tell me that."

No, Coll could not. There was something remarkably nonuxorious about Davy. But for Tom it had been otherwise, and for himself too; wild boy he might once have been, but after his marriage he had derived the keenest pleasure from the small things of home: the holding of a child upon his knee, the sight of washing on the line, the smell of cooking, the knowledge that there would always be someone there to welcome him. They told him he would grow bored. It was not true. He had never been bored except on the rare occasion, and even boredom had provided its own contradictory pleasure. The thought of Jean again tugged at him, yet he experienced a comfort now in the sight of this young woman kneeling there in the dim light, her head bent over his shabby jacket.

"You need a new coat," she said, without raising her head.

"Aye," said Coll, drawing down his face, "and new breeks. And new stockings. And new shoes. Give me the money, mistress, and I'll buy them first thing tomorrow. With some fine duds for yourself."

"My name is Grizel," she said, snapping the thread with her teeth.

"And mine Coll," he returned gravely, then laughed as she extended her hand as if for a formal introduction. He kissed the back of her hand, as if he were a court gentleman, then went on, "Now we are introduced, may I ask you to give me the pleasure of dining with me?"

She raised her head at this. She gave him a long, sorrowful look. Then she sighed, saying, "I suppose one must eat," and at this he set the bread and cheese before them on the floor, with himself in front of her, his long legs wide.

They ate in silence, moistening the dry food with the last drops of wine. Coll saw that despite her previous remark she ate almost as if she were starving, and probably she was, poor lass. The fare was hardly inviting but it was at least food, and she could not have had much stomach for anything during the past twenty-four hours.

When the meal was done, they looked at each other a little warily, as if this sudden enforced domestic intimacy astonished both of them. They were both silent, and it was Coll who broke the pause by demanding in a quick voice, "How did you first meet Tom?" Then he flushed up, horrified by this outrageous lack of tact; this was no question to put to a young girl so newly widowed. But then he realized that his instinct had been wiser than he knew, for almost before the words had passed his lips, there was a softening of her features, a light in the swollen eyes. This was far better for her than any conventional condolence: Tom was so much within her heart and mind that she longed to speak of him, for that moment he was alive again.

She did not, however, answer immediately. She was still kneeling there. She had insisted on his taking the only chair, and he lowered himself cautiously into it, for he was a big man, and one leg of the chair was already cracked.

She watched him, then said quietly, "Did he never tell you?"

"No." This was not entirely true, though he only had a dim memory of Tom's story, but he would have lied himself into hell to see her as she was now, half-smiling, back for a while in her brief happiness. Tom Ryder lay in his pauper's grave with not so much as a cross above him to signify his presence, but he did not after all need a memorial, he was lodged in Grizel's heart. And the smile, which up till now he had not seen, revealed that once she had been a well-looking lass, with both bone and spirit that were more lasting than beauty.

Tom had never told him all she was telling him now.

She said, her voice soft with dreaming, that strange, deep voice that sang with love, "Oh, he was a soldier. With the English army. He came across the border to capture our prince, to bring us all to heel. That is what he said to me. To bring us all to heel. We lived not far from Gladsmuir, that the English now call Prestonpans, for my father wished to come down from the Highlands. He said he could not endure the rain; he wanted a wee farm where he could retire in peace. And then in September the battle was fought, and of course we won, and the English were so angry and they roamed the moor to find food and shelter, and sometimes they behaved badly, very badly indeed. But not Tom—" She turned shining eyes on Coll. They were fine eyes, but the light was not for him; for that moment she had forgotten his existence, she was happy again. "He came to us," she said. "Oh, he was in a terrible state, terrible, and we were all so feart; we thought he would kill us or burn the house down, do the dreadful things we had heard of the English. And my poor old father, he was sick, and my mother was greeting. She said we would all be dead by the morning, so I had to go down to him in the kitchen. He'd come in by the back door, and we heard him falling around, we thought he was drunk. So I took my father's pistol—"

"Pistol!" repeated Coll.

"To protect my honor," said Grizel proudly, and she announced this with such a dramatic air that he too forgot the occasion, and burst out laughing.

The sound of his own laughter shocked him back to the present, and her too, for the smile was struck from her face, and she put her hands against her eyes, falling silent.

When she spoke again, her voice was dragging. "He laughed too," she said. "He laughed and laughed to see me standing there, aiming my pistol at his breast. He laughed so much that he nearly fell over, and him with his fine red coat in ribbons, the hair plastered over his eyes and the blood trickling from his shoulder where they'd hit him. And when he'd done laughing, he fainted, and there he was, lying flat on the floor, and me all alone with him, with a pistol in my hand that I'd no idea how to use. We married a week later," said Grizel.

"So quick!" said Coll, bewildered.

The great eyes were raised to his again. "Oh, yes. Oh, yes. I think perhaps I knew there was not much time for us. I have always had the *taibhse* that the English call the sight. I married him, my Tom, and he turned his coat for me; he said nothing mattered as long as he could spend the rest of his life with me. He did not mind if he served under prince or duke, for he was a fee'd soldier, fighting was his profession. 'They don't care for me,' he said, 'and I don't care for them.'" She must have imagined some condemnation in Coll, though indeed there was nothing of the sort, for she cried out fiercely, "He was right. You cannot deny he was right. All war is a bloody business, and it makes no difference what side one is on, it's the same, it's killing, it's murder. But of course they all tried to stop me. The women—"

She broke off, a strange look of shame and contempt on her face.

Coll, curious, persisted, "The women? What women?"

"They took me from the house. They came for me in the evening." Her lips twisted into a bitter smile. "They stripped me and tied me to a post in my own backyard, while the minister himself watched, then turned away without offering help. They tarred me and emptied the midden over my head."

He half-rose, horrified. He exclaimed, "The bitches! If only I'd been there... but your mother, your father surely—"

"Oh, my father, poor silly old man, he drove me from the house, and I've had no word of him since, nor from my mother neither. They'd not have raised a hand to help me. It was Jenny, the lassie from the kitchen, who waited till the women were gone, then she crept out and untied me; she even sent word to Tom and he came to me." Then she whispered, "He was so angry—I've never seen a man so angry. He would have murdered those women if there had been time. He would have gone looking for them if I hadn't stopped him. He said he would have swung for them any day."

"I would have murdered them too," said Coll savagely.

"What good would that have done?" She sighed as she spoke. "With Tom at my side, can you really believe I cared? The muck and the filthy names, they could no longer touch me. And it was all such nonsense, to say that I was wicked to marry an Englishman. After all, there is no difference between Scot and English, they are both men, they are both human beings."

He rose to his feet, and walked over to the window. He found that he was still shaking with rage at the thought of Grizel tied to a post, with the harridans screaming at her and befouling her. The horror of it roughened his voice, as he said, his back half-turned to her, "That is rank heresy, and well you know it, my girl. For such a remark you could be burned at the stake on both sides of the border."

She took this seriously. He thought that she was a literal-minded girl who would always take things seriously. She demanded with great vehemence, "Why? I think you're talking nonsense," and her pale face was quite flushed with anger, as if this were something of great importance to her.

He repeated, half-derisively, "Why?" Then, remembering, "I think few people would agree with you. But of course that is no excuse for those abominable women—"

"Ah, forget those women. I don't want to remember, I don't want to think of them again. You can tell me why what I said is rank heresy. I thought you were a sensible man. I was sure you would agree with me."

He made himself answer her. He saw that one section of her mind and all her heart was with Tom, perhaps would always be so, yet that in speaking in this fashion she was herself coming to life again. It was almost as if they were conducting two separate conversations, one above ground and one below. He said, "At this rate you might as well say there is no difference between Catholic and Protestant."

"And is there?"

"Oh!" He shook his fist at her, turning back from the window. "Now this is mortal sin, Grizel. Both of them would run to provide a gallows for you, and vie with each other to tie the noose the tighter. Why, girl, you are undermining the most important precept in the world. No! I will continue and you are not to interrupt. If there were no such difference, you and I would not be here at all, so the difference is all we have to hold onto. For the sake of humanity there must be at least a dozen different gods, each nodding in his own corner. If you achieved this absurd equality, we would have nothing left to fight over, and so the world would come to an end."

She said quietly, "The world has come to an end."

Coll wanted to contradict this, and violently, but how could he, for what she said was true; her world had ended with a gush of blood, and his perhaps had finished on Culloden Moor. He remained silent, all the desire to argue stripped from him, and it was she who spoke again, in a calm, acceptant voice, though what she said was neither.

"I will tell you something," she said, "that is nothing to do with this at all. My Tom is dead, Coll, I cannot argue against that, but it has left me so afraid. I was never a coward, I have not feared much in my life, but now I am so afraid, I do not know what to do."

Coll said immediately, "You have no reason to be. I will look after you. We will all look after you."

"You don't understand." She spoke coolly, as if no one except Tom had ever understood. She looked straight at him. "Do you never think how unreal everything is?"

"What do you mean?"

"The life we lead here. I think sometimes we are none of us real people anymore. What kind of a life is it, after all?" She rose swiftly to her feet, as she spoke. He saw again how thin she was, her pregnant belly seeming unnaturally distended.

"Tom was real for me," she said. "And I for him. He said once that most of us were not living, we were pretending to live, making a game of it. Everything about us is a kind of shadow. Gossip and scandal and drinking, meeting in that Club of yours, always making plots that can never come to anything, but nothing real, no background, no family, no friends. When Tom was with me," said Grizel, "then everything was real. This is no kind of place I could have called home in the old days. It is mean and cold, and the people here are so unfriendly, but when we were together, I didn't care, it was the best home I have ever had. I couldn't imagine being anywhere else. But now I am alone. Oh, yes. Having someone with you makes no difference. I think I will always be alone. And I'm afraid, oh, so afraid. What sort of life is this going to be for the bairn?" She broke off, making a resigned gesture. "You poor fellow! You come here on an errand of mercy, and all you get is a sermon. I'd not blame you if you walked out on me. You must have better things to do than dealing with an hysteric female."

"I'd not call you hysteric," said Coll. "And I should be accustomed to such things. I am after all a married man."

"Are you?"

"Very much so. I have two children. There is Amy who is ten, and wee Donald. But he's still only a baby, he is just four."

"And will your wife soon be joining you?"

"My Jean?" He paused, then looking up unexpectedly saw with anger the unmistakable censure in Grizel's eyes; he heard too the undisguised contempt in her voice. Of course she would be instantly up in arms against a woman who had not joined her husband in exile. And because he was aware of this, because he knew that nothing would have kept her away from him if she had been married to him, that she would have begged, borrowed or stolen her passage money simply to be at his side, he grew as furious as if she had spoken the criticism aloud.

"Of course," he said, overloudly, "naturally she will. She'll be with me any moment now. But you must understand, there is a great deal of business to see to first. We own land and cattle, and of course there's the house—we have a big house by Loch Maree. It will have to be sold. I believe the matter is actually in hand."

"Then that will provide the money for her fare," said Grizel. Her voice had roughened, her face was stiff with disdain.

He exclaimed, "You talk as if it is all so easy. It is almost impossible to sell a house just now; no one has the money to buy, and few want to live in the Highlands."

She did not trouble to answer this, so he was forced to continue. "The Rising has left us all so poor," he said. "We are lucky to have a roof over our heads." He was floundering now. It was as if this damnable girl, who was as plain as a pikestaff, who had none of Jean's glorious beauty, were consolidating in his mind all the doubts and fears that blew about him. He would write at once to Jean when he got home, a long letter, longer than usual. He would try to force some definite answer from her.

He said to Grizel, "And of course the bairns . . . it is hard to travel with two bairns, and Donald only four." The confidence was returning to him. Everything he was saying was perfectly true. Scotland was a beaten country, and the beaten and defeated do not buy large houses and acres of land. Besides, traveling with children was almost impossible. Amy would certainly be seasick, she always had a queasy stomach, and the baby might catch some infection from the crowd of passengers.

"It will not be long now," he told Grizel triumphantly, and believed the words as they fell from his lips. "She's a fine lass, my Jean. We have been married for fifteen years, you know. It has been a success from the very beginning, no one could ask for a better wife. Even when I came out—and mind you, she was not entirely in favor of it, but then it's different for a woman—she stood by me. Oh, it will be a grand moment when she comes. You must meet her at once. You will love her. Everyone loves my Jean."

To all of this Grizel did not say one word. It was only too plain that everyone loved Jean bar one. She was kneeling again, staring into the empty grate. And Coll too fell silent, the longing for Jean stirring within him so that he did not know how to endure it, and the damnable doubts following thick and fast. Not once had she mentioned joining him, though in every letter he said, "When are you coming? Come soon, I cannot wait much longer. I am longing for you, oh, Christ, how I'm longing to see you again." There was always a charming reply, little tales of the children, what Donald said in his prayers last night, and Amy—"There's a little fool prattling by me who will needs have me to offer her humble duty to you"—always affectionate, sympathetic, always offering to send him the money that she could bring over herself, which would keep them all in comfort for a long time.

But never offering to send herself.

He had had enough. His head was thick with his emotion and her sorrow, also with a savage, unreasonable resentment, for all this took him back, back to a place where he longed to be and wanted to forget; it made him think of a wife and children and home, with the sewed-on button as a kind of symbol. He could not bear to be with Grizel any longer. He rose abruptly to his feet from the chair where he had sat himself down again, towering over Grizel who did not so much as raise her head.

"I must away," he said. "Will you be all right now? I'll see that someone comes to see you. I'll have a word with Dr. Tullideph. I'll come myself when I can." Then he said hesitantly, for his conscience was biting him, "Are you sure I can't speak to Madame—what's her name?—the concierge? I'm sure—"

Grizel now raised her head to look at him. "Madame Thierry? But I told you. She'd not help if I was dying, except to stamp on me."

"She is after all a woman—"

"Is she?"

Coll reflected on what he had seen of her, and it was true, he could not see her helping anyone. She would be more likely to throw Grizel out into the street, for fear that the baby would become a nuisance. She was, poor lass, in the same situation as all of them: Each led so separate a life that the paths never crossed when help was needed. But he could not remain any longer with this pregnant girl who twenty-four hours ago had a husband, and now had none. Even her pregnancy, the belly so vast in that thin frame, half angered him, reminded him of other pregnancies when he had been wild with delight, when he had felt that the world could hold nothing more for him. Her grief, her condition, Tom's death, all these now stifled him so that he longed for the outside street, for people milling about him.

He said almost roughly, "Are you sure there is nothing more I can do?" and prayed that she would not answer, seeing immediately even in his anger and disturbance that there was indeed something he could do, must do. She had shaken her head, almost, it seemed to him, as if she understood, and he fought with himself, angered even further by her strange acquiescence.

Then his conscience won. He said abruptly, "I'll take the sheets off that bed for you. I'll make it fresh." He turned on her a resentful smile. "I'm a good bed maker these days, though faith, I seldom trouble with my own."

She said, "You are very kind." She added, "Your Jean is lucky to have such a man."

He did not answer this. The innocent remark—was it so innocent?—aroused his anger again to such a pitch that he who was not a violent man could almost have struck her. This plainly implied once again a criticism of Jean, a criticism that he refused under any circumstances to accept, especially from this plain, matter-of-fact girl, so devoured by sorrow yet who turned so keen an eye on his affairs. He turned violently toward the bed, and proceeded to remake it, expending his rage on it so that he pummeled the pillows, wrenched at the sheets, and banged everything down with the flat of his hand, to make it smooth. The bed was a miserable affair with half the springs gone, but he had to note that the linen was of fine quality. Grizel must have brought it over with her as a tocher. It was oddly incongruous to see such delicate material in this wretched slum room.

His temper lessened as he worked, and when he had finished, he turned a little penitently toward Grizel, to see that she had once more sunk into her grief. She sat huddled there, staring down at the floor.

The pity and exasperation warred within him again. He told himself that he had done more than could be expected of anyone, even an intimate friend; after all, she was in no way his responsibility. He bade her an abrupt good night, but this time she did not seem to hear him; she made no attempt to reply, nor did she raise her head as he went toward the door.

He said weakly, "Grizel—"

But she remained silent, and at this he gave it up, shrugged and shut the door behind him. His last sight of her was the bowed shoulders, head sunk upon her breast.

It was only when he was down the stairs that he realized he had left his newly mended coat behind. He hesitated, then decided it was not important, and stepped into the courtyard. It was after all a warm night, and he had another coat at home, even shabbier but good enough to wear for a brief while.

Madame Thierry was in her doorway. She looked sourly at him. He wondered if she ever smiled. She remarked in a strange, automatic way, as if such remarks were jerked out of her by some reflex action, "One day your kind will pay for our sufferings."

Coll stared at her, astonished. He could see no point in this remark. He thought that her sufferings could hardly be very grave, for he could see the cozy little room behind her, and she seemed to have nothing to do except grumble at the tenants and presumably collect the rent.

He repeated, "My kind?" then suddenly realizing what she meant, burst out laughing. No one in his senses could take him for an aristocrat. He was in his shirt sleeves, the ruffle was torn, the cuffs frayed. If this old bitch really believed him to be one of the rich who battened on the poor, she must either have bad eyesight or be out of her wits. It was true that Paris mumbled and grumbled continually of revolution, but not even Jean-Pierre, who related such terrible tales of what happened in feudal country mansions, had ever accused Coll of being one of the oppressors. This woman was plainly ridiculous and not worth worrying about, but he wished all the same that she were kinder and more feminine. He toyed with the idea of entreating her to go up to Grizel, then, looking at her bad-tempered, vindictive face that seemed to grudge the whole world a living, decided against it.

He merely said again, "My kind?" and waited.

She nodded her head at him, her eyes moving over him as if she took in every dangling thread, every shiny patch, and still found it all a deliberate attempt to mislead. "You'll see," she said, then, as they all did nowadays—the meaningless phrases of verbal revolution!—"*Ça ira.*"

He asked in genuine interest, "Do you really believe there will be a revolution?"—and perhaps this scared her, for she suddenly went an alarming red and screeched at him, "Get out! We don't want your sort here. Why don't you go back to your own country? You just come over to scrounge and live on us, like the rogues you are. It makes me sick to think we pay you a pension. I expect you're rolling in it, and you'd still rob a poor old woman of her last penny. If you don't go this instant, I'll call the watch."

Coll laughed again as he turned away, then realized that the old she-devil seemed to know one hell of a lot about him. His laughter stopped as abruptly as it had begun. This was after all only the second time he had called at Tom's lodgings, yet she seemed to have found out that he was a foreigner, and as for the pension—if so miserable a sum deserved the name—this was not the type of thing he would ever have expected her to know. He reflected, as he made his way back to the Club, that this was an oddly sinister world where everyone seemed to know about everyone else; there was always the uneasy impression of someone at one's shoulder, listening, reporting, repeating, filing away.

Chapter 3

COLL COULD not bear the thought of his dank, lonely room. His conscience moreover was still nagging at him. He had after all done everything he could and more than most would have done, but the picture of Grizel kneeling there was somehow painted on his eyelids. He decided to go to the Club; he was longing for masculine company, and there would be someone to talk to, perhaps Aeneas, with whom he could discuss how to procure help, food and money.

It was by now just after ten o'clock.

The theaters were empty now, the fashionable ladies and gentlemen paying short social calls before their supper. Here on this warm June evening the streets were crowded, and round the corner a fair had opened up, with its covered galleries and illuminated stalls. The Parisians loved fairs, and Coll himself liked to wander through them, looking at the puppet shows, the giants and dwarfs, the performing dogs;

sometimes if he had the money, he bought himself a tartlet, and ate it with his fingers as he strolled about.

But now he was not in the mood; he elbowed his way past the crowd and, when someone touched his sleeve, swung sharply round, his hand clenched, believing it to be a pickpocket.

Then he said in exasperation, "Paul!"

They all called her Paul, sometimes Paul *la tricoteuse*. They seemed to regard her more as a good fellow than a woman, and perhaps that was the secret of her trade, for not only was she plain but she was also middle-aged, and she carried her knitting with her everywhere she went, so that she almost gave the impression of being a decent housewife who had slipped away from home and would then return, after her illicit glass of wine, to feed her husband, bath the children and become a good French bourgeoise again. Almost—for despite the dowdy black clothes, the hair pulled back into a bun, the roughened fingers knitting away and the pale, inscrutable countenance, Coll knew exactly what she was the moment he saw her, and so did everyone else, for she never lacked customers.

Once he asked her, half in joke, "How is it you're so successful?"

She replied without a smile, "They think I am their mother."

This so astounded Coll that he did not laugh anymore. It also rather revolted him. But he saw that her words were perfectly true, for her clients were mostly young boys who, wanting adventure but secretly terrified, recovered their confidence at the sight of this respectable-seeming, middle-aged woman who wore no paint on her face, who knitted constantly at some indefinable garment, and who never made the first approach, always waiting until spoken to first.

He realized then, with no pride in himself, that he too had spoken to her because she in some way seemed safe. The whores came frequently to the café he patronized, and seeing this good-looking young man who was always on his own, and whose clothes, however shabby, indicated that he must have some money, at once sidled up to him, sitting down at his table, asking for a glass of wine. Sometimes he wanted them, and always he disliked them; some innate fastidiousness was revolted by the paint slapped on their faces, their bold eyes, coarse speech, their frank invitation. He had in any case no money so what with this, the furtive desire within him, and his instinctive revulsion, he answered them rudely, telling them to get out, in the gutter French he had by now acquired.

Sometimes they laughed, sometimes they were angry. One of them asked him if he preferred little boys. He turned an enraged, shocked face on her, and at this she screamed with laughter, the other girls joining in. It was at this point that he became fully aware of Paulette, who sat in the corner as she always did, with that confounded knitting of hers, her fingers moving with such rapidity that one felt the garment—it always seemed to be the same—must end by being a mile long.

She must have been aware of him too. She stopped knitting for a second, and looked at him. He thought she must be about forty, though possibly her trade, in addition to snatched meals at all hours, had prematurely aged her, and she could be younger. There was no beauty in her face, only a massive, rather disturbing, calm. He could not imagine her screeching abuse at him as the girl had done, but he was aware nonetheless of some intense reserve of violence within her. She was not bad-looking, with regular features and steady gray eyes, but there was no movement there; it was all static, though somehow the personality was so strong that it did not matter.

He had already seen her with customers, and found it almost obscene that young boys should be attracted to her; for him at thirty-five any woman over thirty was well on the shelf.

Now he himself came over to her and, his voice embarrassed and self-conscious, asked if he could buy her a drink.

She did not answer him, only jerked her head at the proprietor. When he came over with two glasses of wine, she carefully laid her knitting on the table, fumbled among her skirts and produced the money to pay him.

Coll, protesting, half-rose. He said angrily, "But I asked you—"

"You have no money," she said, surveying him calmly as if he were a silly child.

"I have enough to pay for a glass of wine!"

"Then you can buy yourself an extra glass tomorrow."

Coll was defeated. Afterward he found it amusing, but not at the time. He was more preoccupied in working out how it was that he was sitting opposite this extraordinary woman who seemed older than himself, and drinking her wine. With no idea of what to say to her, for he had never met anyone so strange in his life, he said at last in desperation, "What are you knitting?"

Her lips twitched. It was hardly a smile, but it was the first movement he had seen in those calm features. She answered, "It is nothing. Do you wish to see it?" And without waiting for a reply she laid it on the table.

He saw that it was simply a length about six inches wide, it might have been a muffler. The wool was very coarse and of a dun brown. He did not know how to comment, took a gulp of wine and said unconvincingly, "It looks very nice and warm."

"I unpick it every evening," she said, "then I start again."

This really was too much. Coll burst out, "But why?"

"It gives the clients confidence," said Paulette.

Coll saw that he was doubtless included in the noun, and of course it was true, it had given him confidence. If she had not looked so respectable and knitted so fast, he would never have come over to speak to her. For the first time that evening when he had already felt battered and grossly slandered by the accusation of pederasty, he found himself on the verge of laughter. It was all grotesque and absurd. If this had been some beautiful young girl it might be understandable, but this female, who in some extraordinary way reminded him of the minister's wife at Loch Maree, baffled him not because she was so plain but because he had to admit he desired her.

He gave it up. Afterward he was to talk freely to her, indeed say anything that came into his mind, but now he could find nothing to say at all. He drank his wine in silence, made no protest when she bought him a second glass, went home with her and presently into bed, while a large, fat cat, which seemed to be her only permanent companion, watched with the air of one who had seen this many times before. She then cooked him a meal—a surprisingly good one, despite the poverty of her room—and he emerged into the street on a cold, early morning, a little shocked by himself, bewildered and released, not knowing whether to laugh or swear, but resolved not to mention this to a soul, even someone like Davy.

The episode, repeated many times, always remained unreal for him. He had brief moments of shame and embarrassment when he thought of Jean, but it was all so remote from his own life that he could not coordinate the two ways of living; they came from different worlds, and what he did with the one did not touch the other. Paulette made no demands on him, indeed would probably have kept him if he had permitted this. Sometimes when he was angry and shouted abuse at her, she said nothing at all. If he had struck her she would certainly have accepted the blow as one of the natural inevitabilities of life. The only time she betrayed emotion was sometimes in the café when he went there to look for her, and one of the other girls approached him. Then her whole face changed, and he saw what he had already dimly perceived, that she could be dangerous; those knitting needles might perhaps serve another purpose than producing that ridiculous length that was unpicked every evening.

She was at this moment the last person he wanted to see. He had had enough of women, he wanted the company of his own sex, and this strange, almost perverted creature, with the knitting tucked into the bag she always carried, suddenly sickened him. Indeed, he was growing more and more aware of a revulsion that made him want to kick her aside; the awareness that this was both ugly and ungrateful only made it worse.

She said simply, "I have made a *blanquette de veau*."

This exasperated him more than ever. Paulette held the simple conviction that men wanted two things only: sex and food. The first she supplied automatically, and Coll had to shut his mind to the obvious fact that not only was he one of innumerable clients, but that he was probably living on their proceeds, all of which totted up to a total he preferred not to acknowledge. The second she made only for him, or so he believed; she was a good cook, and her cooking was extravagant, of a type he had not tasted for a long time. And because he was hungry and lonely, he ate it without compunction, and even now, when he had no desire to be with her, he grew aware that except for a miserable bite of bread and cheese he had eaten nothing today. The thought of the *blanquette de veau* brought the saliva to his mouth.

He said, "No. I have business to see to."

She asked, "Who is that woman?"

"What woman? I don't know what you're talking about. And I have to—"

"You took her to the graveyard. You went back with her."

He had turned to walk away. Now he rounded on her, a little white. This no doubt was where Madame Thierry got her information. He did not like to think of the silent, invisible shadow that must have been tailing him for some hours, that must have waited for him in the street. He said with the softness of repressed rage, "Have you been spying on me?"

She raised her eyes to his. They were large and they should have been beautiful, but it seemed to him, looking down at her in the dim lamplight of the courtyard, that they were the eyes of a blind woman. There was no light in them, they seemed opaque as if she had a cataract. They made him shudder, though he could not have said why. Those eyes would look on death as they looked on life, they would watch a man tortured and not even flicker, there was no humanity in them.

She answered simply, "Yes," then as if this were an automatic reaction, opened her bag and took out her knitting. It was the same length as always. He wondered irrelevantly if she knitted her lovers into it; if it were short it meant she was unsuccessful; if long that she was well in pocket.

As she knitted she leaned against the wall. The incongruity of it reduced his temper to something childish and ridiculous. It made him say what he did not intend to say.

He asked her, "Are you one of the revolutionaries, Paul?"

She made that strange mumbling movement with her mouth. But she only answered, "I don't know what you mean."

"Oh, it don't matter. I don't know why I asked." His temper was rising again. "But I don't like being followed. What I do is no business of yours."

She did not answer. Her fingers moved swiftly. Then she turned the strip around; another row was done.

He began to shout at her. He felt as if he were beating a feather pillow. "Don't ever do it again!" he cried, then, "Do you hear me, damn you?"

She still said nothing, knitting away. She must have received a great deal of bawling in her time and worse. Coll, baffled almost to the point of hysteria, was filled with an unexpected urge to ask her all the things he never mentioned: Why do you do this? What sort of a life is it? What do you think of us? Are you not sometimes afraid? What will happen to you in the end?

He only said, a little more quietly, "What I do with my life is my own affair. I don't after all meddle in your business. If I ever catch you following me again, it will be the worse for you." He added like a child, "And I don't want your *blanquette de veau*. Give it to the bloody cat."

He began to walk away.

She called after him in her flat voice, "Is she your wife?"

"Good God, no!" The words were jerked out of him before he knew what he was saying. Then he found he could endure all this no longer, and he walked on again so fast that he was almost running. At the corner of the street he was impelled to turn his head. But Paulette was gone. Perhaps she had found herself a customer, though it was unlikely in this district where the only people who roamed the streets were also on the lookout for clients, if of a different kind. He decided that he was finished with her for good and all. He thought of Jean with her beautiful body, the clear, clean profile, the dark hair that swept back from her brow, and the comparison with this ugly, middle-aged whore brought the vomit up in his throat.

Yet he knew he would be back. The shabby, drab little

room, with its fat ponce cat the only opulent thing there, was all the home he knew. There was nothing in it that pleased him, much less Paulette herself, but it was in its way a mooring, somewhere where he belonged, could relax and be himself.

He came into the wineshop where he bought himself the cheapest bottle possible, then climbed the stairs with only a brief exchange with Jean-Pierre. The shop was full as always. These Parisians never seemed to do any work; they spent their time boozing and talking scandal. Coll, repelled by the noise and heat and smell, came thankfully into the Club room, to find that it was apparently empty. One candle still guttered in the broken cup that supported it, and presently, his eyes growing accustomed to the dim light, Coll became aware that he was not alone after all.

Dr. Tullideph stood by the window. He was staring down into the alleyway. The noose swung an inch away from him. He did not turn as Coll came in; only when Coll spoke did he raise his head.

"Well, Tully," said Coll. "I thought by this hour you were always tucked up in your bed. Have you changed your habits? Then change them a little more and be Jock-fellow-like. Drink a glass of wine with me. Here's the bottle. There's nothing to pay. I'm so poor already that it'll make little difference, a crumb less tomorrow rather than the day after. Take the candle out of that cup, and I'll fill it for you. It will do you good."

The doctor turned slowly round. A passing lantern below illuminated the pale, round face and, as he opened his mouth to speak, the lack of teeth. It was ugly. God knows how he ever managed to chew his food. He said coldly, "You know perfectly well that I never touch any kind of alcohol. Why do you plague me with such foolish invitations?"

Coll sat himself astride a barrel, in his usual fashion. He said, "I do not care to drink alone."

"Then don't drink at all."

"You would deprive me of one of life's rare consolations. What's the matter with you, boy? Are you Papist or Quaker that you so despise the few good things that are left to poor devils like ourselves?"

"That is like asking a man to choose between gout and the gravel," replied Dr. Tullideph, and this seemed to Coll so out of character that he broke into an astonished laugh, saying, "Why, you're human after all, Tully."

"Did you not believe I was?"

"Sometimes," said Coll, drumming his fingers on the barrel, "you do not give that impression."

"You only say that," said Dr. Tullideph, speaking into his chest as if the words were distasteful to him, "because I do not drink, gamble or whore."

"What else is there to do? But that is not what I want to talk about. I am glad you are here, Tully. You're the man I want to see. I have just come from Mrs. Grizel," said Coll.

The doctor merely nodded, not so much as asking how things were, and Coll persisted with some irritation, "She will need all the help you can give her, sir."

"We all need help," said Dr. Tullideph, then, as Coll, exasperated by this platitude, was about to burst into speech, added, "We do not get it."

"For Christ's sake!" exclaimed Coll, banging the flat of his hand on the barrel. "I thought for one moment you were human, but now I see I'm wrong. What is the matter with you? Have you no heart at all? The poor lass is far gone with child and her man is dead, she is completely on her own. She'll need a doctor any moment now, perhaps at this very minute. You are a physician, are you not?"

"Yes," said Dr. Tullideph. The word plummeted into the dark. It sounded to Coll as if it had some terrible significance, a finality, but he could not accept this, and continued more quietly.

"Then you must help her, sir. You must surely want to help her. She is a Scot as we are Scots, she is alone in a strange country. The physicians here," said Coll, speaking from the memory of a time when he went down with a fever, "do not provide for Scots' constitutions. They do little but purge and bleed and force filthy concoctions down one's throat."

And as he spoke, he opened the bottle and drank from its neck, as if to wash some nasty taste away.

"They say," said Dr. Tullideph with a sudden little giggle, "that four thousand here die annually from blood lettings."

There was a pause. Then Coll said very carefully, as if to curb his mounting pulse and temper, "Tully. I am not interested in the four thousand, nor should you be. I am not talking of four thousand people. I am talking of Tom's widow. Would you force her to go to some back-street midwife who will surely kill the bairn, when you are here, her compatriot, her husband's friend, a qualified man who can be kind to her, speak her own language, be with her when she so sorely needs a friend? You must go, Tully. Good God, man, you have no choice. How can you stand there doing nothing when the poor creature's in such trouble? Even if there's little you can do, at least you'll be there so that when the child comes she'll have a friend at her side, someone to help her."

"I cannot go," said Dr. Tulideph.
"You bastard! You mean, bloody bastard!"
At this the doctor raised his head again, but he did not utter another word, and presently Coll, struggling to control himself, for after all it would scarce benefit Grizel if he alienated this impossible man, said as calmly as he could manage, "Well, I suppose there's no point in calling you names. But just tell me this. Why can't you go?"
"You'd not understand," said Dr. Tulideph.
"Then explain it to me."
"Why should I?"
"It might prevent my throttling you," said Coll.
"Do you believe I'm afraid of you? There comes a point," said Dr. Tulideph to his chest, "when you have been so afraid that you can no longer be afraid of anything."
Coll received this in silence, then said quietly, "That's not true, friend."
"What do you mean?" The doctor's voice suddenly roughened.
"Of course you're afraid. You're afraid of your own bones. You have as much courage in your carcass as—as teeth. You are feart to death. You always will be. There's no one walks with you, Tully, except fear, and that you take home with you every night. You're running away so fast you'll soon knock yourself into hell. You'd best tell me about it. I could scarce think less of you than I do, but maybe I would at least understand. I may not know much," said Coll, speaking with a soft savagery, "but I too have been afraid in my time, and I know a frightened man when I see one."
Then he began to sing, smiling at the doctor who stood there motionless, his head down. He sang:

And we ran, and they ran,
And they ran, and we ran,
And we ran, and they ran awa', man!

Dr. Tullideph said in a choked voice, "You have no right to ask me."

"Oh," said Coll, slapping his hand down on the barrel, "I have no rights, we none of us have rights. You need not answer, after all. But perhaps we need a touch of reality, Doctor. I have spent the entire evening with Mrs. Grizel, you know. She is a very brave girl. I buried her man with her, and then I came back and made up the bed for her, while she sewed on my buttons. But that's no matter. She said something strange to me that sticks in my mind. She said we are all shadows. There's no reality in our life. And she's right, Tully, by God, she's right. We are not real. Perhaps we don't exist at all, which is an interesting thought. What do we do with our lives? We walk and we talk and we drink and we whore—if we have the money—then we go back to our little dark mouseholes and sleep half our life away, to come out in the morning and start all over again. Perhaps, with luck, there's some juicy bit of scandal to brighten our day for us—Charlie with his leman, or the king eating himself into a vomit with his fine dinner of two of everything. Or the Pompadour slapping a face here or there, or some old butterfly sweetening his boy with kisses and louis d'or. It gives us a reason for breathing, but that's about all. We have no home, Tully, no wife, no bairns, no real friends. Faith, if we examined what's left of our souls, we'd find that we hate each other's guts, as I hate yours, Doctor, and you from the mealy look of you hate mine. So let us admit it, we are not real, but just for the one moment, let us be real, then we can both forget about it. Tell me, Tully, why you have forsworn your oath to Hippocrates, and why you elect to let a fellow countrywoman die with her bairn, rather than lift one podgy finger to save her. It'll pass the time, if nothing else, and when you have done, I shall probably get drunk, and so will pass another day."

He did not really believe Dr. Tullideph would answer. He even wondered if the doctor might try to knock him down, then walk away. It was difficult to imagine him behaving with violence, but he could not have been more grossly insulted, and he was presumably a man. But he did none of these things. He began to speak, his head so sunken that there must surely be a bend in the collarbone, to receive so solidly that unhappy chin.

He began strangely, "You talk of the drink—"

Coll, astonished, protested, "But I do not. I—"

"You talk of the drink," repeated Dr. Tullideph. Compared with the rest of them who talked almost nonstop he was a morose and silent man, but it was plain that once he decided to start talking, nothing would deflect him. Coll made a gesture of resignation with his hands, as the French did, and gazed into the half-darkness that, now the doctor had moved away from the window, revealed nothing of his features and gave a strange sonority to his voice.

"There was in my town," said Dr. Tullideph—it was Aberdeen, Coll remembered, but the name was not uttered—"two brothers who drank so much at their mother's burial that when they set out for the churchyard, they forgot the corpse altogether." He broke off as Coll made a faint choking sound. "You are not to laugh! What I am about to say is not amusin.'" Then, as if half to himself, "But maybe it is, maybe it is."

Coll, ignoring the last remark, said gravely, "The way you

recount it, sir, does not entirely lack humor, and after all, the old lady was presumably in no state to take offense. Did they go back for her, these wicked boys, or did they bury themselves?"

"If," cried the doctor in so wild a fury that the laughter was knocked out of Coll, "you make mock of me, I'll not continue, I'm done, I can speak no more."

"I apologize, Tully. Though you must admit it's an interesting situation. But I'm sorry. I'm sorry. Go on. I'll not laugh anymore. Only I don't see the relevance of this at all. Who were these two brothers? Of what importance are they to you?"

"I was one of them," said Dr. Tullideph.

And this time Coll remained silent, and the desire to laugh left him; it was so strange that Dr. Tullideph should be speaking in this fashion, so extraordinary that he should describe himself as a drunkard, that he waited as passionately as at the playhouse to learn what all this could be about. And how right poor Grizel was; the doctor might be speaking reality as he knew it, but the setting in this dim, barrel-filled room was completely unreal, bearing no resemblance to anything Coll had ever known.

"I drank," said Dr. Tullideph. "I was as drunk as a beggar from morning to night. Upon my soul, I believe I was as near mad as any sane man could be. There was always a bottle to my hand, and it never remained empty."

Coll opened his mouth to protest at what was beginning to sound like a confession before a synod of ministers; then something of Dr. Tullideph's horror and grief penetrated his bones so that for the first time compassion stirred within him. This, he sensed, was not so much a confession as a deliberate and prolonged self-flagellation. Dr. Tullideph was, for reasons of his own, choosing to crucify himself, and he must be allowed to do so, undisturbed. He raised the bottle to his lips again, hesitated, finding this in the circumstances unseemly, then thought, "What the devil, why not?" and swigged a vast mouthful, rolling it round his mouth in defiance.

He did not believe the doctor noticed; he was away in his martyrdom. The heavy voice went on, "They all knew about me. I was notour in the town."

"It is a venial offense," said Coll gently.

"Not in a doctor. But for a long time I managed to practice. Oh, it was sometimes difficult, and sometimes my hand betrayed me, but the devil looked after his own, there was no disaster. But the judgment awaited me, as sure as the fires of hell. Those who fall into the devil's hands will have their souls torn out as ravenously as a set of hungry lads tear out the hearts of bawbee rolls."

Coll reflected that Dr. Tullideph had plainly chosen the wrong profession, then wished he had found another simile so as not to remind him of his own growing hunger. But nothing would have moved him now, so he pushed away these shamefully material thoughts, took another gulp of wine, and waited.

"There was a girl," said Dr. Tullideph.

Coll forbore to remark that there always was. He was not an unkind man, nor at this point did he wish in any way to mock this unhappy devil, but there was a humorlessness to Dr. Tullideph that provoked the levity in him, almost as self-defense; the lives of all of them were so devoid of tenderness and light that what was plainly to be a stark, naked narrative was almost unendurable. He remained silent, and the doctor went on again.

"She was pregnant," said Dr. Tullideph. He was speaking

more loudly now as if some of his self-confidence had returned. "By a soldier. A common Highlander who had been pressed to be a drum and who ran away. The lass took him into the house, and he lay with her, to give her a bairn by way of payment. But the soldiers found him and took him, they hauled him out of bed, naked, fettered and tied between them, and presently they hanged him to a tree, so that was the end of him."

"Did you watch all this?" demanded Coll, bewildered again, for the doctor was recounting his tale in the most dramatic manner imaginable, yet as if it in no way concerned him personally.

"Ay," said Dr. Tullideph, adding with a kind of contemptuous surprise as if Coll were stupidly missing the whole point, "It was my house."

Coll gave it up. None of this made sense. He waited for the tale's conclusion.

"The poor lassie was in a great state."

"That is surely understandable for both of them," said Coll a little angrily, and wondered what it could be like to have your lover snatched from you in the very act of sex, and bundled out to a shameful death.

"Oh, him," said the doctor, as if he were following Coll's thoughts, "I do not give a merk for him. He was a rebel and a thief, a sly, cunning sort of fellow who deserved the hanging. But the lassie was pledged to another, she was to be wed in a little while, and there she was with child by another man, and the only thought in her mind was how to rid herself of it. Only women are such silly creatures, she tried the country ways which are no use, and then it was too late." He paused to rub his hand over his forehead, which was shining with sweat.

"She was a sonsy lass with red hair, but not much there—not much there."

"And you," said Coll, "helped her."

"I did a great deal more than that," said Dr. Tullideph. "I killed her."

Coll said after a long pause, "I see."

The doctor cried out, his voice soaring to falsetto, "No, you do not see. You see nothing at all. What can you know of such things? I was drunk. Don't you understand? I was drunk, or I'd never have done it. It's not my job to take life. They tried to bring me into this damned rebellion, but I'd have none of it. I once refused to drink the Prince's health and they forced a glass of wine down my throat. They told me I was a traitor, a follower of King George. They threw stones at my windows. They told me they'd hash me to pieces, given half a chance. Oh, they all hated me, but I'd not go into the war, I said so, and they waited for their opportunity. I gave them the opportunity," said Dr. Tullideph grimly. "I cut the bairn away from her, but I was filled with wine, my hands were shaking, and so I killed her. She died four days later, and she died terribly, poor lass, and there was nothing I could do for her, nothing at all."

Coll said at last, "At least you wished to help her. Why should you blame yourself? Who was this lass? Was she your maidservant?"

"She was my daughter," said Dr. Tullideph, and at this Coll could find nothing more to say, only looked away from him, for the pain in his voice was as sharp as broken glass.

The doctor said, after a silence, "They came for me. They told me I was a murderer and deserved hanging. I wish they had hanged me. But they did not. I daresay they felt that doctors were needed, even drunken sots like myself. They sentenced me to be whipped and drummed through Aberdeen, Old Meldrum and Strathbogie; they knocked my teeth out with a hammer, then told me that unless I joined the army as physician, I would be hanged."

The doctor seemed to have calmed himself with the horror of his own story. He looked across at Coll who was again drinking from his bottle, and Coll believed he smiled, though it was hard to tell in the half-light, and it was at the best a death's-head kind of grin. He went on, "You have my story, sir. You are the first I have ever told it to. You know my secret. Now you can tell all your friends and laugh about it together; you can say you backspiered a murderous old physician who drank his own daughter to death, and now lives out what remains of his life away from his own land and from his fellow human beings."

Coll said calmly, "I will give you Mrs. Grizel's address. I do not know how far gone she is, but I suspect she is very near her time, and the shock of Tom's death may bring it on sooner than she expects. She is very young, Tully, perhaps only twenty-two or -three, and it's her first bairn. She lives in a filthy tenement, with a bloody old limmer for a landlady who'd cut anyone's throat for a ha'penny. Perhaps you could find a sister from a convent or someone who would give her woman's care. She should not be alone at such a time. We'll all see to it that she does not starve, but we are not physicians, and you are. The very fact of your being there will comfort her."

Dr. Tullideph cried out in a screaming whisper, "You did not listen to one word I said!"

"Oh, ay," said Coll, revolving the bottle in his hand, and

studying the label as if this were the most important thing in the world, "I heard every word." He raised his head. "You were drunk, you accidentally killed your own daughter, and you have been most savagely punished for it. You are very sorry for yourself, Tully, and so you are taking it out on the whole bloody world. But you are still a physician, and now you do not drink and your hand is steady. This Scots lass needs you more than you've ever been needed in your life. You cannot in humanity's name send her to the Hôtel-Dieu, for that too would be murder, she would doubtless catch a fever, and then both she and the bairn will be dead. Do you want another death on your conscience?"

"You don't understand," whispered Dr. Tullideph. "You do not understand at all."

"I understand perfectly. Go to Mrs. Grizel. You should be there in a quarter of an hour."

"I cannot!"

"You can. You have no choice."

"I cannot," said Dr. Tullideph again.

Coll rose to his feet. He said as if he had not heard, "Tell her I shall come when I can. And—" He rummaged in his pocket and pulled out a handful of small coins. "This is all I've got in the world. It's not much, God knows, but at least you can buy her some milk and eggs."

"Take them yourself," said Dr. Tullideph like a pert child; the rudeness came out oddly in his heavy voice.

Coll looked at him. "Tully," he said, "you are still a doctor. I do not give a damn what you did, and frankly, I do not give a damn either what has happened to you. I only know that here we are all strangers, we are all away from home. It is the only thing we have in common. You cannot refuse, you cannot, to help this girl who is as lonely as you are, who has just had her man die in her arms and who this afternoon buried him. You cannot. Why, because you made one mistake—"

"Mistake! My own daughter—"

"Ah, for Christ's sake!" exclaimed Coll, suddenly angry. "Stop blethering, man. Go to Mrs. Grizel. Do you have to kill her as well? See to it that the bairn is delivered, and that both of them are looked after. If you do not, Tully, I swear by whatever oath you like, I'll put you out of your misery, I'll even swing for you, though much good that'll do me—"

"Here," said Dr. Tullideph, with a disconcerting plunge to normality and reason, "they use the ax."

Coll gave a faint laugh. "One baby or one rolling head then. I think when you drank, Tully, I might quite have liked you. It is a pity that now you are sober, you have become such a dead bore. But then all sober men are bores," said Coll, who was by now a little drunk himself. "The brain needs whiskey to stimulate it, though wine will do at a pinch; the one certain thing is that it softens on milk and water. Go to Mrs. Grizel, Tully, and buy yourself a bottle of *rouge* on the way, to wet the baby's head after the cord is cut."

"I think you are out of your wits," said Dr. Tullideph in a dazed way.

"I think you are perfectly right," said Coll, "and to prove your point I'll tell you one thing more, Tully, just one thing more. I am a respectable married man, Doctor, with a wife I love with all my heart, and two bairns who are half my life to me. Nonetheless—nonetheless, Tully—forgive me if I repeat your name so often, but then I am fou. I drink, Tully. I am given up to the bottle. It blurs one's natural longings—Where the devil am I? Ah. Nonetheless, Tully, I have taken to myself a whore. She is ugly, she is old. There is nothing about her to please me except that I do not have to pay her and she cooks like an angel. She also knits, Tully. She knits us in during the day, and undoes us every night. I met her this evening and I told her I would never see her again. I am now going round to her, Tully, to eat something she calls *blanquette de veau*. I don't know what it is, but I have no money, I have just given you my last sou, and I am famished. It is a sad comment on human frailty, but when morals war with the belly, the belly always wins. I wish you good evening, boy," said Coll with the utmost dignity, and strode a little erratically in the direction of the door.

Dr. Tullideph stared after him as if he could not believe his ears. He heard Coll crashing down the stairs. He still stood there. His eyes were tightly closed. There was within his mind, his agonizingly sober mind, the mind that had seized on his experiences and knotted them into a hard, sick, painful lump, the sound and sight of a hand that slipped, an instrument sliding out of his control into the butter-soft flesh, and blood and screaming, though whether the screams were his or Mary's, he could no longer say: a cacophony of dreadful sights and sounds and himself running, the agony of the lash, the ceaseless beating of the drums.

He flung his hands to his toothless mouth and whispered, "I cannot bear it, I cannot bear it." His eyes, now wide and staring, moved to the noose that swung above the window. The next moment he had recovered his composure, and he followed Coll down the stairs, making for his own room where he still had his case with its drugs and instruments; there was even in it a half bottle of brandy.

Coll went straight, if his progress could be so described, to Paulette's, where she received him with the patient air of a woman expecting her man back from work. The cat sat on her knee; the pan simmering over the fire gave out a warm, savory smell. She did not display the faintest surprise at seeing him, only tipped the cat off her knee and at once served him his dinner.

He ate till he could eat no more. He thought he had never eaten anything so good in his life. Then, because he was a little remorseful at treating her so cavalierly, he tried to make some kind of conversation, but she hardly responded and, when she did, only in monosyllables. She made no further reference to Grizel. He did not offer to sleep with her, nor did she seem to expect it of him. Indeed, she was so remote and cool that he was a little piqued; he had to wonder what the devil he meant to her, for he refused her hospitality ungraciously, turned up when he pleased, expected her to cook for him, and had never once brought her so much as a bunch of flowers.

He said to her suddenly, "If I were you, Paul, I'd kick myself down the stairs."

She merely shrugged, the strange, opaque eyes fixed on him as if she could read his mind.

He persisted. He said, "I make fine use of you, don't I? Why the devil do you put up with me? I don't even give you any money." And as he spoke, he was amazed afresh that two human beings could make so little impact on each other; he had after all spent two hours here. He said curtly, "I'm going now. I must write to my wife." Then, because her continued silence angered him, he added in a rough voice, "Do you want me to stay?"

But she only picked up that confounded knitting of hers, and answered placidly, "You must do as you please."

He exclaimed, "Oh, for God's sake!" She disconcerted him, in some odd way even humiliated him. Yet for all she was so calm and acceptant and nondemanding, he had the feeling as always that there was something buried deep that was not calm at all. Perhaps it was this awareness of danger, this kind of evil excitement that brought him so regularly to her side. It was hardly soothing to retreat to this alien atmosphere where there was no communication between them, but in an odd way it invigorated him, even gave him, as Grizel might have pointed out, a little reality, if of an ugly kind. As for her, he could not understand what pleasure he gave her; the sexual side must mean so little to her by now. Perhaps when she had done with her innumerable boys who slid in and out of her bed, she needed someone to sit quietly at her fireside, for whom she could cook enormous meals; perhaps for her it was reality too.

Yet, as he looked back at her before closing the door, he found her more unreal than anything else; this strange creature, so plain and drab and middle-aged, who was more successful in her profession than the younger, prettier girls around her, came as much from a twilight world as himself, eternally a stranger.

He did not write to Jean after all. There was a letter from her awaiting him when he returned to his room. One of the little Savoyards must have slid it under his door. There was money inside. It was the first time she had ever sent him money. Coll fingered it in a kind of longing fury and resentment. God knows he needed it, his pension was not due for a week yet and it was always late, he would be lucky to have it within the month. And what with Grizel and the baby to be, he needed money more than he had ever done, and he had just handed over his last coins to Dr. Tullideph. But it hurt savagely that Jean should be sending it to him when he so longed to be able to post off the fare for her and the children. She had offered innumerable times, and he had always refused. Now he knew he had no choice, he had to accept it. It seemed to him a sorry reversal of rôles. Once again there rang in his heart a bell that tolled the ending, that she would never come to him, that he might never see her again.

He lay flat on his bed, and read the letter. The money, wrapped in a little oilskin packet, was on the floor beside him.

It was all lively, gay and affectionate. In his present mood of passionate disillusion everything about it seemed to him unnatural and wrong.

There was a long story about the three-year-old little girl of a friend of theirs, a true Jacobite baby. "Whenever she hears the word 'Whig' she girns and makes faces that would frighten a bean, but when her mama names the prince she kisses her and looks at his picture."

The father of this little rebel was, as Coll knew, in Rome, an exile like himself, and the wife was seven months gone with another child, but Jean did not refer to this situation, which was a traditional one, on both sides. Few gentlemen had their wives with them and almost all of them kept a mistress, while equally often the wives at home took lovers. Coll's mind flickered wildly for a second over the possibility that this might have happened with Jean; he could not believe it because he would not, yet after all she was still quite young, and she too must be very much alone.

He went on to read about Amy, who had apparently found herself a beau. "He is two years younger and will not so much as look at her, but she swears she is dying of love for him. I give the passion two more weeks." And Donald, "our bonnie little pet who is perfect well and sends Papa his fondest duty." And, "We have fine weather, promising well for the harvest, the good white meal sells at sevenpence the peck." And, "The minister last Sabbath had a fine discourse on the two first and three last verses of the Sixtieth Psalm."

So much and so little, and never a word, never one word, to say that she hoped to join him, that she missed him and loved him, and never the question that he could not answer, yet longed to receive: "When are you coming back?" or, "When may we come to you?"

The letter, when he had read it over three times, dropped from his fingers, and a splash of salt water landed beside it, the water from the stream of loneliness and self-pity. Coll did not pick the letter up, only continued to lie there, staring at the ceiling, arms beneath his head. The room was chilly and damp, even on this June night, and the stench of the urinal outside came through the window, which he had been compelled to close tightly; one pane was broken and he had stuck a piece of paper over it.

He thought dimly as he had thought before, that he might after all join Lochiel's regiment from the court of France. It would at least give him something to do, restore a little of his dignity; some of the exiles had already done this. It would save him from growing into the querulous, grumbling, self-pitying creature that no money and nothing to do had made of many of them. But he was a lazy man, as he knew very well; he felt he could not make the effort. What he really wanted to do at this moment was to write back immediately, to say, "I love you, I want you, I can't live without you. If you cannot come to me, I must come to you, and never mind if it means spending the rest of my days skulking in the hills."

But he did not, though the very thought of it made him so sick with longing that he believed he might die of it. To feel the heather beneath his feet once more, to see the hills purple in the twilight—And to have Jean running to meet him, her hands outstretched, the children ahead of her, leaping into his arms. He could feel again the weight and firmness of those small, wriggling bodies, smell the sweetness of them; it was almost as if their wild, damp kisses lay on his cheek and brow.

"God damn everybody!" said Coll aloud, and did not know whom he was swearing at, perhaps it was simply the whole wide, bloody world. And then he thought irrelevantly of Grizel and was for some reason a little comforted; now he would be able to buy proper food for her. And he wondered if Dr. Tullideph would go to see her, or if he had lost his courage at the last moment, and retreated into his fear and outrage, to sit with ugly ghosts in his lonely room.

He heard the church clock striking. It was three in the morning and sleep was a league away. He realized that it was not only that poor devil, Tully, who had his ghosts; he too had them girning and mouthing at him, and he must not stay here, otherwise there would be nothing but to drink himself into a stupor, and then all this beautiful money would be gone, with nothing left for Grizel and emergencies. He swung his legs off the bed, to get out of this room, walk himself into sleep again, stop this lying there being sorry for himself. His drunken exhaustion had left him, his head was clear, he felt wide awake. And meaning to carry Jean's letter with him as a talisman, he picked it up to slip it into his pocket, then saw that there was a postscript on the back, written so hastily that it might have been penned by a stranger.

Jean wrote: "I received your last which gives me great pain. I plainly see you labor under that disease of longing for your country. You must not. Raise up your courage and act like a reasonable man. Don't think of coming home, whatever may happen to us." And then, underlined, "You must not."

That was all. Coll sat down again on the edge of the bed for a while, the letter on his knee, then slowly, like a drugged man coming out of his stupor, he tore it across, then across again and again. Then he got up and walked down into the street, with no idea of where to go, but wild with anger, murder-mad with anger, hating everything about him from the stinking little room to the cold, hard words that still shifted in his mind, like music out of tune.

He wondered momentarily if he should call on Dr. Tullideph to find out what had happened. There was an insanity and despair in the doctor that suited his present mood. But this was hardly the time for a social call, and certainly poor old Tully must have had more than enough of him; it would be surprising if he even opened the door. Coll had never visited him, Tully not being a man who invited callers, but he knew where he lived, for he had once out of pure curiosity walked down his street. The doctor must have mentioned the address, and Coll had a good memory. It had interested him mainly because it was of a far better class than the places the rest of them lived in. It was not of course an aristocratic quarter, but it was cozy and middle-class, filled with pleasant small cafés, and a few shops, over one of which the doctor lived. Dr. Tullideph must have brought something more than bitter memories over with him, though he never mentioned his money and never offered help or a loan. And this was surprising, even in an egotist like the doctor, for however much they might dislike each other, they were still misfortune-bound, and in crises always joined forces.

But then Dr. Tullideph had always been the odd man out. Absorbed as he was in his own disaster, he was probably not aware of other people's existence.

Coll walked along with the violent speed of temper, and as

he walked came a little to his senses. He saw now that what Jean had written, if not at all what he wanted to hear, was undeniably true. It did not necessarily signify that she no longer loved him; it was even a proof of her love that she thought so fiercely of his safety. At the beginning of it all—what a long time ago it seemed!—when he was dazed with shock and loss, when he did not even speak the confounded language, when he was completely disoriented, he had been seized a dozen times a week with the idea of sailing back to Scotland, to spend a few days with her if no more. But there was a sharp lookout for returning exiles, and it would help nobody if he were transported to the West Indies or, as was only too possible, hanged. If he did return it would certainly be for more than a few days, and it would have to be planned down to the last detail. Aeneas spoke little these days of the Loch Arkaig treasure, but Coll knew well enough that there was something in the offing, even though it might not evolve for a long, long time.

No, Jean was reasonable, but he did not want reason, and the coldness hurt him. She had not always been so reasonable or so cold. Why should it give her pain to know that he longed to see her? She could surely have said, "I long to see you too, but it is simply not wise. A husband overseas is better to me than a husband dead."

Not simply, "You must not."

The minister had spoken to him once before he came out. It was at the beginning of August, 1745. "You would not be wise, Coll," the old man said—perhaps he was not so old after all, but then Coll was young, and to the young anyone is old. "Never engage too warmly in any kind of party matters, and"—here the finger of damnation was raised and prodded into

Coll's midriff—"on no account be concerned in any rebellion against a settled government."

Coll had irreverently laughed. "I doubt, sir," he said, "if your own Lord obeyed any such injunction."

The minister exclaimed, "But that is blasphemy!" and Jean, standing beside him, hastened to explain that her husband had meant no such thing; presently the matter was forgotten, with the help of Amy, whose prattling served to tide it over.

But when they came home, Jean, in the fashion of wives who assumed a meekness abroad that they did not practice in the house, grew angry and repeated the minister's warning. Perhaps women were after all the detached and reasoning sex; they were only concerned with home and family, with no interest whatsoever in pretenders and risings and lost causes.

Coll, who owed his present lamentable state to all three, could almost at this moment of disillusion have agreed with her.

And so he continued to walk the Paris streets.

Chapter 4

HE STRODE around for some time, falling now from rage to self-pity. He did not think of calling on Grizel again. In his present mood he could not endure the additional burden of her grief. He knew that it was something far worse than what he was suffering. Jean at least was alive and there was still the hope that he might see her again, but Tom was gone for good and all. He would gladly give her all the money he could afford, he had done his best to persuade Tully to go to her, but in his heart there was no room for her at all, it was already filled to overflowing.

He was of course ashamed of himself, but this did not dispose him to behave any better, it never did, and he rolled the self-pity, blended with self-condemnation, round in himself, almost enjoying the pain of it.

"I daresay," he once said to Aeneas, "this is how all heroes end."

"I deduce from that," said Aeneas, with that ironic smile of his that tinged his most amiable-seeming words, "that you consider yourself a hero."

"Good God, no! When I say hero, I mean merely some poor fool who goes tilting his lance for lost causes. If he succeeds, then he is indeed a hero, or so the world calls him, but if he fails he is an idiot and a fool. That goes for Hector and Achilles and all the lot of them. And what the devil are we left with? The answer is easy—the rags of our vainglory, regret, grievance and self-pity. Why," said Coll, engulfed in his own verbiage, "look at all of us in the Club. A fine heroic army! One lecher, one self-pitier who talks too much, and one who has cut himself entirely off from the world. And of course—" He stopped.

"And?" repeated Aeneas.

"Ah, there you have me, sir. Sometimes," said Coll, "I believe you do not belong with us at all. I do not know if you were even in the scrape; we all take it for granted you were, but you never mention it. I think you play your own game, and it isn't cavagnole, though you always seem to beat us when we try it."

A secretive look came upon Aeneas' face, but he only said coolly, "You make of me what I am not. You have too much imagination. One day perhaps I'll enlighten you."

Coll remembered this as, turning aimlessly a corner that led into the main boulevard, he almost knocked against Aeneas, who was sauntering along, dressed as always far better than the rest of them, and wearing the air of one preoccupied with his own business. When he realized it was Coll, he smiled, and held out his hand, as if this were broad daylight, not the small hours of the morning, as if this meeting were the most natural thing in the world.

"You are the man I particularly want to see," he said.

"Am I?" said Coll rather sourly, very much aware of his shirt sleeves and battered appearance, but still interested enough to wonder what the devil Aeneas could be doing out at such an hour, for he looked as if he had come from some select dinner party, and it was now just after four o'clock, an odd time for so respectable a gentleman.

"Of course. Come and drink a coffee with me," said Aeneas, and it was plain from a flicker in his eyes that he thought it would be inadvisable to suggest wine. He added, "There is a little bistro, a few yards down. I go there sometimes. It is open all night."

"I do not even have a coat—"

"Oh, what the hell does that matter? You've become *bon bourgeois*. These are Parisians here, not holy west coasters. Nobody minds how you dress, and neither do I. Besides, I want to talk to you, and in the Club there are always other people there."

They sat down in the bistro, and Aeneas, who seemed to be in the highest of spirits, ordered demitasses for the pair of them, together with little cream cakes, which made Coll's bleared eyes open wide, for the price was well beyond his means.

They talked for a while of Grizel.

"There is a convent near," said Aeneas, "of Saint Vincent de Paul. I know the Mother Superior. I am sure one of the sisters would be willing to look after the poor lass."

"I am hoping that Tully will also help," said Coll.

"Tully?" repeated Aeneas sharply. "Have you been talking to Tully?"

"Tully has been talking to me."

"He'd not lift a finger for his own mother."
"Then I'll cut his throat for him," said Coll.
"You need a cognac, man."
"I have already been drinking too much."
"Ah, you must have sobered up by now. A cognac will set you right. And forget about Tully. What I have to say is not to be repeated to Tully, Davy or anyone else. Above all, not the girl. A woman is incapable of keeping a secret, she is the best town crier in the world. Tell her something in strict confidence today, and the whole world will know it tomorrow."
"Not with Mistress Ryder, I fancy."
"I doubt she's any different from the rest."
Coll thought of Grizel with her plain, serious face, her directness and honesty. He could not imagine a better confidante, he could not visualize her tattling to anyone. But at long last the weight of an exhausting day was beginning to fall on his shoulders. He did not trouble to argue the point, only sipped his brandy, and watched Aeneas, reflecting how strange it was that a man could have everything that totaled good looks and charm, yet somehow be as cold and inhuman as a statue. In the overtired state when body and soul are longing for sleep, the eyes grow unnaturally sharp, everything assumes the kind of clarity that comes just before day turns into night. He saw a face that could have been termed beautiful, with its straight nose, finely curved mouth, deep-set gray eyes and stubborn, cleft chin. But there was an almost feminine air of grievance to it; the mouth in repose was sullen; the eyes shifted before one's gaze. It was somehow the face of a disappointed man who had never achieved what he believed he deserved.
"Are you a married man?" Coll asked him suddenly.

"No!" The answer was almost affronted. Then Aeneas, eyeing him sideways in a suspicious way, demanded, "What makes you ask me such a thing?"

"Oh, I don't know. Curiosity, perhaps. I am a married man myself," said Coll, "though much good it does me. You are in a way fortunate. What's the point of loving a woman who is a hundred miles away, whom you cannot touch or talk to or even see? It's worse than being a widower."

"You are in no way bound to her," said Aeneas. The gray eyes raised themselves to Coll. "She don't seem to be much bound to you. If she wished to join you, she could surely do so."

"Could she?" Then Coll grew angry, raising his voice. "How could she? Tell me that. There are the bairns. What have I to offer her? I live in one room that stinks like a badger's set, and half the time I do not have enough money to feed myself, much less the three of them. At least they live in reasonable comfort, at least they have clothes for their backs and enough to eat. And," added Coll after a weary pause, his temper cooled, "they breathe sweet, fresh air, not the smells of a cesspit like ourselves." He looked intently at Aeneas as if he were trying to make some personal contact with him. "You are Johnny Lackland like me. Do you not sometimes long for home? Do you not dream of the heather and the hills and the soft, fine rain? Are you not sick to death of this stinking city with the filth running through the gutters, people shouting instead of talking, and nothing for us to do but die?"

"I shall never go home," said Aeneas.

"What! You say that so calmly. You cannot believe it. Even I cannot believe it. Sometimes at my worst I believe I shall be an old, old man with a long, white beard before I see my own land again, but if I really thought I'd end my days here, why,

I'd end them quicker. I might even swing on the rope that Davy fastened to our window."

"Oh, you talk like a fool," said Aeneas calmly, and beckoned the waiter to bring them two more cognacs.

"Where do you come from?" asked Coll, ignoring the last remark.

"From the Highlands like yourself."

"Is that all the answer you're giving me?"

"Ay," said Aeneas, and smiled.

"And you believe you'll never go back?"

"Why should I? Here it suits me fine. You prate of the hills and lochs and it all sounds gey and romantic, but Scotland is not all like that, you know it as well as I do. There's the scourge and the brank and the stocks for those who do not comply, and the chieftains still have hanging powers when they choose to exercise them. There's nothing there for an educated and ambitious man."

"And you are educated and ambitious?" said Coll, a little derisively.

Aeneas answered with pride, "I am that."

And indeed, it was plain that he was. Resentful, perhaps disappointed with unfulfilled hopes, he might look, but there was still an air to him, and it seemed to Coll that here was someone who would not care overmuch what he did to get what he wanted.

"So you are staying here," said Coll. "And what is it this country gives you? A revolution, perhaps?"

Aeneas blinked. It was momentary, so much so that Coll half-believed he was mistaken, yet for that brief moment his eyes flickered as if the question had caught him on the raw. But he only answered, as if the matter bored him, "It is true that Paris for some time has talked of little else."

"Oh, Paris talks!" said Coll. "Paris always talks, but does nothing about it. The French are born grumblers, but I doubt they do much except swear, brawl and drink."

"Don't be so sure," said Aeneas. "They are souls not yet weaned, but the day will come."

"*Ça ira!* They all say that. I believe they satisfy themselves with slogans. But it takes more than slogans to create a revolution."

"It takes personal suffering. And of that there is plenty."

"It also takes greed and grievance and a thirst for revenge," said Coll dryly. "Of that there is plenty too. Our landlord talks of precious little else. But he serves his wine as he spits damnation, and so it will go on. It's still Papa Louis after all, they'll never bring themselves to chop his head off. Though faith," said Coll, "it would make little difference to the world. But I daresay he's no worse than anyone else, for all his cats and silkworms and La Pompadour. I am very nearly an honest man myself, having no possessions to encourage dishonesty and only friends who are as impoverished as myself so that I cannot sponge on them, but occasionally a faint revolutionary twinge seizes me, especially when I think that Mrs. Grizel's bairn may starve, while each time the king goes visiting, he spends a few millions. In excess, naturally, of the twenty-five million needed for the upkeep of the royal houses." He saw Aeneas' look of surprise, and grinned. "But I am still not quite a revolutionary, sir. This is Jean-Pierre speaking. I get the figures with my bottle, every time I go near him, so they have remained in my memory. I doubt it means much to either of us. When you have a thousand francs at your annual disposal, the odd million here or there is remarkably insignificant. It is just that since we are talking treason, I feel in the mood to add my own quota. I am after all dispossessed. Do not the dispossessed make the best revolutionaries? They have nothing to lose and so much time to talk; all revolutions start with talk, even if they end in murder."

"I have never heard you hold forth like this before!"

"I am tired beyond exhaustion. If tomorrow you remind me of what I have said, I shall certainly deny it, and equally certainly will not even remember it. What did you want to see me about? You have now stood me three brandies, which is almost my monthly budget, sweet cakes and coffee. I do not believe this is entirely for the charm of my blethering conversation."

The strange, secretive look once more masked Aeneas' face. He did not answer immediately, so Coll, finding that he was too fatigued to keep silent, started again.

"At least our personal revolution has ended with nothing but words. And drink. Do you ever see our little Sobieski-Stuart? 'A sair, sair altered man, Prince Charlie cam' hame.' Is that not what they say?"

"It's not true." Aeneas frowned at him, as if he were an admonishing schoolmaster. "It is foolish to talk like that."

"After three brandies," said Coll, "I talk as I please. Of course it's true. He is grown gross, like myself he drinks too much, and his amours are a public scandal. This does not promise well for the new Rising. If there is to be one. . . . We are still after all a Calvinist people, for all we toy from time to time with Popery. Do you really believe the Scots will welcome a debauched lecher tottering onto the shore at Moidart, and doubtless falling flat on his royal face even as the standard is being uplifted? With of course one of his innumerable ladies in tow. Oh, no. It is not in the tradition, sir. We all have our vices, but we like our heroes to assume virtue even if they do not have it, and above all, we do not like being made ridiculous. A drunken prince with his whore behind him! Besides, I think the day of pretenders is done, and so do you, if you would bring yourself to admit it."

"You are talking nonsense," said Aeneas. But for some secret reason of his own he looked amused, as if he did not take even his own remark seriously.

"It's not what the English would call it," said Coll, and broke into a brief, loud laugh. He realized at this point that he was very drunk indeed, and grew instantly grave again.

Aeneas seemed unaware of his drunkenness or, if he were aware, chose to ignore it. He looked at Coll for a moment, then said, "If I told you that there was indeed a chance of a third Rising, would you disbelieve me?"

Coll was about to answer with derision and rudeness when the full impact of these words struck him. It was as if a wheel of chance revolving in his brain suddenly whirred to a stop at the winning number. He did not think of Charles. He never had really thought of Charles whom he had only glimpsed once or twice in battle and heard his brief speech after a victory. He thought only of Jean and the two children. He did not give a damn for a third, fourth or fifth Rising, though he had still just enough sobriety in him not to say this to Aeneas, but the words, the thought of it, brought before him a vision of Loch Maree, of home, of a life worth living again, that dried his mouth with longing and inaptly brought the water to his aching eyes. He did not speak, only looked; he did not quite believe but dared not disbelieve.

Aeneas began to speak, softly and swiftly. "I cannot go into details here. But this is not a dream, friend. This is something that could be a reality for all of us. We speak of the Loch Arkaig treasure—"

"Again?" said Coll in savage disillusionment. Was hope to

depend on something that had become like a fairy tale? "Again. Why do you say it like that? It is still there. I have information—no matter now. In any case, it is too soon for us to go. The English are always waiting for us; they have already captured some of our men who hoped to return home. We will have to go at the worst time of the year, when they will never expect us. We have planned the expedition for December."

"December!" exclaimed Coll too loudly, for Aeneas at once hushed him. He continued in an enforced conspiratorial whisper. "But this is absurd. There will be gales and storms, we could never survive the crossing. What chance would we have of ever reaching the Scottish coast?"

"Some. There is always some. Now there would be none at all. There are ships waiting for us, and soldiers posted everywhere. But in the dead of winter no one would expect us; it would seem as absurd as you yourself have said. However, I cannot discuss this fully here, only I would wish you to dine with us—"

"Us?" repeated Coll.

"Friends. I cannot give you the names. We are arranging a meeting in the Place des Vosges. I will give you the address nearer the time. Only you must speak of this to no one, no one at all. Davy is as trustworthy as a rattlesnake, and the good doctor—why, we all know so little of him, he might even feel it his duty to report us to one of the government spies. Besides, in such a venture, the fewer people who know, the better. But you, Coll—why, we disagree from time to time, you and I, but I know I can have confidence in you, you would never betray us."

"What you really think," said Coll, who was sobering up fast with the shock of this sudden news, "is that it would not be worth my while, that my need to see my family again is such that I would never dare to work against you."

"Something of the kind," said Aeneas with a little, tight smile.

"I imagine you trust nobody in the world."

"I have never found any reason to. Is that important? The man who trusts people is a fool. But there is one more thing." He was rising to his feet, a fine figure of a man who must look superb in his native kilt. "Never a word to Mistress Ryder. Is that understood?" He bent a fierce, intent gaze on Coll. "You went to see her."

"You asked me to. I could even say that you forced me to."

"You were a long time there."

Coll could have asked how he knew this, but did not. Though he was by now almost sober again, his head was still throbbing with drink and exhaustion, and he was too tired to engage in any further brawl. But he was disturbingly aware that he was being constantly observed, though for God knows what reason, and he thought that perhaps all that Aeneas had said to him was little to do with what lay at the heart of the matter. It seemed to him that intrigue enmeshed him like a fishing net, that in some way that he did not yet understand, he was being used, that Aeneas had some sinister design of his own that had nothing to do with princes or risings.

He replied sharply, "If one goes to condole with so new a widow, one hardly appears to say, 'I grieve for you'—and then go away. I had to attend the burying, and more besides. What are you accusing me of now? I do not like being spied on, and that it seems to me is what you are doing."

"I am accusing you of nothing," said Aeneas in a pacific manner, "and of course I do not spy on you. Only as I have said, I never trust women, and I cannot make Mrs. Grizel an exception. I would prefer you not to see her too much. I have already promised that she will be looked after, and I have arranged that she is not short of money, indeed, the rent will be paid."

Coll surveyed him in silence. He neither agreed nor disagreed. He did not say, as he longed to do, "What confounded impertinence!" He had every intention of seeing Grizel again, as many times as he chose and when he chose. He would certainly not speak to her of this strange matter, but he was convinced that she was entirely to be trusted, perhaps more than any of them. It was absurd that Aeneas, two years his senior, but in no position of authority with regard to himself, should presume to dictate to him what he should do and whom he should see. But it was interesting, and his mind, now a little restored, assimilated this oddity as something to be investigated at length later.

He remembered suddenly Grizel's remark about there being no reality to them. Perhaps she, whom death and birth had made indisputably real, was proving some kind of touchstone for them, perhaps that was why Aeneas did not want him to see her again.

He made his farewell, and walked slowly back to his room. It was almost morning now, but the desire for sleep devoured him so that his movements were clogged with it. It was only when he was halfway that a new and unpleasing thought occurred to him. Aeneas had said that he was to dine in the Place des Vosges. The Place des Vosges was an ancient and fashionable quarter that bore no resemblance to his usual surroundings. And he had become like a woman, to cry out despairingly, "I have nothing to wear!" This seemed so ludicrous to him that he began to laugh. Passersby, on their way to work, glowered at him and moved out of his path, convinced that he was mad or drunk. Coll stopped, for indeed this was no laughing matter. He began gloomily to consider his wardrobe, including the unhappy wig in the cupboard that looked as if the rats had nibbled at it. Perhaps they had. There was not much else for them to nibble at. No doubt Aeneas would lend him something more seemly, for they were after all much of a size, but Coll pushed this idea away; he had no wish to borrow from a man he did not really like.

Grizel seemed to be the only answer. He would go to see her, and perhaps her deft needle would perform miracles for him, though how the poor lass could be expected to make anything of a frayed shirt, patched breeks and a deplorable jacket, he did not know.

He did not, however, call on her for the next three days, chiefly because his mind was totally absorbed with the thought of going home. It did not matter that the whole scheme was in some way a dream. He had pushed hope down inside him for so long that he believed it to be drowned; he saw now that in some strange way it had always been near the surface, and now it popped up, strong, vast, heady, so that he was almost choked with it. In this blaze of hope people and places and things around him became misty and unreal. He did not even, until the third day, go to the Club. He did not write to Jean, he did not dare; she might detect from the simplest words that once again he was alive and happy. He knew she must not know, for all their sakes, and so he did not write at all.

He did not go near Paulette either. He did not even think of her. She was part of the other, unhappy world. In his present mood she was something he never wanted to see again. He spent all his time roaming the Paris streets, as he had done when he first came over, talking to people he did not know, watching everything with new-washed eyes, listening to the rumors and gossip that grumbled everywhere beneath the routine of everyday life.

It was true enough that people talked of revolution. Perhaps the French, by nature an aggressive people, always had done. But there was no consistency in them, they were to him so foreign in their way of thinking and expression that he could never entirely understand them, for all they might be said to have started the scrape by sending over to Scotland a young woman who bred the present prince many generations back.

Once at the beginning he had said idly to Davy, "Davy, how do you like the French, now that you've been among them for nearly three months?"

The little man replied with a grand air of dignity, mouthing the words in a dramatic manner, "I cannot answer your question, for I am not acquainted with any of them."

He had already lain with quite a few of their women, as Coll very well knew; Davy made no secret of it. But he chose to affect great surprise, saying, "What! Not acquainted!"

"Ay," said Davy, "I never enter into conversation with the Frogs, for to tell you the truth I do not understand a word they say."

This was of course a complete lie, even then, for Davy had monkey wits and would have found his way round Turkestan, but it pleased him to affect this lack of understanding, with so superior an air to him that it was obviously a matter of national pride. Now of course he spoke his own brand of gutter French, which consisted of stringing words together without grammar, and the French found no difficulty in understanding him, though what he said was not always of a kind to please the more genteel *faubourgs*.

But whether he understood the people at all, it was hard to say, for Davy lived his own raffish, private life wherever he was, more concerned with a woman to bed or a man to brawl with, than any conventional relationship. And even to Coll, with a far better command of the language and far more interest in people as people, they still remained strangers, and he could never make up his mind how serious their grumblings were, how soon, if ever, the revolution would break among citizens who flocked to royal processions on Monday, and on Tuesday sat in a bistro, swearing at the crippling taxes and recounting terrible tales of what went on in some of the feudal estates.

"Nailed horseshoes to his blacksmith's feet," Jean-Pierre told him. Jean-Pierre with his fine profile and enormous body had a vast encyclopedia of horrors. This concerned some old marquis or other, whose name Coll had forgotten, a gentleman of the most *ancien régime*, with apparently a sadistic pleasure in making the punishment fit the crime.

"Oh, in Paris," went on Jean-Pierre, noting with pleasure Coll's grimace of revulsion, "you do not see such things, it is too open, there are too many people. But in the provinces—ah, God, what goes on there, I should not like to tell you. Such diableries, unbelievable, unmentionable, enough to make you sick—"

They were indeed enough to make anyone sick, and Jean-Pierre, after asserting that he could not bring himself to mention them, recounted them in full detail, aided by a most active imagination, then when he had had enough of torture and murder and rape by *droit du seigneur*, fell into his usual tirade on the taxes: the one grievance that afflicted everybody, except the nobility who were mostly exempt. *Taille, gabelle, censives, terrage*—the words poured from him, then he would give Coll a glass of wine on the house, and invite him to dinner, where his wife, who had never heard of revolution and regarded its mention as a kind of masculine idiosyncrasy, gave him an excellent meal that no taxes could spoil.

"You realize," Coll told him, "that if ever the revolution comes, you'll be one of the first to swing on the nearest signpost?"

"Why the devil should I?" Jean-Pierre demanded.

"Because, my friend, you are an honest man. Revolutions have no time for honest men; they tend to cling boringly to the ideals that are swept away in the first onrush."

But this was not in Jean-Pierre's way of thinking, so being by that time a little drunk, he simply roared with laughter, slapped Coll on the shoulder and told him he was a man after his own heart; if he were not a bloody Scot he would be almost human.

And the next day Coll took up his strolling again, as if movement were the only anodyne, listened to all he could hear, totted it up in his mind and made no understandable total. And the king hunted twice a week in the Forêt de Rambouillet, visited his girls in the Parc-aux-Cerfs, where Madame Bertrand, known always as the Mother Superior, ran a special brothel for him, gambled, ate and took his pleasure from Versailles to Choisy to Fontainebleau, and then back again, scattering a few million francs by the wayside. There were clouds of pamphlets, papers and songs, and somewhere beneath the spending and the grumbling lay a most dreadful discontent, but Coll could not take it entirely seriously; it lacked oddly enough the intense, heartfelt emotion of his own small revolution, where people had given up everything for a young man they did not know.

He was walking now in a shopping street he did not know.

There was great business being done, crowds of people, and the air was filled with the sound of loud, bargaining voices and the smell of wine, spices and food. Coll pushed his way past this all, averting his eyes from the open cafés where the Parisians were sitting eating vast quantities of food, stuffing it into their mouths, wiping up the last drop of sauce with huge wedges of bread. He reflected that it might be easy to become a revolutionary after all, even for a lazy, easygoing man like himself, if revolution were based on the simple question: Why should he have what I do not? When he was newly arrived and even poorer than he was now, with no Paulette to succor him, so that for a while he did not even know where the next meal was coming from, he had one day made his way through a fashionable center where he could see the lords and ladies eating languidly what seemed to him platefuls enough for giants. In his hunger he hated them, grudged them every mouthful, wanted to push them away and gulp up the food himself. The ordinary citizen, staggering under a load of taxes, must view this kind of thing with bitter envy. Someone had said once that in France nine-tenths of the population died of hunger and one-tenth of indigestion. Coll, who until his exile had never known poverty, began to see that the queen's dinner of twenty-nine courses must foment more murder than the wicked marquis who so savagely misused his blacksmith; the one happening was presumably unique, but the other continued all the time.

At least Jean and the children would have enough to eat. Even in a country depleted by war, there was Highland mutton and fresh fish from the loch. Coll, deliberately torturing himself, tried to visualize them with him, living in some mean, small room with Jean, like Grizel, cooking potatoes over a miserable fire. It was not bearable, it was not even possible.

He could not bring himself to visualize his elegant Jean in shabby, darned clothes, growing thinner and angrier, with the children querulous for lack of proper food and warmth. Better, far better, for them to stay where they were, however much his bones ached for them—

He became aware that the noise around him had become ugly and violent. He looked up sharply, dragged from his dream.

It seemed to be a fight. The French were always fighting, the nobility with their swords killing each other for a look or a sneeze, and the people with fists and knives. He prepared to skirt round what seemed to be a struggle among three men; he was not physically aggressive by nature, and in any case, as a foreigner on sufferance, preferred to keep out of trouble. But, crossing the cobbled roadway, he could not out of sheer curiosity prevent himself from glancing back, and suddenly something in the group, with arms and legs flailing, seemed somehow familiar.

As he stared, narrowing his eyes, thinking he must be mistaken, a well-known voice yelled at him, "Coll! For Christ's sake, man!"

It was Davy. It had to be Davy, who must have been in trouble from the day he was born. Coll did not hesitate. This was not from any particular feeling of friendship, for the little man with his fighting and stealing and whoring was a confounded nuisance who did the cause of Scots refugees no good at all, but simply from an instinctive urge to join up with a compatriot in trouble.

He shoved his way through the crowd, and grabbed at Davy who was getting very much the worst of it and, fortunately perhaps, unable to reach his dirk, for both arms were held by burly Frenchmen, and he was being swung to and fro like a pendulum, screaming abuse, his short legs well off the ground. Coll swung out his fist at one of the men, and kicked the shins of the other; disconcerted by the new enemy they both turned on him, and Davy seized his opportunity to break loose. Dancing in rage, for under such circumstances he had no sense at all, his hand dived to his stocking, but Coll was having none of this, he lugged him away, and the two of them crashed through the crowd like a herd of cattle. Then they ignominiously took to their heels, though Davy tugged wildly at Coll's hand to get back into the melee, and at one point even lost his balance so that he was dragged along in the mire.

The crowd followed halfheartedly and soon abandoned the chase, but Coll was taking no chances. He continued to run with Davy furiously on the leash, until they were a couple of streets away. Then exhausted, with the sweat streaming down him, he sat down on a convenient wooden box, while Davy, scarlet with frustration, mortification and fury, swore frenziedly at him in the Gaelic, calling him a son of a whore and more besides, then seeing that Coll was unmoved, dug in his mind for further insults and finally flung at him the accusation that he had personally lost the battle of Culloden, because his regiment had been refused their rightful position and sullenly cast down their arms.

"That was the Macdonalds of Keppoch," said Coll, still breathing in gasps, "and in any case I have never believed it."

"You're a bloody Macdonald!"

"I am not," said Coll wearily, "and it would scarce matter if I were. This is neither the time nor place for clan warfare, Davy. I do not give a damn what the Macdonalds did, and neither do you. In my present state I would shake hands with

McCailein Mhor for half a dozen francs." He looked up at his compatriot who was still hopping up and down with temper, like an elderly child deprived of its sweetmeats. He burst out laughing. "Oh, for God's sake, Davy," he said, "what is all this? Do we not have enough trouble as it is for you to involve yourself in a common brawl? What is it this time? Did the shopkeeper have a pretty wife, or were you simply stealing?"

"Are you calling me a thief?" demanded Davy in a high voice, his hand stealing down to his stocking again.

"Oh, leave that damned thing alone," exclaimed Coll. "What good will it do anyone for me to end up dirked in the Faubourg St. Antoine? Of course you're a thief. You're a whoremonger and a bastard and a bloody idiot. Does that satisfy you?"

"I was not stealing," said Davy sulkily.

"Then it was a pretty wife. Was she bonnie?"

"Na! She was not worth the picking. I might have known she was no good from her wearing so few petticoats." He met Coll's ironic eye, and his sullen look vanished. He too began to laugh, clasped Coll round the shoulders to indicate the depth of their friendship, then crouched down beside him, while passersby eyed the two mad foreigners covertly, and walked well round them.

Coll shook his head at him. "One day," he said, "you'll end up in the Bastille. You'll not like that, Davy. You'll not like that at all. I believe they chain you down and starve you on a bed of straw, and serve you right for the nasty devil you are. Can't you leave the women alone?"

"They'll not leave me alone," said Davy sorrowfully.

"Sometimes," said Coll, rising painfully to his feet, for the battle had not been one-sided, and he had received several blows and kicks, "I wonder how any of us survive. You'll hang us all before you're done. You'd best come back to the Club with me and drink some wine to keep you out of mischief. Have you any money?"

"Oh, ay," said Davy, looking sideways at him with his twisted smile.

Coll suspected that the fight was not entirely to do with a pretty wife. Davy had the pickpocket's fingers; the forefinger and the next one were of the same length. No doubt one hand was up the lady's petticoats or lack of them, and the other in the husband's pocket. Davy did not do anything by halves, and he always had a surprising amount of money.

Coll said firmly, "Then you can damned well buy the wine."

"I'll buy anything for you that you want. You are a true friend," said Davy, performing one of his customary voltes-face. "Two bottles of wine. Three, if you want—"

The shopkeeper must have had excellent reason for his violence. Coll made no comment, however, and the two of them walked on, with Davy, who had recovered his temper and was now in an excellent mood, cavorting beside him, whistling at any pretty girl they passed, winking and grimacing so that some of them giggled and paused to smile back. But Coll merely tugged at his arm, thinking they had had enough drama for one day, and presently they came up to the Club, after having bought from Jean-Pierre a bottle for each of them.

There was no one there but themselves. To Coll, who had not come for two days, it was extraordinarily cheerless. There was no sign of Aeneas, there was not even Tully, sitting wineless on a barrel and reading his book.

"Where is Tully?" Coll demanded.

"That glumpy man? Oh, I don't know. I've not seen him for a long while. Perhaps he's drowned himself in the Seine," said

Davy cheerfully. He was concentrating on opening his bottle of wine. He had paid for it as he had promised. There was an undeniable mean streak in him, even when he had money; no one could call him an open-handed man. But this time perhaps he felt he owed Coll something after all. Indeed, he had produced such a sum from his pocket in the wineshop that Jean-Pierre had noticed and asked him if he had been robbing the Bourse. By tomorrow, of course, he would have nothing again, it would all be gambled away. There was never any tomorrow for Davy. He lived here as he must have lived on his native moors, taking what he could, throwing it wildly around, then sleeping rough and eating drammoch until he could steal some more.

Coll watched him as he fiddled rather inexpertly at the bottle. The graying hair indicated that he was not young, but it was impossible to tell his age; he might be anything from thirty to fifty. They all knew less of Davy than anyone else, except for his present whoredoms and adventures, both of which were certainly exaggerated. He talked enormously when he was in the mood, but gave little away; of his past, except for the knowledge that he had escaped from the hulks, they knew nothing. He was the only one of them to whom loneliness came naturally; one could not imagine Davy with a host of friends or surrounded by family. The clan loyalties that he had flung at Coll meant nothing to him whatsoever; he would as soon dirk his chief as an English soldier, and there was no friend or lover who would not be instantly sacrificed in the name of expediency.

Coll, driven as usual by curiosity, said before he could stifle the words, "And Aeneas—does he too come here no longer?" And he was about to add that he had met him a couple of days back, but did manage to check himself. It was bad enough to mention Davy's most detested enemy without involving him in Aeneas' strange, secret conspiracy.

But the name was enough. The blood rushed to Davy's face, and he slammed the bottle down with such force that Coll protested, "You'll break it—for God's sake!"

Davy instantly picked the bottle up again and examined it with tender care. They could none of them, whatever their temperaments, afford to waste something as precious as wine. Then he spoke, in the thin vicious voice that the mention of Aeneas always provoked, called him every name imaginable in a mixture of Gaelic, English and French, then suddenly checked himself, and crossed the room until he faced Coll.

"Do not trust him," he said. "Never trust him."

"Why not?" asked Coll, refusing to take this too seriously. He himself did not trust Aeneas, though he had so far no particular reason not to do so, but Davy for once sounded almost reasonable, and perhaps the little man would at last give him some excuse for his almost absurd loathing.

But he only said, "He is a bastard."

"We are all bastards here. What particular bastardry has he committed?"

But Davy would not answer this, only concentrated again on the bottle, chewing his lower lip and looking so thunderous that Coll decided to drop the matter.

Then Davy, having opened the bottle and taken a great swig of the contents, astonished him by remarking in a clear, high voice, "Did I never tell you now of my time with the English?"

"You did not," said Coll, instantly interested. Whatever his mood or state of exhaustion, he could always be roused by something as new and intriguing as this. He waited hopefully, sipping his wine, but Davy was not to be deprived of a crumb of his drama. He did not start immediately, only cleared his throat, made portentous faces, surveyed Coll through slitted lids, and made such a meal of all this that his audience at last lost all patience.

Coll exclaimed, "You behave like a lass about to give birth to her bairn. For God's sake, man, get on with it. Tell me of your time with the English. If you behaved like this with them, I am astonished they allowed you any time at all."

Davy gave him a cold look, then remarked to the ceiling, "They are dull, hot men, the English. I think myself they are not entirely human. But I'll admit that though God has not given them over-much wit or sense, they were braw bodies to be with in the hulks, for they were frighted to death of the Scots and could always be persuaded to share their rations with us. Did you know that it was the English who wished to array their hangmen in the Prince's tartan?"

"I neither know nor care," said Coll crossly. "Tell me about the hulks. You wander about like a mountain sheep."

But one might as well try to check a waterfall as Davy in full spate. The little man paid this no attention beyond a scowl, only gulped down some more wine and continued along his own way.

"They crow well enough upon their own middenhead," he said, still apparently on the subject of the English, "and they're fine with their army to protect them, but they're not people I could live with. They're brutish and slow and they have no principles at all, not at all."

Coll surveyed the principled man before him and sighed, but after all he had nothing much better to do, and Davy entertained him, mainly because he seldom believed a word he said. He lay back resignedly on the barrel, his head against the wall, and Davy, with a compelling glance as if to make sure that his audience was listening, continued.

"I'd as soon be with Keppoch's dumbie," he said. "You've heard of Keppoch's dumbie now, the wee deaf-mute who fought at Prestonpans, with not an idea in his poor soft head as to what he was fighting for, or indeed where he was?"

"Sometimes," said Coll lazily, from his recumbent position, "I think that applied to most of the Highland armies."

Davy did not answer this, probably because such considerations did not touch him. He was never a man to consider the impersonal. He had doubtless got caught up in the battle as he would always get caught up in battles, and certainly he had enjoyed the drama of it, suitably blended with blood and whisky. He drank some more of his wine, and began to talk again, somewhat in the tone of one telling a child a story, though what he related was by no means a fairy tale. The soft Highland voice pleased Coll, for it half-took him home; he listened with pleasure and only after a time began to realize what was being said.

"They took me to Inverness jail," Davy said pensively, as if he too were enjoying the reminiscence, however horrifying it was. "I mind that they handcuffed me so tight that the flesh puffed out and the iron was hid. Oh, it was sore—but then I am only a common Highlander, and these were the English. It was, 'Damn the rebel dog and throw him into prison directly.' Besides, I was a private man, not an officer. Maybe they'd have treated an officer better."

"I doubt it," said Coll.

"Ah," said Davy, enjoying himself, "but you're a gentleman."

"Am I?"

"Of course. The world is different for gentlemen."

"You've been talking to Jean-Pierre."

Davy shrugged this off. It was in any case unlikely, for his French was purely of the expedient sort, and he was besides too restless a man to sit down and talk as Coll liked to do; he always had to be up and out somewhere. Even now he could not stay still, but wandered up and down the room, bottle in hand.

"There was a deal happened," he said, "that I'd not burden your gentlemanly ears with. The English at play are a strange people, with what one might call an unusual sense of humor. And it's too long a story. I should naturally have escaped the jail, only the weather was against us all, it was English weather, it was not for Highlanders like myself. And we had not eaten, you'll mind that, Coll; we was famished and weak with it, like kittens. I did my best. I saw a friend of mine killed at my side, then I ran away. But the marshy ground hampered me, and I would have been taken there and then, if I'd not found a riderless horse thirty paces ahead. I tried to mount, but I was too weak, and if a laddie from Lochiel's regiment had not picked me up and thrown me across the horse like a loaded sack, I'd not be here drinking wine with you. I'd be a corpse like the others on Culloden Moor. So off I rode, on the high road to Fort Augustus, and there I spent the night at a public house, where they gave me oaten bread and whisky, fine fare for a starving man. It was the last good meal I was to have, for the English soldiers came and they searched the barn and dragged me out. I was lucky they did not burn me; it was what they did to a great many others. They'd not have found me either but for an iniquitous interpreter of the word of God, who considered it his holy undertaking to carry a pistol under his greatcoat, and who acted as evidence man against his own countrymen. Of course," added Davy with a self-righteous air, "he was an Episcopalian."

Coll refused to take up this theological gauntlet, but shot Davy an expressive look from his half-closed eyes, and swallowed some of his own wine.

"And then," said Davy, "it was the Tolbooth for me, and a trial—oh, a fine wee trial too—and then the hulks, with some strange island at the end of it, if I survived. I do not mind the name, but it began with an insect, an ant, and it was set in a sea a thousand miles away that they call the Caribbean. I had no fancy to go there at all, for they say all the men there are black, with two heads and a tail, and what would I do for women? I could not find it in my heart to lie with a woman with two heads. I could maybe put up with the tail, but two heads on the pillow beside me—"

He must have grown aware of a faint disturbance in his listener, for he stopped to glare at Coll suspiciously. However, Coll made no comment and managed to subdue the laughter rising in him, so he continued.

"I tried to tell myself," he said, "that if I was not there, I'd be in a skulking, starving way, lying on the side of the hills all the day, but, oh, it was hard, man, it was hard—"

Davy paused again, and in a lantern flare from the alley below Coll saw his face change. It was almost as if it had fallen into its bones. He saw at that moment that Davy was indeed an old man, whether from his years or his experiences it was impossible to say, but the youth, simulated by a mobile countenance and a constant change and flicker of expression, had vanished. It was not only the iron fetters that had pressed so savagely into the flesh.

"We was in the *Leith*," he said, "lying off Inverness. There was near two hundred of us died in the first three weeks in our ship alone." Then he fell silent, his face turned away so that Coll could no longer see it.

Coll said at last, "But you escaped."

"Aye." Then Davy's voice grew shrill and fierce. "I'm here, am I not?"

"How did you manage it?"

"I escaped."

Coll did not pursue the matter. He saw that this was Davy's reality. A flight in the heather, a turncoat clergyman, cruel fetters in the jail—all these he could make light of, tell a story about, no doubt make up a great deal that had never occurred, but the hulks, the hulks were something that not even Davy could laugh at; this was what had bitten into his bones, destroyed his youth.

Davy said presently in his former light voice, "Oh, it was not so hard for a clever laddie like me, though faith, I was scrimped for time, and at the last I was nearly betrayed by a *mouton*, a shag-faced thin fellow and a very great rogue. Of course he was a Macdonald."

This at least was something that Davy had brought with him, from some ancestral feud, the cause of which he would not even remember. No doubt if asked in some bistro to drink with a Macdonald, he would call him the son of a whore, and slam his glass into his face. Coll sighed, half amused by Davy's use of local slang. It was somehow typical of him that he should use so idly a word that signified a prison spy, when probably he would find it hard to exchange the time of day correctly.

"I sharpened his throat with my skean," said Davy in an idle way, as if this were of no consequence. "They called him Whisky, I mind that well, though I never could see why a young puppy should wear so grand a name."

"And then?" said Coll, exasperated by the gap that lay between the escape of a starving Highlander at Inverness and his arrival in Paris.

Davy only said, "Paris is not such a bad place."

"Better than Antigua? That must be your island. With the two-headed women."

"Perhaps they have two of everything else," suggested Davy, after some reflection, and it was plain that this entrancing idea almost made him change his mind, for he added with a sudden, brief guffaw of laughter, "I might have done worse than go there after all."

"But how did you get here?" persisted Coll.

"I'm not telling you," returned Davy, and he put his finger to his nose, shutting one eye, as if he were clowning a secret on the stage.

"Why the devil not? Do you think me a *mouton* too? If I were, I could do you no harm. This is ancient history."

But Davy would not answer this, only the familiar malicious look came into his face as he peered forward, saying, "And how's the lassie doing with her bairn?"

"What the hell are you talking about now?" said Coll, taken aback, for his thoughts were elsewhere.

"The poor, poor young lady! Alone here, with her man in his grave. It grieves me even to think of it. How happy I am to know that she has a fine gentleman like yourself to look after her. It must give old Tom great consolation in the other world to know that before the sod is barely turned over him, she has someone to be at her side, to act as father to the poor wee bairn."

Coll met that malevolent, malicious gaze, clenched his fists and struggled to shove his temper down. It would benefit no one to fight with Davy, and he had no wish to have his own throat sharpened, however remorseful the little man might be afterward. He said in a repressed voice, "Why do you not call on her, yourself? It would be an act of Christian charity. Do you not call yourself a Christian?"

"Are you saying a mass in my lug now?" said Davy, with a twitching grin.

"I belong to the Scottish church," returned Coll sourly.

"Ah, she'd not want to see a common laddie like me," said Davy cheerfully, as he had said before, but he did not pursue the matter, though Coll could see well enough that in the depths of his mind he was delighted to smell intrigue, even if the intrigue did not exist.

"Then she'll have to make do with a fine gentleman like me," said Coll, seeing that he must indeed visit Grizel, and deciding to do so tomorrow. He looked up into Davy's bland, wicked face. He wondered if Davy with his women ever had moments of love and affection and sincerity, if sometimes he remained with them, just to be there, to talk, to treat them as human beings. He believed that Davy would never dare be so natural. He prepared to depart. He was suddenly sick of this little man who anticked like a monkey, yet who must have undergone such horrors as the mind could scarcely comprehend; if one could not reach people, one had to let them go.

Davy did not attempt to follow Coll as he made for the door. He would probably stay there, buy some more wine and get drunk. It was the one release available to all of them, except for Tully of course, and that was his own choice. But he called after Coll, who was opening the door, "Buy the wean a pretty toy," and, digging his hand into his pocket, threw a handful of coins onto the floor. Then with barely a pause, he said in a slow, thick voice, "There was two hundred of us died. Of the scurvy, the bloody flux and the fever. Two hundred.

They did not even take the dead away, and we was too weak to throw them overboard."

And with that he turned his back on Coll, and the echo of his words was a coronach that the Prince, doubtless drinking deep or throwing furniture at Madame de Talmond's head, should have heard, perhaps occasionally did hear in the angry, self-pitying recesses of his mind.

Coll picked up the money. It was not very dignified, but the sum was quite large, and he could not, on a matter of pride, deprive Grizel of what she so sorely needed. But Davy, whose moods changed like shadows on the loch, had not yet done with him. He called out again, in that sharp, inquisitive way of his, when nosing out something disreputable, "That quean of yours—"

This was too much for Coll, who would at that moment have risked a dirk in his belly for the pleasure of punching Davy's head, but Davy did not give him time to attack, even verbally, for he went on, "I saw her with your friend, Aeneas."

This so astounded Coll that his temper sank again. He no longer wondered how it was that Davy knew about Paulette at all, for it seemed that everyone here knew about everyone else. He was, however, amazed that Aeneas should even speak to such a woman. In his strange, remote, almost sexless way, it was hard to visualize him with any woman, but if he had one, it would surely be some highly perfumed court lady, not this plain, poor, common little drab, who knitted her lovers into a length of wool that she unpicked when she had done with them.

But he could not argue on this with Davy. He said nothing, only went down the stairs, preparing to go back to his own room. Only the odd fact nagged at his mind, and once again he had the uneasy feeling that they were all watched; they led their isolated, disoriented lives with loneliness but without privacy. It was as if resentfully they intertwined with each other, unable to let go.

In his room that evening he forgot about this, and wrote to Jean. He did not respond to the postscript that had so distressed him. He had somehow pushed it out of his mind; it lodged somewhere with the Loch Arkaig treasure that might in the end bring him home.

"We have all become old women," he wrote to her. "Perhaps men without women become womanish in self-defense. We do nothing but gossip interminably, become malicious at each other's expense, we talk too much, we bore each other and ourselves, and often we are at each other's throats. Yet we cannot do without each other, and every time we swear never to meet again, we reappear at the Club as if nothing has happened. Then it starts all over again. . . . My life, how do the infantry do? Bid Amy from me not to trouble her head overmuch with beaux, but to read history, use, exercise and endeavor a contented mind without bigotry. . . ."

So much to say, and all of it not to be said. The component parts of my life can none of them be set down. I cannot tell Jean of Paulette, she could not understand, she would be revolted. I cannot tell Jean of Grizel, she would be jealous. I cannot tell Jean in detail how we brawl, drink, talk bawdry, fly into tantrums like the bairns and stamp our feet upon the ground. I cannot, oh, dear God, say I may be home again, see her again, see the bairns again, see my native land.

My native land.

"I would like some more books, if this is possible, on religion and philosophy and history. I am a little difficulted at the present time, and in any case it is never easy to find English books here, though I can now read French with comparative ease, and sometimes find volumes that interest me. . . . I miss you, dear, dearest Body, but who knows, perhaps one day soon we will meet again."

Sometimes I believe Sheridan, the foolish Irishman, when he said, "All is over. We shall never come this way again."

"Write to me, my dear Life. . . . My service to all friends. . . . Embrace the bairns for me. . . . Your affectionate husband while I breathe. . . ."

While I breathe. Sometimes I wish I could stop breathing forever, for each breath is such pain, such loss, such bitter memory. If only I could hope. If only I could know. My dear, dearest Body—

All is over. We shall never come this way again.

Chapter 5

COLL SET off to see Grizel the next morning. It was a blazing July day, the sanded streets tawny, harsh and stinking in the heat, the light so dazzling that it made him blink, the roadway filled with people who could not endure their sweaty rooms. Perhaps it was the heat that made him turn down a side passage, to come once more into the cemetery where he and Grizel had buried Tom, or perhaps it was the thought that this might give the poor young creature a little pleasure. Whatever the reason he pushed the little iron gate open and came up the rough stony path, to where Tom's grave lay in the corner.

The long, green grass that could not have been cut for months gave the place an air of coolness, or perhaps that was due to death, marked everywhere in the uneven humps that reminded him of Culloden Moor after the battle; there was certainly no more respect or ceremony. Yet this was not entirely so, for on Tom's grave lay a bunch of flowers, and they were fresh, they must have been placed there that morning. Flowers were cheap in Paris in the summertime, but for a girl who lacked a sou to buy herself bread, this must have been a sacrifice indeed, and Coll would have been willing to wager that this happened every day, even if she had to find someone to do the errand for her.

He stood there for a while, looking down at what remained of Tom Ryder, a tumulus, with the green already frothing round the edges where the earth had been dug up. The bright pink and red of the roses gleamed upon it. It was peaceful as graveyards are peaceful; the sun glinted on the grass, the birds sang in the shadowy trees at the side. It was an oasis from the world. Only Tom had left the world altogether, it would never trouble him again.

Coll moved slowly, almost reluctantly, away. He glanced back, with a twinge of conscience, at the roses. Davy's money rattled in his pocket, he was for once almost rich, he could surely bring Grizel a fairing. The conscience was for both Jean and Grizel; the one would certainly resent a present bought for another woman, and the other might feel herself neglected, for he should surely have come to see her again the very next day, instead of waiting about so long, doing nothing.

He knew, however, deep within himself, that Grizel would not feel neglected at all, it was simply not in her nature. She would never consider herself entitled to attention or a gift from anyone. And this knowledge gave him the final impetus; he stopped at one of the market stalls and bought a few flowers and some grapes. It was so long since he had bought anything for a woman that he felt self-conscious, especially as the young girl at the stall beamed at him, hoped his *belle amie* would like the gift and be kind to him. It made him feel very much the foreigner, entirely the Scot; a Frenchman would have joked back, but he merely went red and could think of nothing to say.

The old limmer—what was her name now, Madame Thierry—was inevitably waiting for him, or so it seemed, for as he stepped up to the entrance, she instantly appeared in her doorway.

He wished her good morning, not wishing to create any kind of situation, but she was obviously a woman who thrived on scenes, for she at once burst into a frenzied tirade. Coll, whose mind ran on revolution these days, could see her only too clearly screaming abuse at some unhappy victim, or summoning neighbors to apprehend a poor devil on the run.

She glowered at the bunch of roses in his hand. They were already wilting in the heat, and any real gallant would have done better by his girl.

"So you're still after her, are you?" she said, nodding violently, her eyes flickering over him. "I thought you'd left her by this time. You look the kind who would. Not that I've anything to say for her, no-good *salope* she is, with her poor husband just in his grave—"

Coll choked back what he longed to say. It would only make things worse for Grizel if he returned the abuse. He was bewildered that the old she-devil should be so malevolent, but then women were entirely unpredictable, though he had always believed that in emergencies they banded together to help.

He pushed past her, in silence. She shouted after him, "I hope you've got her rent, at least. If you haven't, she'll be out on the streets where she belongs, I can tell you that, my fine gentleman. I'm not a charitable institution. I don't take in people for free, especially sluts like that one. Soon, thank God, we'll have your kind where they belong; there's no place for people like you coming into our country, eating our food, living on our money, and making mischief for us fathering bastard brats—"

Coll, though he had heard this before, was as always astonished by such vituperation. But his temper, never stable, could take no more of this. He rounded on her, cutting her speech off with such violence that she was instantly quiet and backing away. He was of course a big man and she of small stature, but he realized now that she was all noise; one threatening gesture from a dwarfish child, and she would run a mile, crying out no doubt that she was a poor weak woman and he had no right to bully her.

He was pleased by this. The thought of her insulting Grizel aroused a satisfied cruelty in him. He would have liked to hit her. He demanded of her, "Are you married, old woman?" and he raised his voice so that it pealed down the dark corridor.

She went quite pale. She really was a poor sort of thing. "My man is dead," she began, but Coll cut her short.

"I am not surprised," he said. "You'd kill off anyone. It's a pity he didn't beat you to death. I hope he did. It's the only treatment for old bitches like you."

She cried out in a gasp, backing into her doorway. "You be careful. I've two sons. They'll make mincemeat of you if you dare speak to me like that again. They don't like foreigners either, taking the bread out of our mouths—"

Coll, entertained by the odd picture this presented, was beginning to feel like the Red Etin, the fairy-tale ogre who once long ago made Amy wake up, screaming. He advanced still further on Madame Thierry, saying in a kind of roar, "Where are they? Bring them out! I'll deal with them—" hoping in a spasm of caution that two hulking youths would not suddenly make their appearance. But no one did, and the old woman merely shrieked in a surprisingly feminine way, slammed the door in his face and—he could hear the rattle—shot the bolt.

Coll, now rather above himself with the general drama of it all, bellowed after her, as the Red Etin would have done, "I'll ding you and dang you with a silver wand," then burst out laughing a little hysterically. But it was not so amusing after all, as he instantly realized while continuing on his way upstairs. On the second floor he began to see clearly what a fool he had been, on the third he knew it, and on the fourth began rather grimly to consider where he could possibly find Grizel a new room. Madame Thierry would probably not let her stay another week after this, would even perhaps, once he was out of the way, go upstairs and throw the wretched girl's belongings down into the hall.

I am a damned idiot, thought Coll, very ashamed of himself, then, what with his temper and the awareness of his own imbecility, found that he had rushed up the stairs at such a speed that he had to pause to regain his breath; if he arrived in this gasping state, the girl might imagine something was seriously wrong.

He stood there. His heart and breathing steadied. Then he heard it. It was unmistakable. He had already heard it twice in his life before. Then it had pricked his blood with an unbelievable joy and excitement. It had been the peak moment of his existence. Now he listened with excitement mingled with dismay. He muttered aloud, "Oh, my God." His hand went to his mouth as if somehow the sound had issued from himself.

It was a thin, mewling cry. For all its thinness it was so penetrating that the old devil downstairs might well have heard it. Coll whispered, "Oh, my God," again, then, forgetting everything in his agitation, pushed open the door without knocking.

Grizel was sitting by the bed. The baby lay in a wicker basket in front of her, and she was gently rocking it with her foot. Coll could see the fists flailing, caught a brief glimpse of a puckered, wrinkled face.

At his abrupt entrance, Grizel leaped to her feet. There was such a look of apprehension on her face that he saw at once that his own fears on her behalf were entirely justified. She could not continue living in such an awareness of fear. Never mind the fact that women were supposed to be kind to the young and defenseless, to love babies by a natural instinct; Madame Thierry, for all she had borne two sons herself, was plainly of the kind to devour infants for breakfast, and this would not do, it would not do at all.

He was overcome for a moment by an almost unbearable emotion. The force of it confused Grizel with Jean, transposed the abominable room onto his own airy, sweet-smelling home, confused the ugly noises below with those of wind and water and gently swaying trees. He stepped forward, took her into his arms, and held her against him, his hands caressing her head and shoulders. Then, realizing what he was doing, he instantly released her, stammering apologies, then saying, "I didn't know. I did not know."

She was to him an extraordinary girl, like no one he had ever met in his life. She seemed to find nothing strange in this wild emotion from a comparative stranger; she seemed in no way outraged or offended. She moved back from him a little unsteadily as if she were still weak, then said in that odd, deep voice of hers, "I am glad you have come, Coll. I am so very glad."

He said, deeply ashamed, "I should have come before."

She smiled at him. She looked very ill, and thinner, if it were possible, than ever, but the smile was a sweet and warming one, the smile bestowed on errant menfolk, the man returning drunk, the man who had neglected her, the man who had forgotten to do everything she had asked of him. It was not—the thought flared through his mind, then vanished—the kind of smile he had ever received from Jean.

"It's of no matter," she said, then with a sideways glance from the fine eyes, "I doubt you'd be much use at a confinement."

He said pompously, "I have already attended two."

"As midwife?" said Grizel, then the baby wailed again, and she bent over to pick it up in her arms.

He gave her an embarrassed smile, and shook his head. He thought angrily how different the circumstances were. Jean had had every attention possible, with a physician fetched from Edinburgh to be in constant attendance, and her mother always at her side. The babies had been born in a warm, comfortable room, with himself waiting frantically outside, drinking too much whisky, and going white at every cry behind the closed door. And the babies had been beautiful, both of them, pink and strapping and bursting with life. He looked at the infant now on Grizel's knee, a minute, wizened doll, the plainest thing he had ever seen, skinny, monkey-faced, with great purple shadows under its eyes. He could not quite understand why his heart was performing such strange antics within him, but he said in a sudden gasp, "Let me hold it."

"Her, please," said Grizel. "We are not to be called 'it,' are we, my darling?" She rose to place the baby in his arms, where it lay, not crying now, the cloudy, unfocused eyes moving past him, the fingers twisting and clenching like little tentacles, the smell of sour milk coming to his nostrils. It seemed to him to weigh nothing. His one hand could have cradled it. The pinched face was that of an old, old woman, but despite all this, Coll was overcome with a passion of love that almost hurt, it was unprecedented and unexpected. The dirt and squalor and barrenness of the past two years receded so that for the moment he felt that he was once again at home. Then he came to his senses, and handed the child back to Grizel almost brusquely, ashamed of the weakness that melted his bones, determined to bring himself back to normality.

He said in a harsh, matter-of-fact voice, not thinking that his face had already betrayed him, the tenderness in his eyes, "I should of course have come before. I know that. There is no point in my apologizing. There is no excuse for me. But I had no idea, all the same. When was this child born? Are you all right? Was there someone to help you?"

"Oh, yes," said Grizel. She looked up into the face that had now settled into determined lines, the face of a man not to be moved by sentimentality. She gave him a half smile. She said, "He was the strangest man, but he was very kind to me. I have never met him before in my life. I don't know how he knew of me. It was you, Coll, wasn't it? I knew that, though he never said so. He arrived. He just opened the door. He called me Mary, though I think he must have known who I was. Even when I told him my name, he still called me Mary all the time. Once he cried. The tears poured down his poor face. I remember that, which is strange, for it was all very bad for me, and I was so sure I was going to die. He told me quite sternly that I must pull myself together, I was not going to die at all, it would be all right, it must be all right. And—" She broke off for a moment, then went on steadily, "It was all right, was it not? We are here, Henny and I, perhaps not so much of us, and we are poor, thin things, I have to admit, but we are here, all the same, and that is the one thing that matters."

"So Tully did come after all," said Coll, half to himself. He reflected briefly on the strange man called Dr. Tullideph, who had done so ill and suffered so terribly, and reappeared to help Tom Ryder's widow. Then he said, "What did you call her? Henny? What kind of name is that?"

"It's Henrietta. That was Tom's mother's name, and I think he would like her to be called that. But it is too vast a name for such a poor wee scrap, so I call her Henny. I doubt if she could carry any more syllables."

Coll said slowly, "I am glad Tully came."

"He never told me who he was. He said he was a doctor, that was all. A tall man, with no teeth at all, poor creature."

"That is our Tully," said Coll rather grimly.

"I believe he is a good man," said Grizel. "And I know he is a good doctor. Without him I could never, never have survived. We would both be dead now, Henny and I. And," she said with one of the rapid changes that he was beginning to see characterized her, and speaking in a rousing voice that came strangely from the frail body, "I daresay you'll believe that I wanted to die, that I longed in my heart to join my dear Tom, but that is not so at all. I am by no means such a fool as you appear to believe."

"I never said any such thing," began Coll, bewildered, but she interrupted him.

"You looked it. Do you think I have no eyes in my head? I could see it in your face, as plain as plain. You were saying to yourself, 'She's a poor thing, she's wishing she was dead, the bairn and all. She thinks of nothing but Tom. All she wants is to lie beside him in the graveyard.'"

Coll gave it up. Women were impossible creatures, they

created drama out of nothing, and Grizel was obviously more dramatic than most. She was speaking now with such ferocity that it was as if he were attacking her, instead of standing there, saying nothing. He watched her in a mixture of exasperation and resignation, compelled to accept the extraordinary remarks attributed to him.

She went on, "Well, I can assure you that you are entirely wrong. You do not even begin to understand me—"

"I'd never deny that," said Coll, but she paid him no attention.

"I do not wish to die, and I do not wish my poor, wee Henny to die either. Tom would not want it. Tom would wish us to go on living, and that is what I propose to do."

"I am delighted to hear it," said Coll, then saw that despite her fierce voice the tears were creeping down her cheeks. He suddenly remembered that she was a very sick girl, after all, only a few days away from a shocking confinement, and he came over to her, to place his hand on her shoulder. He said gently, "Don't quarrel with me, Grizel. I am a foolish and clumsy man, but I mean no harm. Of course you are not going to die. I should not allow it. But I do not think you should stay here, with that old she-devil downstairs. I must find another room for you. Perhaps you could have mine for a time, and I could sleep in the Club. It is not much better than this, but my landlady is a kindly soul, she would not ill-use you. I have money here for you, given me by wee Davy—oh, and the flowers and fruit are for you too. They are poor stuff, I'm afraid, but it was the best I could do."

She took the flowers in a wondering kind of way, as if it were a long time since she had received such a gift. She said at last in a muted voice, "I believe I can still stay here. Aeneas is finding money for me, and he says he will pay my rent, so madame will not be so angry with me. And the man you call Tully—he is a good man, Coll, and I think he must have suffered, he has the look on him—he has arranged for one of the sisters from the convent to call on me, and she comes every day with milk for us, for I have so little and I cannot bear Henny to go hungry. She don't weigh enough. She should take as much nourishment as possible." She blew her nose at this point and seemed to have recovered her composure. Then she said, "Your doctor tells me he can never come again. Why is that? Do you know? I should so like him to come, if only to thank him for both of us. You cannot imagine how kind he was."

Coll was finding this difficult to equate with his image of Dr. Tullideph who, from his personal knowledge of him, seemed to live so isolated an existence, shut away in his own despair, but he could not explain this to Grizel. He said after a pause, "He is, as you said yourself, a strange man. I cannot answer you. I don't know the answer. I only know that you are the first person he has considered worth the helping since I first met him. He seldom talks to any of us, he has no friends, as far as I know. He goes home to his own room every night, and seems to spend his life there, reading. Perhaps you have done more for him than he for you. I did not think he ever thought of anyone but himself."

"You see," said Grizel, "you judge people too quickly. I saw at once how good he was. But I still do not understand why he don't come back. If only to see Henny. I should like you to do something for me, Coll."

"What is that?"

"Go and see him. Thank him for me."

Coll hesitated. He had never called on Dr. Tullideph in his life. He did not believe he would be welcome. In any case, they none of them called on each other; it was almost an unwritten rule in the Club. He had no idea where Davy lived, if he had a room at all, and as for Aeneas, he lived a life remote from the rest of them. He had only called on Tom once, on a matter of emergency. They had no money for entertaining, their dwellings for the most part were simply places to sleep in, and all their social contact took place above the wineshop. He said slowly to Grizel, "I am not sure if that would be wise. He is a solitary man. He is lonelier than any of us. But of course, if you really wish it—"

"I do. Oh, please, Coll, I do."

"Very well. Now"—his voice grew brisker—"I will go out and get some food for you, with Davy's money. I daresay it's ill-gotten, almost certainly stolen, but I think our consciences will support it. And I hope that old beldam soon has her rent. She seems to me quite crazed in her wits, and I don't like to think of her bursting in on you." He stopped, hesitating, then he said very quickly, "Don't be angry with me, Grizel, but I must ask you this. Would you not consider going home, if we could raise the fare for you?" He saw that she was about to answer violently, and held up his hand to silence her. "No. Wait a minute. Hear me out. What I have to say is only common sense, and I believe you are a sensible girl. After all, there is no attainder against you. I run the risk of the gallows if I return, but you do not, there is no danger. I know your parents were against your marriage, but now with Tom gone, and the wee thing here, surely they would welcome you with open arms. Are you not the only child? I cannot believe that any mother in the world would refuse to take you back."

He stopped. He saw that Grizel had gone very white.

She spoke quietly enough. Her hand moved out to cradle the baby's head. She said, "No, Coll. Never. Oh, what you say is sensible, I can see that. It is perfectly true that I could go home tomorrow. I do not think my mother would refuse me, and I am certain they would welcome Henny. As for my father, he is a poor, silly man, he talks too loud, but he is not cruel or unnatural. But I cannot go home. Can you not understand? They hated Tom. They threw me out because of him. They called him wicked names, and if we had not run away so quick, they would have set the English soldiers on him to flush him out. I know he was their enemy, but he was my man and my lover and my husband, Henny's father, and what they did against him, they did against me, and that is something I can never forget. Perhaps one day I may return to Scotland. But not to my home, it is my home no longer." The deep voice roughened. "Tom is dead, Coll. Tom is dead. And for me, they are dead too. I will never see them again. What they said against him, they said against me, and now he will always lie between us. You don't understand, do you? I can see that in your face."

He said, a little helplessly, "No. Frankly, I do not. I think you should consider the bairn. What sort of life will it be for her, or indeed for you? What sort of life is it for all of us? It's no life at all, and well you know it, but we have no choice, and you have. And you're a woman. It's worse for a woman." Then he thumped his fist down on the back of the chair. The baby, frightened by the noise, began to cry again, and Coll looked instantly contrite, saying, "I did not mean to disturb her. I'm sorry." Then he went on, "But you must listen to me, just for this once, and I swear I'll never mention the subject again. Think of Henny. If you take her back, she'll have proper food and warmth and care. You cannot give her these things. You cannot, Grizel. Oh, we'll all look after you as well as we can, we'll see to it that you don't starve—but look at this room.

Look at it! Is this a place for a young child, a child born too soon that is weak and small? Is it a place for you? You have no flesh on your bones, girl, you need the care too, and there's none of us can give it you, however much we want to. We do not have the money or the means, we are too badly off ourselves. You must go home. You must. Swallow your pride, Grizel, for the babe's sake, if not for your own. When you are strong enough, go back to Scotland. We'll find the money for your fare, if we have to knock some rich old man on the head. Go back where you belong. For Christ's sake!" cried Coll, in a fury of desperation. "If I could go, do you think you'd see my heels for dust? Why, lass, I'd be away this very instant, getting myself to the coast, jumping onto the nearest packet, whether they wanted me or not—"

She said sorrowfully, "I cannot go, Coll."

"You're a damned, thrawn, obstinate bitch!"

"Yes. I am all that. But I cannot go. And I think in your heart you understand."

He did and he did not. Deep within him he thought that he might act in the same way. Yet it was impossible for him to accept that someone who could go home would not. The thought of Scotland made him sick with longing, and here was this ridiculous girl with pride her only embargo, staying of choice in this stinking hole, where the child might easily die, where she in her weakened condition might die, herself. The whole business made him so angry that he longed to shake her.

He said in a heavy voice, "I cannot prevent your being a fool. But I do not understand, I do not understand at all."

"Don't be angry with me," said Grizel.

"I am not angry!" Then the sound of his own loud voice

caused an unwilling smile to tug at his lips. He said, "Did you argue like this with Tom?"

Then she smiled too. "Most of the time!"

He sighed. What could he do with her? His eyes moved as if magnetized to the baby, now quiet again; she was making faces, sucking her toothless gums, and a little balloon of dribble trickled onto her chest. He thought he had never seen an uglier, more miserable child, and again the love surged up within him, so that he could have given up his life to protect this wretched scrap who would scarcely survive the winter, unless enough money could be found to provide warmth, food and clothing.

His own vulnerability made him angry again, and he turned to Grizel, speaking in a quick, loud voice.

"What sort of life do we lead?" he asked her. "We are in a kind of no-man's-land. There is no past for us that we dare recall, and no future we dare contemplate. We are landless, we belong to no country. We just live from day to day, there is nothing else to do." Then he forgot his tirade. He wheeled round on Grizel, his hand descending on her wrist. "You have the sight. You told me so. Will we ever go home again? Tell me. You must know."

But she shook her head violently. "Oh, I never prophesy the future. I don't want to. I would be afraid."

"This once. Surely you can tell me."

"No, Coll. You should know, you're a Highlander too, that people who have the sight are afraid of it, they never use it deliberately. It just comes. It just happens that sometimes one knows."

"Don't you know now?"

"I don't want to." She began to cry again, as if her weakness were such that she could not control her tears. She sobbed, "The answer might be never, and I could not bear it. Oh, I do so want to be home, I do so want to be home—"

He gave it up. He said sadly, touching her hand as he did so, "You are the most impossible girl I have ever met. There is no reason in women—I don't know what to make of you. We all want what we cannot have, but you want what you can have, yet you do not take it." Then an idea struck him, and he thought he would try yet once more. "Do you think Tom would wish this? Don't you think Tom would take you by the scruff of your silly neck and say, 'Go home and don't be a damned fool.' He was never lacking in sense, after all. And you are. My God, you are."

She did not respond as he expected. But then Grizel, as he was beginning to learn, never did. She smiled again, almost contemptuously, though the tears were still on her cheeks. "Do you really think," she said, "you know my Tom better than myself? He was as proud as the devil, Tom. He never forgot and he never forgave. I at least do forgive. But he would never want me to go back to people who threw me out. He would understand well enough why I am staying here. And you must try to understand too, Coll. Please try."

Coll did not answer, only extended his hand to Henny, who instinctively clutched it in a grip extraordinary for someone of her size.

Grizel watched the pair of them, then said, "You like children."

"I have two of my own."

"Tell me about them."

He began a little self-consciously; then as the words took him back to where he always belonged, his voice eased and softened. Amy, he told her, was ten, already a young madam with an eye for the lads, pretty, self-willed, adept at getting her own way. Donald was more like himself, a plodding boy, though sweeter-natured, bullied a little by Amy who adored him, but insisted on keeping him in order. And then away now, with the waters of the loch rippling in the breeze, the trees sighing, the clouds scudding over the hills, he began to recount stories of them, what they had said: the silly sayings of children, so foolish to outsiders, so clever and endearing to the parents. He described the mischief they got up to, their intelligence, their adroitness, their love for their mother, their disarming disobedience that he could never find it in his heart to punish.

And Henny slept, and Grizel listened, her face sad and compassionate, until at last Coll broke off, saying in a shamefaced way, "How tedious I must be. Forgive me. When I was young and a bachelor, I found fond fathers a dead bore, talking all the time of their nasty infants, recounting their pretty sayings. I see I am become the same. These things are of no possible interest to anyone else. Only," he added ruefully, "it is so long since I have seen them, and to talk of them makes me feel a little as if I am at home again."

Then for a while he was silent. He did not mention Jean, and Grizel, as he was compelled to notice, did not do so either. He sat there, half in this wretched room, half at home, while Grizel fed the baby, then set about preparing a meal. He watched her vaguely, not fully taking in what she was doing, then suddenly coming to his senses, exclaimed, "I trust you are not cooking for me. You must have so little to spare, and I am going out in a moment to buy you more food and perhaps pay some of the rent. That will calm the old devil's temper, if nothing else."

She answered quietly, "Of course I am cooking for you.

Aeneas brought me in some meat and some money too. Do you not trust me as a cook?"

He protested, "But you are not well enough."

"Oh, I'm hardy," said Grizel, and he dared say no more, though he thought she looked as if a breath would knock her over. And presently they shared the casserole she had prepared, and a great peace came upon him. It was agreeable to sit here in a woman's company, with the baby sleeping in the cradle. It was true that he often ate with Paulette, but that was no comparison, and his own meals were either such things as bread and sausage or eaten in cheap bistros, badly served and unappetizing.

He helped her clear away. "I am a good maidservant," he said, rolling up his shirt sleeves. He saw that she was ashen with exhaustion, but he was beginning to know her a little, and he made no comment. Afterward, when the washing-up was done, he said, "I'll call on the doctor, if that is what you want me to do. But I fancy he will be coming again. As you said, he'll want to see the baby, and besides you still need care and attention."

"I have been thinking about it," said Grizel. "I don't think he will come. I don't think I shall ever see him again."

"But that's absurd. What kind of doctor is this, not to follow his patient's progress?" And at that moment Coll hated Dr. Tullideph, who had behaved briefly like the physician he was trained to be, and a human being into the bargain, but who was now apparently retreating once more into his fastness.

She said, "I have the feeling that none of us will really see him again, at least not—oh, it is hard to explain." Then she said self-defensively as, he was beginning to know, was her way, "I daresay you think I am foolish, that perhaps I believe I have the sight more than I do, and it is true, I know nothing about him, though Tom mentioned the name once to say that he never touched the drink and was a little crazed in his wits. But I believe he came to me because he was in some way driven, though I shall never know the reason, and that to deliver my baby and save both our lives was of enormous importance to him. I do not know why he called me Mary, perhaps she was someone he loved—oh, I cannot say and, when he was here, I was too ill to care, but I cannot forget the look on his face, I have never seen anything like it; it was somehow as if he were defying death, as if this were a kind of mission for him. No doubt," said Grizel in her most practical tone, "you think me silly to talk in such a way."

Coll did not think her silly, and he could have explained the matter to her, but he did not do so; he did not think Dr. Tullideph would want it, and moreover Grizel was hardly strong enough for such a story.

He said, "You say none of us will see him again. You surely don't think he is going to kill himself?"

"No, I don't think that," said Grizel, as if considering the matter, "though there are more ways of self-murder than rope and pistol. But I believe he has done what he had to do, and now he will just go away and not trouble about anyone or anything anymore. I doubt he'll want to see you, Coll, but I should still like you to call on him. And don't forget your coat this time. I have mended it as well as I can, though there was not very much I could do."

"We are all as shabby as rats," said Coll. He fastened up his shirt sleeves and slipped the jacket on. It was neatly sewn, every button was tight, the lining was again in order and there was a patch on the right elbow. It seemed to him as good as new, and he said so. He went on, "I'll be back tomorrow, and I'll bring in more food for us. Are they going to go on paying you Tom's pension? If not, and if you'll not go home, what are you going to do? I'll help as much as I can, of course, but we're none of us rich."

"I shall find myself work," said Grizel. She had Henny in her arms and was rocking her to and fro, while the baby wailed fretfully as if not caring overmuch for the world into which she had been flung too soon.

"Work!" repeated Coll derisively. "What sort of work can you do, may I ask?"

She gave him a look. She made a contemptuous noise. She might be thin, pale and weak, but nothing plainly would daunt her spirit to the day she died, and even then, no doubt, she would make some final protest. Coll grinned at her, saying, "When they at last manage to nail you down in your coffin, my lass, you'll be telling them how to do it, and hammering on the lid if they ignore you."

She shrugged this away. She said, "What sort of work can I do, indeed! What do you think women do with their time? I suppose you imagine we just lie languidly on our beds looking pretty for you, without so much as a hand's turn. The washing, I suppose, does itself, like the cooking and the mending, the gathering of the firewood, perhaps the hens milk the cows, and the cows feed the hens. We do not all, you know, have a flock of servants around us, though of course in your rich home with your fine rich wife, you are all accustomed to doing nothing. Why—"

Coll was trying to calm her down, but she paid him no attention.

"I was not brought up to languish in my room, putting stuff on my face," she went on with an air of pride. "It was I who ran the farm and did the housework too. I doubt any man could have bettered me. Oh, I daresay the grand ladies wash their hands in milk to keep them white, swoon at the merest exertion and sit there to be waited on, but I was brought up to look after myself, and others too. Of course I shall work. I shall do sewing for some fine French madame, who's doubtless no better than she should be, and I shall wash for her too, to keep her clean and sweet. Perhaps I can look after her bairns who probably never see their mama, for that, so they tell me, is the way of society. I swear I'll make a better job of it all than any duchess. Work, indeed! I've worked since the day I was born, and I'll work till the day I die."

She stopped, from lack of strength. She had gone very white again. She met Coll's eye, smiled weakly at him, and sat down quickly as if she could no longer remain upright.

He nodded at her. "I'll not argue with you," he said. "Faith, I'd not dare! But now I'll tell you something, my Grizel. You shall work as much as you please, for it would be an army needed to stop you, but I too am capable of some small exertion, and during this fine speech of yours—you should be in politics, girl, that is plainly your métier, for in politics they do nothing but talk—it seemed to me that I too could work, and that is what I'm going to do, as soon as I can find employment."

She looked so shocked that he burst out laughing. "Why," he said, "what kind of a world is this? Must only women work? You don't think much of me, if I am expected to sit with folded hands while you half-kill yourself to keep me alive."

She said in a faint voice, "But you are a gentleman."

"Ah, God!" exclaimed Coll, made a despairing gesture, then in a genuine fury, "I am a gentleman! What does that mean? I am of good Highland stock, and so are you. I daresay my ancestors were crofters like your own, and I daresay they stole cattle and murdered each other just like everybody else. Look at these, Grizel. Look at these—" He extended his hands to her, palm upwards. "Have they been washed in milk? They've sewn my buttons on—"

"Very badly, if I may say so," said Grizel, recovering herself.

"You may not say so. What impudence! I can sew a button on as well as the next; the only thing is that most of the time I forget to do so. These hands have laundered my linen and cooked my meals. They are as good as yours, and a great deal stronger. Let us have no more of this nonsense. If you can work, ma'am, so can I. Jean-Pierre, who owns our Club, will give me a job. He talks enough revolution to hang us all, he'll not dare to refuse employment to a lazy, no-good son of the upper classes like myself. When you next visit us to introduce us to young Henny, when she's a little stronger, you will see me in the wineshop, opening bottles with the best. That at least is one thing I'm fully qualified to do. It'll not bring me in a fortune, but a few francs here and there are not to be despised. Even by a gentleman."

But Grizel, speaking in a firm voice as if to end the argument, only said, "It is not right."

"You defeat me," said Coll. He gazed at her in honest bewilderment. It was true enough, as he had to admit, that he had never worked in his life at a fee'd employment. But then there had been no need. There had always been enough money, there had always been servants. As tacksman he had walked his lands, keeping an eye on things here and there, often turning his hand to a crofter's job, because it was his own place, because there was nothing degrading in honest work. He believed that he could have run a small farm with the utmost ease; like Grizel he had milked his cows, fed his hens, tended his crops. But he had no academic qualifications, and naturally he had never considered working in a shop, it would have been ridiculous. Now it seemed to him, in his new life, quite extraordinary that he had never had to earn his living, and even more extraordinary that Grizel should think nothing of working herself, yet be shocked at the idea that he too could go out to earn money.

"I think," he told her, "I am becoming a revolutionary."

But this did not interest her; she would never have heard the rumbling, grumbling complaints that rolled through Paris. She said, "You do not need to work. I am sure I can earn enough for Henny and me, even enough to give you a dinner. When she is stronger, I daresay I can persuade the sisters to look after her during the day. They are very kind. I do not see any difficulty at all. I know I am a little weak now, but that is only natural, and I shall recover fast, I always do. I am very healthy, even if I do not look it. Why, in a week's time you'll probably not recognize me."

He looked at the thin face with the bones almost showing through, so pale and luminous was the skin. He looked at the trembling arms that cradled Henny so lovingly, and saw that her skirt was gathered in at the waist with pins as if without them it might fall to the ground. He wanted at that moment to hug her and shake her, but he did neither, only made a stern face at her as if she were Amy in a tantrum, and went toward the door.

"I'll bell the cat," he said. "I'll pay that old beldam some of her rent to keep her quiet. I'll be back tomorrow."

Grizel asked suddenly, as his hand was on the latch, "Who is that strange woman who is always knitting?"

Coll stopped dead. The easy color that always shamed him rushed to his cheeks. It was the last question he expected to hear from her. He had in his usual fashion simply pushed

Paulette out of his mind. It was not an episode suitable for Grizel's ears, and in any case he had decided not to see her again. He saw no reason to have a conscience about this. Paulette must be accustomed to men appearing and disappearing in her life; she could never have believed that this would prove a permanent liaison. This extraordinary reappearance bewildered him.

He stammered, like some young boy caught in misdoing, "What do you mean?"

"Perhaps you do not know her," said Grizel, and fortunately for him Henny stirred at this moment, so she bent her head and did not see his confusion. "I thought you might have seen her. She always carries her knitting with her, I have never seen her without it. She is a friend of Madame Thierry's, and I have met her several times. She is very strange, but she is not unkind. She came up after the baby was born to bring me some soup."

Coll was left with nothing to say. He could not believe Paulette capable of a disinterested kindness; it did not fit in with her character. But he was chiefly dismayed to know that she was friendly with that abominable concierge, and once again he had the unpleasant conviction that he was in some way being besieged; first Aeneas and now Paulette, they seemed in some incomprehensible way to hem him in.

He came down the stairs, resolved to avoid the old woman. He was in a good humor which he felt she might destroy. His last words to Grizel had been, "I like arguing with you. I have not argued with so strong-minded a lass for a long, long time." This had astonished her into silence, which made him laugh; he was still smiling to himself as he arrived at the hall.

Madame Thierry was standing at her door. He prepared to brush past her. But to his amazement she was smiling—it was something of a gargoyle's smile, fit to frighten children into hysterics but it was a smile of a kind—and, as he gazed at her in bewildered dislike, she said, "Why not come in, monsieur, and have a glass of wine with me?"

He was too taken aback to think of an excuse for refusing. She had after all, barely an hour past, shrieked abuse at him and Grizel. He should have shaken his head and gone on, but the pause gave her her opportunity, and in some strange, incomprehensible way he found himself inside her room; his curiosity was such that he was compelled to stand there, staring around him.

It was very much what might have been expected; he had been inside these bourgeois French homes before. Madame lived a cozy life, though the bobbles and bows and drapes and frills would have driven him mad in five minutes. There was far too much furniture and far too little air. Despite the warmth of the day a fire burned in the hearth, and a fat, sleepy cat lay before it, which reminded him unpleasantly of Paulette. These lonely women seemed somehow driven to cats—

She poured him out some wine, and put the glass in his hand. She begged him to sit down, but he refused, saying he had an appointment and could not stay.

"And how is the poor little thing?" she asked, then shaking her head, "Ah, God, she's not long for this world, one can see that."

And she made a tutting noise, while her bright small eyes fixed themselves eagerly on Coll, who sipped his wine and noticed automatically that it was of better quality than his customary *rouge*.

He was not quite certain whether she was referring to Grizel or the baby, but replied stiffly, unable to keep the shivering dislike out of his voice, "Very often these premature children grow stronger than all the rest." Then suddenly he remembered. He put his hand into his pocket. He said, "I believe, madame, that Madame Ryder owes you rent. She has just given me the money to pay. How much is owing?"

A strange look passed over Madame Thierry's face. It was hard to tell with the old toad, but he could have sworn it was regret. She replied calmly enough, "No, monsieur. The rent is quite up to date."

"What!" Coll was astonished enough to speak in his natural voice. He put the glass down. He had hardly touched it. It might be a good wine, but he could not bring himself to drink in such surroundings and with such a companion.

"Certainly," she said.

"But—" He was about to say, "Who the devil has paid you?" but stopped himself in time.

She went on, turning a little from him so that he could not see her face, "I do hope poor madame will be happy here. The room is of course very simple and not really suitable for a small child, but then we are simple people, monsieur. This is not after all a royal palace."

Coll could think of no reply to this prodigious understatement, but he was in any case so taken aback by such a volte-face that he remained silent.

She continued, fiddling with the ornaments on a table beside her—the room was filled with small pieces, all in execrable taste—"I am making arrangements to see that madame is more comfortable. A little carpet, so nice and cozy in the winter, don't you think, monsieur? And a better fire so that the poor little child is warm." She turned to face him. "We don't wear our hearts on our sleeves, monsieur, but we are a kindly people, we look after the unfortunate. You have no need to worry. The poor young woman will be as well cared for as if she was with her own mother."

Coll was beginning to feel as if he were in a nightmare. The words were charming, no one could have faulted them, but the face from which they came was ugly with malice, envy and suspicion. This was some little game being played, but why in God's name, and what had happened to transform a screaming harridan into this seemingly amiable lady so concerned for the unhappy girl upstairs?

He could endure her company no longer. The room choked him. When she begged him to finish his wine and have another glass, he merely shook his head, mumbled something about the mythical appointment again, and made for the door.

She came with him, a small, dumpy figure almost touching his shoulder. When at the door he turned to make some semblance of a polite farewell, he surprised on her countenance a look of such malevolence that it appalled him. The next instant she was smiling again. "You must visit me again," she said. "When my eldest son is here. Such a good boy, and married to the sweetest girl. I am sure monsieur and Victor would get on so well. And you speak such excellent French. It is always gratifying to meet a foreign gentleman who has troubled himself to learn our poor language. Perhaps a small dinner one evening—"

Christ forbid, thought Coll to himself. He answered none of this except with vague, forced smiles, and he came out into the courtyard, taking deep breaths of air as if he had been stifled. He did not stop walking until he was round the corner, well out of sight of the building. Then he leaned against the wall, mopping his brow, trying to gather his baffled thoughts into some kind of coherence. He could understand none of this, but one thing was evident: Grizel, for no logical reason, was for the moment safe and protected.

But he could not rid his mind of Madame Thierry's look of resentful dismay at having to refuse his money. Probably she had never refused money in her life before. Whoever was responsible for this pantomime was someone of authority, and someone who frightened her; moreover it had all happened while he was upstairs.

Coll shook his head, swore to himself, then set off to call on Dr. Tullideph.

Chapter 6

COLL WAS interested, as on the first time he had walked down this street, that the doctor should live in such comfortable surroundings.

Tully had his room over a greengrocer's shop, now doing a fine trade and selling, as it seemed to Coll, vegetables and fruit of good quality. Certainly it was all above his means, but then these days he walked for miles to find potatoes at a sou less than anywhere else, and he was happy now to come home with bruised apples and overripe grapes that the shopkeeper would sell for very little or even give him for nothing. Once he would not have had the faintest idea of prices, but these days he knew exactly what everything was worth.

"I have become a good housewife," he wrote to Jean. "You should hear me haggle over a piece of poor meat, the kind we'd once have given to the dogs, and then I vow they would have turned their aristocratic noses up at it." Then he told her in a kind of defiance that butcher's meat cost fourpence a pound, and feather flesh was very dear. "A chicken," he went on, "costs from ten to fifteen pence in the market." But he did not add that this was well beyond his purse's capacity, and that he mostly made do with sausage, eggs and cheese. God knows what Jean would think of all this, a husband who bargained in the market, and put on his apron to cook his own dinner. Afterward he regretted having written the letter. It offended his pride that she should be sorry for him, and he had the haunting fear that she would not only pity but perhaps despise him. But the letter had gone by then, and when she answered, she made no comment.

He spoke to the proprietor, asking for Dr. Tullideph. He saw the look of surprise flit across the man's face. He was probably the first visitor Tully had ever had. But the man replied civilly enough: *Monsieur le médecin* lived on the first floor, the room on the right.

"Is he in?" asked Coll.

The man looked away, his tongue searching his cheek. He replied after a pause, "Monsieur is nearly always in. Would you like me to go up first to see if—if he is perhaps asleep?"

Coll, not liking this very much, said he would go up himself and, if there were no answer to his knocking, go away again. He climbed up the stairs, aware that the man was watching him. He thought with anger and resentment that the whole world seemed to be playing a cat-and-mouse game.

He found Tully's room easily enough. There were only three doors on the landing. The place was clean and a window was open. Perhaps it was for this reason that he did not immediately notice the smell of brandy but, when he came up to Dr. Tullideph's door, he grew aware of it at once.

He knocked on the door, prepared to go away at once if not

answered. After all this was Grizel's daft idea, some woman's whim; he had no particular desire to see Tully, and Tully, unless he had radically changed, had certainly no desire to see him. He heard the sound of movement within, then footsteps coming to the door. The doctor did not call out to ask who he was. The door opened and with it came a reek of brandy that nearly knocked Coll backward. The room smelled like a distillery. Dr. Tullideph's face and presence, now filling the doorway, seemed on the other hand remarkably sober, and his voice, when he said in a calm, acceptant manner, "You had best come in," was steady and unslurred.

It was only when Coll, feeling rather like a spy, stepped into the room and looked the doctor full in the face that he realized how extraordinary a change had taken place.

It was as if a brush had passed across the doctor's countenance. All the lines were gone, it was as smooth as a child's, yet the overall effect was that of a vast old age. It was a face that Coll had seen in the dying; so unruffled were the features that they were almost obliterated, and the visage that smiled into his—Tully smiling!—was inhuman as if blurred by some disease. And then Coll knew that, despite the steady gait, the even voice, the strangely smiling countenance, Dr. Tullideph was monstrously drunk, so drunk that the liquor washed over him, drunk so that in all likelihood he would never be sober again.

He stepped inside, feeling that he confronted a stranger, shocked yet still inquisitive enough to stare around him. Dr. Tullideph, drunk or sober, was a methodical man. The bed was made, the floor was swept. A coat was neatly folded over the back of a chair. But the bottles were everywhere, though they too were tidily stacked against the wall. They were all brandy. There must have been over a dozen of them.

The doctor watched Coll's glances, and seemed amused; the smile was still painted on his lips. He motioned his visitor to a chair, then moved back to the window, leaning against it so that Coll could no longer see clearly the smiling, toothless mouth, and the eyes, which alone betrayed him, for they were sunken and bloodshot.

"Well?" said Dr. Tullideph.

Coll found himself unaccountably nervous. He began, "I have just come from Mrs. Grizel." He paused, but the doctor said nothing. He went on, "It was handsome of you to go, Tully. She tells me that you were very kind, that without you both she and the bairn would have died." He paused again, then continued with an edge to his voice, for the doctor's silence was beating on his nerves. "But she still needs your attention, sir. I think she has not had enough to eat for a long time, and the babe is small and sickly with not at the best much chance of survival." Then he could no longer restrain himself, and his voice soared up. "For God's sake, man, do you propose to leave the job half done? The very fact of your asking for her might help her. She has just lost her husband, the child was born too soon, and she is a stranger here without friends—"

Dr. Tullideph replied calmly, "It is a life for a life."

"What the devil do you mean by that?" demanded Coll, rising violently from the chair, and coming across to the window. He could see now that the damned man was still smiling. He had a sudden desire to hit that toothless mouth. He said, struggling to control himself, "Does this mean you are not going near her again?"

"It is a pleasure to deal with an educated man," said Dr. Tullideph derisively. "I mean precisely that. But if you are proposing to use violence on me, sir, you are not as intelligent as I believed you to be. It will do no good. You can beat me to death if you wish, you will change nothing by one iota. I have done what I had to do. The child is alive. The other was alive too, for a little while."

Coll said helplessly, "You are talking in riddles." Then he said, "You're fou, man. You're drowned-drunk."

"Ay," said Dr. Tullideph, always smiling, "and that, with or without your leave, sir, I propose to remain to the end of my days."

"But you would never drink with us—"

"It was a grave mistake," said Dr. Tullideph. "But it makes no difference now. I am back where I was before. Only this time the child remains alive."

"Not for long, unless it receives proper care. If that in any way concerns you."

"It does not. I delivered it alive. The other should have lived, if it had been permitted."

"So you keep on saying. What other?" demanded Coll, bewildered and furious, then he remembered and grew silent.

"I threw it into a bucket of water," said Dr. Tullideph, in even, measured tones. And he made a strange gesture with one of his hands as if casting something away. The hands, Coll noticed for the first time, were big and powerful. "It was alive. I held it under till it drowned. It did not take long. But she was drowned too." For a second his voice faltered. "She screamed so. I hear her sometimes, even now. But the drink keeps her away. When she starts screaming, I reach for the bottle. I cannot stand the noise. I see no reason why I should have to endure it."

Coll said at last, "You have already told me most of this. Do you have to tell me all over again?"

The doctor's voice grew suddenly querulous and high-pitched. The smile vanished. He cried out peevishly, "Oh, you are so stupid, so ignorant. You know nothing. One has to tell you everything twice. And even then you don't trouble to listen. You really are a very tiresome young man. I want you to go away. I never invited you here. This is my home, after all. I don't like people coming into my home uninvited. Go away. Go away this instant."

Coll said steadily, "I want you to visit Mrs. Grizel again."

Then Dr. Tullideph smiled, himself again, the smooth, inhuman look back on his countenance. "I have done," he said, "what had to be done. There is nothing more for me to do." He turned a face on his interrogator so filled with malice that it caused Coll to take an instinctive step backward. He knew at this moment that Dr. Tullideph was mad, devoured by his own demons and the demons of cruelty and destruction. He could think of nothing to say or do. Every instinct bade him leave as fast as possible, yet he remained there while the calm voice continued.

"I have tried to explain to Mary," said Dr. Tullideph. "In time it may stop her screaming. But I am growing used even to that. One becomes accustomed to anything. Even you, sir, will grow accustomed, though I believe that by the end you too will be split into pieces. It is prodigiously interesting," said Dr. Tullideph, speaking now as if he were addressing a class of students, "but the human being, man as one might say, is so dependent on his own environment. In his own surroundings he will behave well enough, for there is something to hold onto, there is a familiarity to act as staff and support. You are married, sir, are you not?" He did not wait for a reply. "There was your wife and the bairns, and I daresay you was quite a wealthy man, you have the air to you. One can always tell. But now you are stripped and divided, and no man can brook a permanent division, for he will go mad." He pointed a finger at Coll. "You believe me crazed in my wits, do you not?"

"I do," said Coll, tight-lipped.

"Ah, but you are mistaken, sir. I am sane. I am entirely sane. But only with the brandy in me, for drink is a unifier, drink obliterates the other world that we are all trying to forget. Oh," said Dr. Tullideph and, as he spoke, reached down for a bottle of brandy which he proceeded to open with great speed and dexterity, "I have watched you all the while you believed you were watching me. And while I watched I saw it all so plain how you changed, disintegrated. I could have told you then that there is no hope for you, none at all. Only the woman perhaps—but then women are simple creatures."

"Do you really believe that?"

"Certainly. But you would be too stupid to appreciate why. A woman after all has her home, her man, her child. She does not ask for more. It is only men who want so much. She may even manage to survive, though for what I cannot say; there is little to warrant survival, we would all of us be better dead. After all, here we live in the past because the present is unendurable. We spend our time dreaming of what is gone, because there is nothing else to do. Tell me," said Dr. Tullideph to Coll who, listening to this meandering, was beginning to feel entrapped as if in a nightmare, "do you not sometimes consider as, if my memory don't betray me, the English bard puts it, shuffling off this mortal coil? I am well read, you know. I derive great pleasure from reading, particularly philosophy —but then, as you will certainly have gathered, I have a keenly philosophic mind. Nonetheless, even I, with my capabilities and intelligence which are of the highest order, have several times considered the possibility of putting a term to my existence. Have you not done likewise? After all, life can hold so little for you, yet you seem to me reasonably healthy, a trifle choleric perhaps but not dangerously so, so there should be a long period before you take your departure. Oh, I am sure you have many times thought of doing away with yourself. Why not? I believe I would encourage you. I might even be persuaded to provide the means. There is no point in simply living just for the sake of it. Do you not agree with me?"

"I do not," said Coll.

"No? You astonish me. I thought you more intelligent." And at this point Dr. Tullideph put the bottle to his lips and took a great gulp of the contents. Some of it ran from the corners of his toothless mouth, but he paid this no attention. He went on, "I gather you are infected with the sin of hope. You should dispense with it instanter. I have done so a long time ago. There is no hope. It does not exist. There is simply nothing, and we live in that nothing, insignificant, useless, contemptible creatures who would be better off in the middle of the ocean. I can only pray that in time you will learn wisdom. Perhaps not, some people never do. And now," said the doctor, waving the bottle at Coll, "I must insist on your leaving. You have already taken up too much of my valuable time. Indeed, you are boring me, and if there is one thing I cannot endure, it is being bored. Go back to your Mrs. Grizel. I am sure she will welcome you, and then you can play with the infant and make a pretense of being home again in what I believe they call the bosom of the family. Bosom indeed! Such a foolish term. But then you are a foolish man, I have always despised all of you, and it amuses me very much to think how you despised me."

Coll moved toward the door. The doctor watched him with his superior, spiteful smile. He said with difficulty, "I am to take it then that you will not call again on Mrs. Grizel, even if the bairn is sick to death?"

Dr. Tullideph did not answer immediately. The bottle clutched in his hand was shaking from side to side. Then his face changed; the calm cracked across like a fissure in a rock. He screamed in a thin, high whine, "Get out! Get out! If you ever come here again, I swear I'll kill you." And with his other hand he dug into his pocket, to produce a pistol. Only what with this and the bottle and his state of confusion, he did not seem aware of what he was doing; one moment the bottle was pointed at Coll, and the next he was glaring frantically at the pistol as if he would drink from it. It was a Highland pistol, the kind called over-and-under. It could fire two shots, and Coll, having no mind to be punctured by this lunatic, ingloriously fled, slamming the door behind him.

But he heard Dr. Tullideph's voice again, raised in a shriek: "Stop that drumming! Ah, Christ, stop that drumming!"

Coll paused on the landing. The sweat was thick on his forehead. He had to stand at the window for a minute to regain his self-control. Then rather cautiously, as if he could not quite trust his legs, he made his way downstairs again.

The proprietor was arranging his fruit and, in the fashion of his kind, making sure that all the finer specimens were on the outside. He looked up as Coll brushed past him, shot one glance at his white face, then said briskly, "Perhaps monsieur would like a glass of wine?"

Coll felt he would like nothing better, and accompanied the man into his office, a small room at the back of the shop. He accepted the drink, then said, "How long has this been going on?"

"He does not harm anyone," replied the man indirectly. "Naturally if he made trouble, I should have to get rid of him. We run a shop, as you see, and I could not have the customers annoyed. But, no, I cannot complain. We seldom see him at all, he is very quiet, and it's only once in a way he becomes hysteric and makes all this noise. It only lasts a moment. He hasn't been like this for several days."

Coll repeated, "How long has this been going on?"

The man, seated on the edge of the table, swung his legs and considered. "It's very strange," he said, "but when he first came here—let me see, that's nearly two years ago—he would never so much as touch a drop. Oh, we asked him in once or twice, the wife and I. You have to be friendly, and he's English, he's a long way from home. Like yourself, monsieur."

Coll did not feel this was the moment for a chauvinist discussion; he accepted the label with a faint smile.

"He'd never come. He wouldn't even accept a coffee, much less a glass of wine. So, well, if folks want to be on their own, they want to be on their own. It suits me, I'm a busy man, I don't have much time even for my own friends, what with getting up at three every morning to go to the market. It's a hard life, monsieur. So we just left him alone and, as I said, he never made any trouble. He used to come back to his room every evening, no women or anything like that, and as far as I know, he spent all his time reading. So many books, you can't imagine! My wife used to say she couldn't think what he did with them. All over the place they were, though he was quite tidy in his own way, he piled them up against the wall. The only time he went out was to some club or other. I never knew where it was exactly, but I expect you know all about it, monsieur. But a few days ago he was out all the day, and when he came back, he was in a fine old state, I've never seen anything like it, shaking and crying, tears rolling down his cheeks they were, and his face white as a sheet. We thought he must be ill and suggested calling a doctor, but when my wife said that, he looked at her, and he said—I remember the very words—he said, "I am a doctor, God forgive me." And then he went upstairs, and we never saw another glimpse of him for two days, so that I began to think he was dead. I went up to him and I was even prepared to break the door down. But it wasn't even locked, and when I went in, I found he'd passed out cold with half a dozen bottles of cognac around him."

The man paused dramatically. Coll thought he was enjoying himself, though he plainly had a kind enough heart. He had no doubt retailed this extraordinary story to all his friends and customers. He concluded, "Before God, monsieur, I don't think he's ever been sober since."

Coll, preparing to go, said grimly, "I have an idea, sir, that he will never be sober again."

"But why? I mean, I like a drink as well as the next, and I daresay on Christmas Eve and on fete days I take a bit more than I should, but what sort of life is it to be dead drunk from morning to night? He must have quite a bit of money, that's obvious. I couldn't afford all that brandy. But can you explain it?"

"I think," said Coll at the door, "that a man comes to the point when he cannot any longer face reality, so that when reality suddenly smacks him in the face, he disintegrates. It's his phrase, not mine. Leave him be. You say yourself he's no trouble. Let him drown the rest of his life away."

"You don't think—You think he may do away with himself?" The shopkeeper had grown a little pale; it was all very well having a fine story for the customers, but a corpse with perhaps its throat slit was a different matter.

"Do you know," said Coll, "I doubt he will." And his own words astonished him, for it was Tully himself who had suggested he should put a period to his existence. He said, almost to himself, "I don't think he any longer has the courage. I think he's finished already; death would be redundant."

And he went out of the shop, buying a bunch of grapes as he did so, feeling this was his duty but selecting the cheapest fruit there. He need not have troubled himself. The proprietor refused to accept his money. He stepped out onto the road, thankful to be away, yet still seeing that room upstairs, where Tully, whom they had all laughed at, drowned the screams and the drumming with his brandy bottle, so that the memory of those terrible days could float away. They would return with the tide, then there would be more brandy, and more and more. Soon or late the day would come when the doctor would choke himself into the final stupor, and that would be the end of Dr. Tullideph of Aberdeen who had no doubt started off with the same hopes and ambitions as everyone else, and who had somehow lost them on the way.

The sin of hope.

Coll, in his own lodgings, which for all they were dark and dirty, seemed somehow paradise compared with that bright, brandy-strewn room, sat on his bed and looked closely at the hope within his own heart. It might be dwindling a little, but it was still there. But Tully was right in his own way. No man flourished without a wall to lean against, without the everyday comfort of friends and family. If Tully, instead of involving himself in a war that he derided and despised, had returned to his own hometown on the Border whence he came—was it not Melrose?—he might eventually have settled back into his practice, doing what he was trained to do. Perhaps he would have taken to the drink again, but the work would have prevented excess, and by degrees he would have forgotten the screams and the drums and the violence of hate and revenge.

But he had chosen otherwise, and loneliness, evil memories and alien surroundings had finished him. Coll turned his thoughts to his own hope, to Jean and the children; the cold within his bones made him shudder, huddle the blanket round his shoulders.

Will I ever go home again? Will I ever see Jean again? Will I ever be able to look around me and say, "This is mine, this is where I belong"?

And if the word is never, not ever, what will become of me? Will I take to whoring like Davy, drinking like Tully, or—Aeneas? I do not know what Aeneas does. Perhaps I will never know. He of all of us is the one who has brought himself with him; whatever he does is what he would always have done, and so he has not disintegrated as the rest of us are beginning to do. But what he does I cannot say—

This reminded Coll of the dinner in the Place des Vosges, but this faded away again; it was somehow not important for all Aeneas had hinted that it might mean return to home and Jean. Coll could only see them all, Dr. Tullideph, Davy, himself and the coughing ghost of Tom Ryder leading a phantom existence, drinking wine to blot out the skeletal truth.

Then he saw Grizel, so plain that for a second it was as if she were in the room with him. A tall, plain girl with a rough, deep voice and a heart as high as a steeple, nursing her poor, ugly little brat who had come too soon, and might leave too soon also. In that moment she seemed to him as if she were the only real thing in the world. He did not love her, he did not even think of her as a lover, but she was home and reality and truth, and he longed for her company so passionately that, had it not been late, with Henny certainly asleep and not to be disturbed, he would have got up that very instant and gone round to her.

Tully knew about Grizel too. Tully, somewhere amid the roaring brandy seas, knew a great deal. Only he had said that women were simple and stupid, which was not true. There was nothing simple about Grizel, and nothing stupid either, only she knew what she wanted, and she did not trouble her head with foolish regrets and recriminations. Grizel had wanted Tom, and Tom she had had. Tom was dead, but there was Henny, and now she was struggling to put strength and life into a poor little scrap so frail that a breath could topple her; she was making plans to earn money for Henny, work for Henny, looking always into the future. If Coll came to see her, she would first make him a meal, then she would mend his clothes, and the thought of this warmed Coll, made him long to help her. He saw himself taking care of her as he had done with Jean and the children, nursing Henny, helping with the rough work, arranging the room for her, doing all the hundred domestic tasks that he longed for, something to fill his days and his empty heart.

And he went to bed, to tide over the dark hours, so that early in the morning he could set out for Grizel and the baby.

He dreamed of home, only Jean was not there. He remembered that in his dream he was angry because she was not there. But he awoke happy, which was rare nowadays, and he made himself the French breakfast he had grown accustomed to: half of a stale *baguette* (he always bought yesterday's bread because it was cheaper) and a cup of coffee that he brewed on his little smoking stove.

Then he came joyfully down the stairs, and twenty minutes later was banging on Grizel's door.

The concierge did not come out either to greet or revile him. Coll had the impression that she was aware of his arrival, was probably watching at the door, which was slightly ajar.

He was thankful not to see her, for the thought of her always made him uneasy: he could not understand her sudden change of heart, and it disturbed and bewildered him that she should know Paulette. Paulette for him was in the past; the thought of her made him a little sick; he could only hope that he never saw her again. But he could not completely dismiss the picture of her, with her impassive face, and the eternal knitting that she made and unmade every day, though now it was almost impossible to believe that he had ever slept with her, spent hours in her company. That dreadful, joyless room with its fat cat, and oddly expectant air as if she were always wanting from him something that he could not give—

He pushed the thought of Paulette away from him, then knocked on Grizel's door.

Grizel showed neither astonishment nor particular pleasure at the sight of him. He had, however, the impression that she was expecting him; it was true that he had promised to come back, but then he had done so the first time and not come near her for several days. She had her hair screwed into a knot on the top of her head, and she wore an apron. She said, "Don't make a noise, please. Henny is asleep."

He came in, as quietly as he could. He looked around him, then down at the baby asleep in her cradle. God knows it was nothing of a room and not much of a baby, either, but the joy flooded within him like a sexual release; he could not have believed that he would ever again feel as happy as he now did, to be here with this plain girl who spoke so severely to him, the sad little creature so waxen as to seem dead, and the depressing room with its broken chair and battered bed in the corner.

Madame Thierry had kept her word. There was now a thin, torn carpet on the bare boards. It was the only improvement.

He looked at Grizel, who met his gaze without a smile. He said, "Tell me what I can do."

She answered at once; the blessed girl seemed to understand exactly what he wanted. There was plenty for him to do. It was like his dream. There was firewood to chop. There was rubbish to take down to the courtyard. There was a window to repair. There was shopping—

Here she paused. A faint color came into her cheeks. She said suddenly in a more nervous manner than he would have expected of her, "Do you not mind, Coll?"

"Mind? Why should I mind?"

"It is not a man's work."

Then he began to laugh. He forgot about the baby, and the laughter woke Henny who at once began to cry—poor Henny, she always cried, as if craving the warmth of the womb she had left too soon. Then he was remorseful, not very, just a little, for after all the remark in the circumstances was an absurd one; anyone would have to laugh at it, and if it woke the baby, well, the baby had to wake sometime.

Grizel at once rated him. Standing there with Henny lifted instantly into her arms, she exclaimed in her rough voice, "Oh, have you no sense at all? The poor wee bairn needs all the sleep she can have. I have just got her quiet, and you have to make these braying noises and wake her up. I am ashamed of you, Coll. You should know better, and you a father too."

"Ah, be quiet, you silly woman," said Coll, still grinning at her, and at that she made a cross noise, looked down at Henny, now bawling her lungs out, up at Coll again, and suddenly laughed herself.

"Go and do the shopping," she said, "or I'll take the broom to you."

He did the shopping, spending all the rest of Davy's money. He could not remember enjoying himself so much for a long time. Shopping, something he had never done before in his life, was a task he had always hated, though he sometimes derived a perverse pleasure from bargaining, finding something a sou cheaper than anywhere else. But now, with Grizel and Henny in mind, it was different. He grew extravagant, though, God knows, they could not afford it; too lavish a meal today might mean nothing tomorrow. But somehow he no longer cared. He bought some veal, which was plainly ridiculous, salad, fresh bread, eggs, butter and milk. Then in a market at the corner of the street he saw some little wooden dolls. Immediately, with what was left of his change he bought one of these too, to place it proudly in Grizel's hands when he had dumped the rest of the shopping on the floor.

He saw the slow tears crawl down her cheeks. He cried out, "I did not mean to distress you. I thought perhaps the wee girl—"

"She is a trifle small for dolls," returned Grizel collectedly, but she smiled at him through the tears, and it was a sweet smile that transformed her face, that made him see as once before that she had been a bonnie lass in her day before death and privation took her looks from her.

She placed the doll in Henny's cradle, and they both watched as the minute fingers curled round it, unaware of what it was, but seizing on something to hold. And Coll felt again the warmth he believed he had forgotten, and crouched down by the cradle to lift up this small, ugly little creature, for Henny showed little signs of putting on flesh, and the white face with its purple shadows was still that of some wizened old woman about to die.

He held the child to him. So had he done with Amy. So had he done with Donald. So had he hoped to do with others; both he and Jean had wanted a large family.

He looked up to give Grizel a rather embarrassed smile. He was a little ashamed of his own emotion. Henny lay quietly against his shoulder. She was a mewling baby and cried a great deal, but now she was quiet, the heavy-lidded eyes half closed.

He said as if in apology, "I daresay you find me foolish, but I always liked children. I used to sing them songs. I used to come home early so that I could play with them." Then before she could reply, which he saw she was preparing to do with some energy, he went on, "I saw—" He checked himself. He could not tell Grizel about Tully. "I saw someone who said that people like ourselves, people so far away from home, change, fall apart. I think that has been happening to me. I never realized how much I needed my own home and my own family. I thought I was the protector. Now I believe I was the protected. I still need that protection."

"And Henny is to give it to you!"

He gave a faint laugh, looking down again at the sad little monkey face. "Poor Henny. But, yes, why not?" Then he raised his eyes to Grizel and saw clearly that it was not Henny who would help him but Grizel herself, poor Grizel with no husband and no home, thin, half-starved Grizel with nothing at her disposal but an indomitable spirit. He did not say this. He thought she would resent it, think it patronage, and he was ashamed too that he a full-grown man, still young and strong, should even contemplate requiring help from her. He said, "My friend exempted women from this fate. You, it seems, are the stronger sex."

"Of course we are," she said.

"You say that so calmly!"

"It is something I have always known. You should know it too. Oh, we are all brought up to believe that man is the stronger, and at once we look for a husband to support us, to provide the strength and courage we are supposed to lack. And we marry and we think we are settled for life—and what happens then?" Grizel spoke these words in a positively militant voice. "I will tell you, Coll."

"I am listening," said Coll gravely.

"Oh, you're laughing at me!"

"No."

"Of course you are. And you will laugh even more at what I am about to say, because you'll know it's true, even though you won't admit it. There we are, with our fine, strong husband, all our troubles ended, every burden put upon his manly shoulders. And then? Why suddenly he is so sorry for himself, the poor fellow, and before we know where we are, the whole beautiful six foot of him is weeping all over us, and we are patting him and kissing him and saying, 'There, there, it don't matter. We'll look after you. You can depend on us, never mind, never mind.' That's how it is, Coll."

"I do think you are exaggerating."

"I never exaggerate."

"You should have been on the boards, Grizel. You have a fine dramatic declaration to you."

She only said calmly, "Then I can earn money for Henny and myself."

He said rather crossly, "You are something of an Amazon, are you not?"

But at this she violently shook her head. "No. Oh, no. I do

not like fierce women." And seeing his ironic look, she raised her voice. "I tell you I do not. I cannot abide these women of Paris who talk all the time of revolution. Oh, yes, I have heard them. Madame Thierry is one of them, and so is that strange woman with her knitting—"

This time she did see Coll's change of expression.

She asked in innocent surprise, "Why, do you know her?"

"You have mentioned her before," said Coll, without answering her question, then he bowed his head over Henny.

She accepted this. He knew with relief that it would never enter her head that Paulette was a prostitute, and that he had solaced himself with her. Grizel understood a great many things, and was less afflicted with feminine vapors than any woman he had ever met, but this was not the kind of thing that the world she came from understood. She only said, "I find I cannot like her. I don't know why, but somehow she always frightens me. She never smiles. Perhaps she has had a very hard life. But these fierce women . . . there are so many of them. I meet them sometimes when I am in the market. I hear them talking. Their faces look so cruel. One cannot imagine them loving a man and bearing children. They talk of death and violence and heads rolling. They seem to hate so much. You cannot believe I am like that. Oh, I can hate too, but I would never want to kill anyone. Do you really believe me to be so horrid?"

He said gently, "No, of course not. I was only making fun of you. You must forgive me. You must not take me so seriously."

"I take everything seriously," said Grizel. Her face was sorrowful. Then she looked at Coll, with the sleeping baby in his arms, and smiled; the smile as always made her instantly young and vulnerable. "I used not to be like that. Once I never took anything seriously at all. You'll not believe this, Coll, but when I was young I was quite foolish, I thought life was easy and gay and delightful, and I never thought of the morrow, only of the day and how I could best enjoy myself."

He said, moving across the floor and depositing Henny back in her cradle, "Dear lass, you talk as if you were a hundred."

She answered him gravely as if she took this remark at its literal value. She said, "I don't feel as if I were young anymore." Then she said, "Do you know when I stopped being young?"

He thought she was referring to Tom's death, but she went on, not giving him time to reply, "It was when those women dragged me out and stripped me. I could never have believed that such a thing would happen. Their faces—that is how the women here look. And, Coll, these were women I had known all my life. They were my neighbors. Some of them I had been to school with; some of them were mothers of my friends, even mothers of young men who had courted me. They spat at me. They struck me. They laughed in my face, and called me bitch and slut and whore. I believe they might almost have killed me. And for what? For loving. For loving a man worth a dozen of them, for all he was English and a soldier. I grew old then, Coll," said Grizel. "I grew a hundred years. You tell me I talk as if I was a hundred, and that is precisely how I felt. Oh, when Jenny untied me and took me in, I thought I would die, I felt so ill, not because of the blows and the dirt and the cold, but because of the hate. All I wanted was to be with Tom and to get away from my own home and never, never come back again. You told me I ought to go home. Now you will understand why I can't do so, not even for Henny. I think I would be sick if I ever saw the place again, and as for meeting those women—You see," said Grizel with a bitter smile, "I am not so fierce. I am a coward. I am frightened of hate."

He pushed down his own anger, the rage that this story always aroused in him. He longed to have those women here so that he could beat them down with the same savagery they had shown to this young girl, but he knew that his fury would frighten Grizel as much as the violence had done, so he choked the words down.

He said, "Don't be afraid anymore. I'll look after you."

If she remembered her own words, she did not betray it. She said, her voice low, "You are a very kind man."

He said, stung into truth, perhaps by her gentleness or by the memory of Tully's words, "I believe I once was. It is easy to be kind when you have everything, it is far easier than being unkind. But now I am not so sure." And still consumed by a strange desire to be candid and frank, he said, "Don't trust me too much, Grizel. I believe I am a weak person. Don't depend on my kindness. You are giving me something I desperately need, that I hadn't realized till today how badly I needed it. You are giving me back a home."

"And a ready-made baby," she said in her normal voice. He had noticed many times already that Grizel never remained subdued for long.

"And a ready-made baby!" But he did not pursue this. This might be dangerous, and at the moment he was too happy to consider danger. "Now," he said, "what more can I do for you? I am at your disposal. You may make a packhorse of me. I'll fetch and carry for you. I'll do anything. I'll work for you, I'll speak to Jean-Pierre about the job as I promised, and you will cook for me, and it will be very domestic."

"And that will make you happy?" she asked in a wondering voice.

"Yes. By God, yes!"

Then she said something so strange that he thought he had

not heard her correctly. She said, stooping to pick up the meat he had bought, to prepare it for the pot, "This is not real, you know. It is a fantasy."

"What?" he said, bewildered. "What did you say?"

She repeated the words as if they hurt her: "It is a fantasy."

"I don't know what you mean," said Coll, suddenly angry. But he remembered that she had said something like this before, at their first meeting. He felt as if she were deliberately destroying his pleasure. His face fell into sulky lines.

"No," she said, very calm now. "I know you don't. One day you will." And she began chopping up the meat spread out on a board which was placed over her knees.

"After all," he said, recovering himself, "we are in the same situation. We have to look after each other. Is it so strange that I should want to help you? It seems quite natural to me. There is surely no harm in it."

She raised her head. She looked at him, and he saw in that look a compassion and a sadness. "No," she said, "there is no harm in it, none at all. Until the fantasy is broken."

"Ah," he said, "you're talking nonsense, woman. I don't know what you mean, and I don't think you do, either."

And he began to sing softly to Henny, who had wakened, and was not quite sure whether to cry or not, one of the songs he used to sing at home, a silly song that Donald always demanded before he fell asleep, and which always made him sleep before it was ended.

He sang:

> Hush-a-ba, birdie, croon, croon,
> Hush-a-ba, birdie, croon.
> The sheep are gane to the siller wood,
> And the cows are gane to the broom, broom.

>   And it's braw milking the kye, kye,
>   It's braw milking the kye,
>   The birds are singing, the bells are ringing,
>   And the wild deer come galloping by, by.
>
>   And hush-a-ba, birdie, croon, croon,
>   Hush-a-ba, birdie, croon.
>   The gaits are gane to the mountain hie,
>   And they'll no be hame till noon, noon.

And Henny slept, and Coll sat there, watching her. He did not see the tears on Grizel's cheeks.

Chapter 7

THE MONTHS went by and the summer faded; the autumn came and departed. The hot Paris streets were moistened by rain and cooled by wind. The dirt and smells remained, and Coll liked them no better than he had ever done, but he was extraordinarily happy. For the first time since his arrival two years ago, he did not wake up in the morning thinking drearily that it was another day, wondering what the devil he would do with it, the only brightness the hope of a letter from Jean. Now he jumped cheerfully out of bed, looked in on Grizel to see if she and the baby were all right, then worked for several hours behind the counter of the wineshop. In this he enormously improved his French, his knowledge of local politics and scandal, and earned enough to buy food for what, half in jest, he now called his family.

He always came back to his own room at night. Very occasionally it crossed his mind that this was strange and even unnatural. Once or twice he thought of staying, believing that Grizel would not rebuff him, but then he remembered Jean, and a kind of self-righteous warmth flooded him, for indeed she had a good husband; there were not many men who would display such self-control.

If he had ever worked it out as an equation, it would have been that to sleep with Paulette meant nothing and therefore was no kind of betrayal, but to sleep with Grizel would be gross treachery and infidelity. He did not naturally consider Grizel's views on the matter, for it was not a subject he ever mentioned to her. It never struck him for a moment that the situation might be difficult for her; if he thought of this at all, it was that she was fortunate to have a man to look after her.

But occasionally her strange words—"It is a fantasy"—came back to him, and because deep within him he was not as unaware as he pretended, he did not like the sound of them. Then for a while afterward he would be surly, forget to do some of the shopping, grumble at Henny if she did not stop crying. And he would go home earlier than usual, and irrationally be irritated because Grizel never protested; then he would settle down to writing a long letter to Jean.

He wrote to Jean more than ever. Indeed, he wrote so much and so often that sometimes he did not notice how infrequent her replies were becoming. But many of the letters he never posted; the ones that spoke of Grizel and Henny were all torn up. If he suspected that this was part of the fantasy, he pushed the thought away, ignored it until he had forgotten. He knew that the situation would certainly be misinterpreted. Jean would instantly be suspicious and angry. Her mind, which was a practical one, held little place for casuistry; Coll's involved reasoning would seem nonsense to her, and perhaps it was, though he seldom admitted it. The only time he mentioned the matter to her was when he told her that the Englishman—"Tom Ryder, you mind Tom Ryder, Jean, I have mentioned him before"—had died, and that they were all trying to help the widow and her child.

But in the unposted letters he told her almost everything, and it was like making a confession, it appeased his conscience.

"It is like home to me," he wrote. "It makes me think always of you and my two dears, my infantry. I would never have believed I could find so much happiness again, but of course it is all on your account, it is because when I nurse this child—so ugly, poor wretch, oh, God, so ugly, and she does not do well at all; she is still so small and weak and pale, sometimes it frights me to death—but when I nurse her, it is like being home again, it is somehow as if you were by my side."

Then after that he wrote so fiercely that his pen dug into the paper, "This shows that a man can be friends with a woman, almost as if she were another man. We are friends, no more. I believe she will always mourn her Tom, he has only been under the earth for a few months, and as for me, I always think of you, my dearest Body, there will never be another woman for me. Grizel and I are united by our love and our memories; it is a bond between us that any other kind of love would break. If ever this changed in the smallest degree, I would leave her at once. I could never be unfaithful to you."

Then he would read through these absurd, exaggerated words and dislike them. The next day he would catch himself watching Grizel as she moved about the room, noting the soft pliancy of her body as she cradled Henny, averting his eyes from her breast as she held the baby to it. Sometimes he quarreled with her, and she was as quick of temper as he; they shouted at each other and he would storm out of her room, to come back shamefacedly the next day with a bunch of flowers, or a little gift for Henny.

To him she was still part of his dream, she was essential to his happiness; she moved in his mind as if that were her only place of existence.

There was no further word of the dinner in the Place des Vosges, and Coll no longer went to the Club until one morning in early November when, having finished early in the wineshop, he went upstairs filled with an idle curiosity to see if the place still held any memories for him.

Aeneas was waiting there as if expecting him.

He looked up at Coll as he came in, inclined his head but said nothing. Coll looked around him. He wondered how he had ever endured spending his days here. The room was icy cold, it could not have been cleaned for many years, and the only trace of former occupation was a pile of cobwebbed bottles, and Davy's noose still swinging from the window.

He went over to this, touched it, swung it out and back. He said, "I swear this will be here when we are all dead and gone. Perhaps it is our memorial. We should drink a toast to it, the last reminder of the Stuart cause."

"Take it down," said Aeneas.

"No. Why should I? It pleases me. There is not much about Davy that amuses me, but this does." And in a sudden fit of absurdity, he placed the noose about his own neck. But the sensation of the rope against his throat was disturbing, and he removed it quickly so that it swung back against the window again.

Aeneas exclaimed, "That's a damned imbecile thing to do. Are you a schoolboy to behave in such a way? When you've heard what I have to say, you'll not be quite so eager to hang yourself, for the job may well be done for you."

"Are you become hangman?" asked Coll. He had seated himself on a barrel as he used to do in the old days. He wished he had some wine, but could not summon up the energy to go downstairs for it; besides, the money on him was for Grizel and Henny, not himself.

Aeneas, to his surprise, smiled at him. "No," he said, "that is not my métier. I am perhaps become intriguer. Or loyalist. Or royalist. But these are only labels. I have come to tell you that you will be dining with us next week."

"Us?" repeated Coll warily.

"Friends. This is the reunion I have already spoken of, in the Place des Vosges." Then Aeneas, with barely a pause, said, "You see a great deal of Mrs. Grizel."

Coll answered in a quiet, pleasant voice, "You may tell your spies, sir, that if I catch them, I'll knock their teeth down their bloody throats."

Aeneas did not seem to be offended. "I'll tell them, if you wish," he said, "but I doubt the occasion will arise."

"Why the devil are you spying on me? What does it matter to you what I do?" And Coll, suddenly very angry indeed, jumped up from his barrel and came over to Aeneas, his hands swinging menacingly at his side.

Aeneas, still unmoved, replied gravely, "I cannot tell you the details now, but you will learn something about this when we have dined together. I do not spy on you, Coll. But on what we are planning to do depend the lives of hundreds of men. No. Let me finish. It is for this reason that I must know where you all are, whom you contact, who are your acquaintances. It is for this reason too that I want Mrs. Grizel to continue living where she is, especially as she is so close to you. It would be dangerous for all of us if she moved and I did not know where. Oh, friend, drum some sense into your thick head. Do you not wish to see your wife again?"

"That's a daft sort of question to ask me," said Coll sullenly, then in a burst of words, "For Christ's sake! Do you ask a famished man if he wants food? Do you ask a dying traveler in the desert if he wants water? What kind of creature do you take me for? Do I wish to see my wife again! No, I need to—need to, otherwise a part of me will die. Now, are you satisfied?"

"I've told you already," said Aeneas. "You will see her in December."

"You say that—"

"It is true. God willing."

"And if God is not willing?" asked Coll, tight-lipped.

"Why, then the trees will bear fruit with thrawn necks. Are you too feart to risk it?"

"You know I am not." Coll's voice sank. He could not believe it. It was not possible. Then he said, "You talk of the Loch Arkaig treasure—"

"Not here," said Aeneas quickly. "Not here. When we meet again. You will not speak one word of this to Mrs. Grizel. Or indeed to anyone."

"I do not have so large a circle of acquaintances," said Coll, and thought of Tully with the brandy waves almost over his head, and of Davy who would leap joyfully into this new adventure, but whose discretion was a doubtful quality. Then because Aeneas' calmness irritated him, because he still felt that he was being manipulated like a puppet, he demanded abruptly, "What dealings have you with Paulette?"

The calm remained, but Coll thought he saw a momentary

flicker. However, Aeneas spoke coolly enough, as if the matter did not interest him. "You mean that whore with her knitting?"

"That is who I mean."

"I have no direct dealings with her at all."

It was the first time Coll had actually caught him out in a lie, and his smoldering suspicions burst into flame once more, though he would have been hard put to explain what the suspicions were.

Aeneas said, "She is a friend of the concierge, and a fine pair of old she-devils they are too. I believe she offered help to Mrs. Grizel. I don't know why, but sometimes these loose creatures have a kind heart."

Coll, who did not believe that Paulette had a kind heart at all, said nothing.

Aeneas went on, "Why do you ask? Do you know her?"

It was his second mistake. Aeneas, if he conducted his spying methodically, must be well enough aware of Coll's acquaintance with Paulette.

But Coll only said with a sigh, "Ay, I know her."

"She is a poor, harmless thing," said Aeneas, adding with a little laugh, "I daresay John Knox would have her burn, but I myself find these creatures innocent. Indeed, I am sorry for them. She's old, she's ugly, it cannot be much of a life for her, and what life there is will not go on much longer. I sometimes wonder what happens to these unfortunates in the end. But that is neither my concern nor yours. My concern just now is that you come to meet my friends, discuss the matter with no one, and keep in touch with me. Oh—" And here he looked full at Coll. "I think it would be best if you did not continue working in the wineshop."

"You'd organize my very breathing for me," said Coll.

"Are you short of money?"

"We are all short of money. Or are we not?"

"I believe I could make you a loan."

"I should prefer to go on working."

"I should prefer you not to."

"I shall still go on working," said Coll.

He saw again a flicker of that impassive countenance. In that second the good looks vanished, to be replaced by something brutal and hard. But then Aeneas laughed, saying, "You are an obstinate devil, like all Highlanders. You must do as you please. Only remember that one indiscreet word could lose you not only your own life, but the lives of a great many others."

"I am scarce one of your rattles," said Coll, and that indeed was true, for though he talked enormously, it was seldom of his private affairs; even to Grizel it was only within the past few months that he had mentioned his home and family.

Only, as Aeneas opened the door, he suddenly asked, "Do you really believe to put a Stuart on the throne again?"

And he thought of Charles as he was now, drinking heavily, brawling with his mistresses, ignoring the continual requests from the French court that he should leave the country, not even answering his father's letters from Rome. He moved his shoulders uneasily, filled with anger and pity. The gallant boy, who had won all hearts by his youthful charm and beauty, was now a debauched disappointed man, who would not raise so much as a thistle, much less a standard. He should have died in battle; no one would lift a finger for a drunkard and a roué, he would only make himself a laughingstock.

He said, "I believe if the Prince came back to London now, nobody would even recognize him. I think he could walk through Piccadilly with the Scottish lion on a leash, and passersby would scarcely trouble to turn their heads. He is no longer dangerous, he is not even important."

He saw Aeneas' face tighten. "Does this mean," he said, "that you are no longer one of us? For indeed, it is a little late to tell me so. I have always believed you to be loyal."

"I think," said Coll, a little wearily, "you believed me to be a fool. I don't know exactly what you mean by 'one of us,' Aeneas, but you can keep your pistol snug in your pocket, for I shall not betray you. I shall cross the Channel with you. I shall even scour the loch for your damned treasure. But don't believe it's all for Charlie or you or anyone. I want to see my wife and bairns again. That is all. I have grown too old for causes and pretty, bright-eyed heroes. I lost my wife for one such hero, and I see now what a fool I was to do it, though I daresay if I were young enough, I might do it again. But now Charlie can go to hell for all I care, only if I must follow his standard to see my Jean once more, I will do so. I would follow the devil's standard if necessary."

He bestowed a grim smile on Aeneas, who for once looked taken aback. He said, "You can depend on me all the more for it. Why, for God's sake, man, you must see that. If it were only for your gallant Prince, you could never be sure that I'd not slip across the border to the other side. But for my wife and children—oh, you can depend on me to the death. I only hope it is not to the death, but I am prepared to take the risk, for indeed it seems to me I have no alternative."

And with this he pushed past Aeneas, came down the stairs, then, instead of going to see Grizel, went back to his own room; he felt he must be on his own to consider dispassionately the unbelievable possibility that in a few weeks he might be with Jean again.

There was a letter from Jean waiting for him.

He read it at once. Then, when he had finished, he read it again, dwelling on every word set down in her neat, thin script.

And it seemed to him a nothingness, a void, like a person who talked incessantly but who had nothing to say.

"The bairns are both well. Your son gives you his service and desires you'll send him some bonnie thing. . . . I tell him Papa cannot send much now, but perhaps later." There was someone, a neighbor, an old man who fell and broke his leg; there were forty-eight splinters of bone taken out of him, and his case was desperate. Coll could not so much as put a face to him. There was a gay account of a lady being married, whose wedding Jean had attended—"a stout lady who eats a great deal less than many a lean one. These are convenient wives in either war or famine. . . ."

Ah, God, God, God, I don't want to hear any of this. Why should I read about some old man who has broke his leg, some fat woman with no appetite who has found herself a husband? This means nothing to me, nothing. I want to hear more of the children, more of Jean herself, how she looks, what she wears, what she does with her day. And that she loves me and misses me—

Then there was talk of some distant relative, a wealthy man who made a rule of asking friends and acquaintances to dinner once only. "It is treating them like beggars at a burial who get their alms in rotation." And a tale of a maidservant who was got with child. "I keep her, for servants are hard to find, but she is a poor thing and, I believe, has no idea of the father." And, "It is showing signs of a hard winter. The rowan is scarlet with berries. We have, thank God, enough wood to see us through, but we will all be thankful when the spring comes again. . . ."

When the spring comes again.

Coll let the letter—it was a long one, three pages—drop to the floor. She wrote because it was her duty, and Jean was a woman who would be compelled to do her duty, but he knew, as if the words had been spoken in his ear, that the love was gone. Then instantly he began to argue against himself. It was surely not possible after all. She could not be expected to send him a love letter when they had been married for fifteen years and had two children into the bargain. The fact that she wrote of everyday things, the small events of her life, did not mean she had no more feeling for him. They had been apart now for over two years. For a young girl this might be unendurable, but Jean was no longer a girl, and their marriage had been a seasoned one; the bonds that tied them were of affection, friendship and understanding. And children. Yet the pain continued to rage within him against all reason. He huddled himself against it; it was so strong that he feared he would disintegrate as Tully had prophesied. He forced himself to think that in a month or so he would be back home, he would see her, all difficulties would be forgotten, their differences as if they had never been. If only he could tell her. . . . But of course he could not; letters were far too frequently opened.

Then, in the thought of his homecoming, courage and hope returned. He picked up the letter, put it in his pocket, then set off for Grizel.

The baby was awake and for once not crying, poor soul, though Grizel's milk was thin and insufficient, and the child would take nothing else. She lay there in her cradle, looking as always a hundred years old, but Coll declared that the spindly arms and legs were a little thicker.

"They were like sticks," he told Grizel, "and now at least they are two sticks put together."

She did not answer this. Only for a second as she looked down at Henny, and expression of terror crossed her countenance, her eyes moving over the pinched face to the little body as frail as a doll's. There was a fire burning in the grate, with the wood Coll had procured for her, the little carpet was under the cradle, and the curtains were tightly drawn. Coll had stuffed all the cracks with rags and paper, but there was still a chill to the room, and at night the bugs crept out on the walls, for all Grizel fiercely washed them down every day.

Henny's cradle was by the fire, and Coll knelt down beside it and began to sing softly one of his songs. The baby looked as if she were listening, and once or twice made little cooing sounds, joining in, in canon.

"You see," said Coll triumphantly, "she understands. She's a good Scots lass." And he sang in his light tenor voice:

> There was a wee bit mousikie,
> That lived in Gilberaty-O,
> It couldna get a bite o' cheese,
> For cheatie-pussy-catty-O.

Grizel gave him a half smile. If there had been that brief, violent terror within her, she no longer betrayed it. She too, Coll thought, could do with some more weight. The face was fine-drawn to its very bones, and the waist, with the tight-drawn apron-strings, gaunt to the point of ungainliness in so tall a girl.

She said in mild mockery, "Of course she understands every word. We'll have her speaking broad Scots within a week or so."

"She's bright," said Coll. "She'll talk early, and girls always speak sooner than boys. We'll have her speaking the two tongues, Scots and French. She'll be a credit to you, Mrs. Grizel."

Grizel said under her breath, "If she lives that long."

"What do you mean?" Coll was instantly on his feet, his voice sharp with anger as if this were a personal affront.

"Oh, perhaps it's foolish of me," said Grizel, turning her face away, "but the thought is always with me. I daresay I am not yet quite recovered, but sometimes at night I cannot sleep for thinking of it."

Coll said with the fierceness of fear, "You are ill-wishing your own bairn."

She cried out, "How dare you say such a wicked, cruel thing to me?" and began to cry so that, filled with instant contrition, he rushed across to her. He would have put his arms round her, only she pushed him away, then blew her nose and began to make a great business of tucking Henny in more cozily, putting the little hands beneath the blankets.

He said, "I don't know why I say such things. But, yes, of course I do. I am afraid too. I love Henny."

"I know that," said Grizel. She was still bending over the baby. He could not see her face, only the knot of shining hair which, strong and beautiful, seemed to weigh down the frail body.

"She is putting on weight," said Coll.

"Ay."

"She is a better color."

"Perhaps," said Grizel, straightening herself, "she is like me, she is hardy."

"It is you who should eat more. I'll bring in more milk, and you must drink a full glass every night. After all, I am now earning money," said Coll, then quickly, as if it hardly mattered, "I have just had a long letter from Jean."

The very mention of the name was enough to bring a curtain down on Grizel's face. She could not, as Coll knew only too well, hide her feelings. But she replied distantly, "I hope she is well."

It was not very encouraging, but Coll persevered. In some strange way it was important to him that Grizel should love Jean as he did, have trust in her. "I gather," he said, "that it is proving a hard winter. I am afraid it must be very difficult for her."

"The poor lady," said Grizel, and her expressive eyes moved over the room where the damp seeped up from the floor, and the wind, November-cold, blew in through the joints of the window.

He shot her an ugly look, but dared not take up the challenge. He went on, deliberately moderating his voice, "The children are well. Donald wants me to send him some bonnie thing. It is hard for a child to realize that his father has no money for gifts. I must try to find something. A small thing for a boy of four years—"

Grizel looked at him sideways. Her voice was more propitiating. "I could make him a wee shirt," she said. "I could use one of Tom's."

This reminded Coll of something else that was more important. He cut in, thankful that the quarrel was averted. He could not understand Grizel's attitude to Jean, which seemed to him both feminine and unreasonable, but he did not want to war with her; both she and the room were too precious to him. Besides, there was always a warning at the back of his mind that in their situation as strangers and exiles quarreling was dangerous; it might take on a permanency that he wished at all costs to avoid.

He told Grizel of the dinner party, then looked down at

himself ruefully. His clothes nowadays were beautifully laundered, pressed and darned, the buttons were all sewn on, the ragged ruffles mended, the frayed edges to his breeches bound, but there was no denying that everything he had on was shabby and mean. As for the celebrated wig, he had pulled it out to look at it, and found that what the rats had left of it, the moths had finished; the wretched remnants were only fit for a mophead.

She said calmly, "Oh, I can help you, Coll. There is a drawer full of Tom's things. I would be glad for you to wear them, and I know he would have been glad too."

Coll, taken aback, reflected on Tom Ryder as he had known him, tall and emaciated. There was nothing emaciated about Coll who had, with Grizel's cooking, been putting on weight, and he could not see any of these garments meeting more than halfway.

Grizel appeared to follow his thoughts. She unexpectedly smiled. "Ah," she said, "you don't know what a fine man he was before the consumption struck him." Her eyes moved up and down Coll in an uncomplimentary manner. "He was a big man. Bigger than you, sir. Handsomer than you. A finer figure than yours. You are developing a paunch on you, Coll, and that Tom never had."

"I am not!" protested Coll, indignant, then could not prevent himself from glancing down again. It was true that his belly, once so flat, was beginning to protrude over his belt.

He saw she was silently laughing, which made him crosser than ever. But he watched her open a drawer at the far end of the room, and presently after much rummaging she began to lay a handful of garments over the back of the chair.

They would not perhaps have done for an audience with the king. There was nothing grand about them. But the shirt was silk and without holes, the breeches were not shiny, and the stockings—"I gave him them for his first birthday after our marriage," said Grizel—were far finer than anything Coll had in his possession.

Grizel said, "He has scarce worn them here." Then after a pause, "He grew so thin, they would have hung on him."

Coll hesitated, then said, "Do you not mind?"

"Oh," she said in a flurry, making a haughty face, "you think I'm foolish like all women. Men always think that—"

"Now, look—"

"Of course they do. Do you think I don't know that? You expect me to burst into tears, to grow pale, perhaps to fall to the ground in a swoon."

"Grizel," said Coll, "you are a silly bitch."

Then she laughed. It could almost have been said that she giggled. But when he tried the clothes on—they fitted surprisingly well, though the waistband of the breeches needed a trifle letting out, and the coat a little shortening—he pirouetted round as if he were a woman himself, then caught sight of Grizel's face and stopped. She was neither weeping nor swooning, but something had happened to her features as if they had slipped out of alignment. In that one brief moment she looked as old as the grave, her cheeks sunken, her mouth drooping, her eyes huge with grief. The next she was smiling at him again, then around him with pins in her hand and mouth, fixing him here and loosening him there, scolding him for not standing still, while her neat fingers performed the necessary alterations.

"You will do me credit," she said. "I cannot have you eating with the fine gentlemen—"

"I don't think they are particularly fine gentlemen."

"Then you will be the finest among them. Stand still! That shirt looks well on you, Coll. Only the cravat—I will make you one. No, leave it to me. I am skillful with my fingers. I will turn you out well dressed if it is the last thing I do. I cannot have Henny's uncle looking unseemly."

He was touched, astonished and grateful. Before he had considered what he was about, he pulled her toward him and kissed her. She did not repulse him, but her body stiffened, and she moved her head sideways so that his lips touched her cheek, not her mouth as he intended. He thought from this she must be offended, but she moved backward and turned a quite saucy look upon him, saying in her rough little voice, "Well, now! The gentleman is grateful—"

"The gentleman is very grateful," said Coll gravely, "and perhaps if he were more of a gentleman he would have said so a long time ago."

"You hear that, Henny?" said Grizel, picking the baby up in her arms. "You hear what your uncle Coll says? He is grateful. You see? Grateful. Perhaps we are grateful to him, Henny. What do you say? He's not such a bad man, after all. What do you think, poppet? Tell me now."

And Henny, in one of her better moods, made little crooning noises, while Coll changed back into his own shabby clothes. He could not help wondering what Jean would make of this situation, but was relieved that Grizel had taken his kiss so lightly; if there had been danger, it was averted.

He set out for his dinner five days later. He had no wig— this Tom could not provide—but then he was a poor exile, so what the devil did they expect? His red hair was sleeked and pomaded, and Grizel, who seemed able to turn her hand to anything, had cut it for him so that it no longer fell over his collar. The suit of clothes fitted excellently, the stockings were so beautiful that he had to glance down at them with pride, and the newly made cravat was a masterpiece.

Grizel and Henny saw him off at the doorway. She waved and made the baby's hand wave too.

He glanced back at them, and Grizel called out, "Now look where you're going, you daft creature. Those stairs are dangerous, and well you know it. I've not taken all this trouble for you to fall head over heels, halfway down. You tear your breeks and I'll kill you."

"In the old days they'd have put a brank on you," said Coll ungratefully.

But there was something heartwarming in the sight of them, and Coll had to pause yet once again to look at them: Grizel with the baby on her hip saying good-bye and good luck to him, while Henny gazed at him solemnly from her enormous caverned eyes. And as he looked, a strange thought came to him, that perhaps this was the last time he would ever see them in such a way; this sent a chill through him and he hesitated, on the verge of turning back.

But this was plainly absurd, and he at once forgot about it, sailing jauntily past Madame Thierry's room in the hall. The old devil seldom appeared these days, but as the rent was paid, it was probably not worth her while. He was glad to be able to avoid her, and he came out into the courtyard.

It was a bright, cold evening, with a bitter wind blowing. The courtyard looked ugly and foreboding, with its one small lamp in the doorway, and the urinal at the end of it. He quickened his footsteps, then sensing the presence behind him, suddenly wheeled round. The sight of Paulette was almost a physical shock to him. It seemed to him as if she brought a shadow and a coldness with her so that the lamplight diminished and the building grew black.

She came up to him. Her face as always was expressionless. She was dressed with the utmost neatness, a dowdy little woman with her hair scraped back, the inevitable knitting protruding from the reticule she carried; it was quite extraordinary how with every mark of bourgeois respectability about her she still contrived to appear so disreputable.

He wanted to walk past her but could not, for she blocked his way. He said roughly, "Well, Paul?" Then, furious that the nickname had slipped out, "I'm in a hurry. Let me pass."

She did not offer to prevent him. The strange opaque eyes moved up and down the fine clothes. "You look very grand," she said. "Too grand for a poor woman like me."

He said suddenly, "You've been spying on me."

She made no attempt to deny this. She merely looked at him.

"You can stop it," he said. "I will not be spied on by you. Our acquaintance is finished. Do you understand? I never want to see you again." Then because her impassivity frightened him, he spoke more violently than he intended. "You disgust me," he told her. "The very sight of you makes me sick. Get the hell out of here."

And he used a phrase he had acquired from the gutter, words that went oddly with his fine new clothes. "*Chienne!*" he called her, but it would have made no difference if he had spat at her or struck her, for the words seemed to slide over her like water.

For the first time since he had known her, there was a movement of her mouth that might almost have been a smile. To his amazement she picked up her respectable skirts and made him a low curtsey, displaying a great deal of her legs which, though covered in thick, woolen stockings, were elegant and slim.

"Monsieur," she said, then in an exaggerated accent, "Milord!"

He could not miss the mockery. He wanted to hit her, to strike her down onto the cobbles. The force of rage she aroused in him seemed even to himself absurd. He strode past her, shoving her aside as he did so. He did not pause for breath until he reached the street. Then he looked back. There was no further sign of her. Perhaps she was recounting the incident to Madame Thierry. He moved his shoulders, feeling as if he had touched something unclean. The thought that he had touched her, slept with her, brought the vomit up in his throat. He was thankful to be away from her, and could only pray that she never went near Grizel again; the thought of the two together appalled him.

But presently in the novelty of it all, he forgot about Paulette, and when at last he arrived at the Place des Vosges, and saw from his fob watch—pawned innumerable times but now fortunately in his possession—that he had a little time to spare, he paused for a while to take stock of his surroundings.

Chapter 8

THIS WAS not a part of Paris that Coll knew well, though when he first arrived, having nothing else to do, he had traversed the whole city, taking in every *quartier* from rich to poor. He remembered those days now when, sore, angry and frantic with loneliness, he had walked and walked; he had existed on wretched scraps of food, understood nothing of what was said to him, and waited always for the pension which never seemed to come. In those days the Club had been his only place of refuge; without it he believed he would have gone mad. He went there every evening, with Davy, Tom, Aeneas, Dr. Tullideph and others. The barren room was the only home he knew, and he would return reluctantly as late as he could to his own room, where he at once wrote long letters to Jean.

He surveyed now this beautiful place with its elegant seventeenth-century houses, where the nobility of France had once lived. He realized with something of a shock what a long way he had come. Once, as the Scots country boy who had never seen anything like this in his native land, he might have admired and envied; now he simply felt out of place. The elegant entrances, the finely carved doors, the serenity of the surroundings, all seemed to him unreal. This was the world that Paris railed at, this was what the women who so frightened Grizel wished to destroy, this kind of thing formed tediously the eternal substance of Jean-Pierre's tirades. The people who lived here now were no longer the nobles, but lawyers, doctors, literati, yet there still hung over everything the smell of privilege and money, the atmosphere of ancient rights and laws. Coll could see, as once he would not have seen, how the cool mockery of this place must anger the people who starved and withered under the taxes that the inhabitants of this *place* did not have to pay; it was as if the very stones said, "Do not touch me, this is my world. You are poor, ugly, dirty. You are intruders whom I do not choose to know." The rich lived graciously, the poor froze or sweated and were buried in a pauper's grave.

Then, a little contemptuous of his own reflections, Coll gave his newly made cravat a tug to right it, shifted his coat into place, and pulled the bell of the house to which he had been directed.

He saw, when they sat down to dinner with Aeneas at the head and some twenty guests around him, that he need not have troubled about his clothing. It was a strange gathering, and something about it disturbed him. It was as if the guests were divided into two distinct sections, and the two halves did not meet. There were a dozen or so of his own compatriots. They all wore the fierce, shabby, battered look that he had come to recognize, that was doubtless on his own face, but they had no Grizel to sew and darn for them; their garments, though they had plainly made some effort, were shabby, shiny and torn.

He knew most of them by sight, though none intimately. One was a distant cousin he disliked, and they bowed to each other in the fashion of men who had nothing in common but a clan name. A couple of them had served with him in the same regiment; all of them had been at Culloden. Their faces were resentful, and they eyed each other with suspicion. The one thing they had in common was that they were attainted. For all of them one false step on their native land would mean the rope, the block or transportation. It was not a friendly bond, but it was an unbreakable one, like a gallows noose, and occasionally they bestowed on each other grim, mocking smiles, as if to say, "You and I, friend, are among the damned, let us make the best of it."

It was the second group that disturbed Coll, for he could not understand its significance. They were all French. They seemed to him worthy citizens, certainly not the nobility, but professional men perhaps of the lower grade—schoolmasters, lawyers and the like; a few of them, he thought, might be shopkeepers. They wore an air of quiet prosperity, much in contrast to his own compatriots, but they were dressed soberly, and they seemed equally astonished by the grandeur of their surroundings. They eyed the lavish dishes set before them with suspicion, and drank a great deal of wine. What they could possibly have in common with exiled Scots, Coll could not imagine; they were indeed of a class that normally despised foreigners.

Coll talked uneasily to his neighbors. One was a taciturn Frenchman, the other a burly Highlander who was drinking far too much and would shortly end under the table. The dinner was magnificent, served by silent, efficient lackeys, the food was almost exaggerated in its quantity, and there was enough wine to sink a regiment. Coll ate better nowadays, with Grizel's careful cooking, but his stomach was no longer accustomed to such luxury, indeed had never been so, for meals at home were plain and plentiful, without all these extraordinary sauces and garnishes the French poured onto their meat. He had starved enough to feel reluctant at not eating what was set before him, but after the third course, with a different wine for each, he found he could eat no more, and he began to grow suspicious of the way his glass was being so relentlessly filled up.

The conversation was poor, mumbled and uncoordinated, almost nonexistent. There was none of the brilliant salon talk here. Coll, falling into silence and noticing that several of his countrymen were well away, turned his attention to Aeneas, who sat there dressed impeccably, with rings flashing on his fingers and a white rose in his buttonhole. How had he procured such a thing in November? He seemed in no way perturbed by his ill-assorted guests, and when one of them, a Macpherson, banged on the table and bellowed rudely for more wine, turned an amused eye on him and at once directed a waiter to his side. Only Coll noticed that his gaze moved from face to face; he seemed less like a host than a puppet master, gently but relentlessly gathering them all toward him on their strings.

Coll had to wonder where all the money for this came from. What this dinner must have cost, he could not even begin to imagine. The room they were eating in was paneled and gilded in the style of Versailles, the pictures, though he had no knowledge of painting, looked good, and the frames alone must have been worth the prince's ransom. The carpets were

Aubusson, the hangings silk, the furniture splendid in the overornate way of its seventeenth-century kind. It was the strangest setting for such a gathering, and Coll, refusing some sweet concoction piled high with whipped cream, waited impatiently for the curtain to rise on a drama that, he was beginning to suspect, was most carefully organized.

At last it was over. Bowls of fruit were placed on the table, and Coll surreptitiously popped a pear into his pocket for Grizel, as he might once have done for the children. Brandy was passed round, and this he accepted, though his head was already muzzy and his stomach warning him that he had overeaten.

Aeneas rose to his feet. The handsome face surveyed them all. Coll saw that despite his calm appearance he was deeply excited. His breath was coming fast, and the one hand on the table gripped so tight that the knuckles were blanched.

Then he spoke in his fluent French.

"I think," he said, "you all have some idea of why we are here. But I will tell you again as best as I can. It is simply this. In a couple of weeks' time, next month, we will, with the help of Providence and these good gentlemen here who are prepared to find money for us, set foot again on Scottish soil."

The words fell into a silence. Coll saw the faces of his countrymen change, and to his dismay felt the tears prick his eyelids. *Set foot on Scottish soil.* He looked around him almost with fear, and saw the rough, angry faces dissolved, blurred by yearning and longing, suffused with an unbelieving hope. It was as if the pibroch sounded about them. Each one of them was saying to himself, "Home." Home might be a clachan in the hills, some small croft, even a whisky house, a girl, wife, children, the gold of the whins in May, the purple of the heather in September, but to all of them, lost, violent men as they might be, it was a tenuous slit into paradise. The glory of it caught at his throat, he wanted to leap to his feet and shout and sing, then he knew it was only a dream, it might never be realized, and he slumped back in his chair, not noticing even that his brandy glass had been refilled.

"The treasure," Aeneas was saying—he must have been talking for some time, but caught up in their dream they had not listened—"still lies in Loch Arkaig, where Achnacarry Castle stood before Cumberland burned it down. The French hid it there to help us restore our rightful King, forty thousand louis d'or of French gold. It is a treasure with a curse on it, for men are greedy, but by the grace of God we will remove that curse, and the money will at last put a Stuart back on his throne. Once it may have divided clan from clan and brother from brother, but now we will see that it joins and unites. It is for us to find it. We have money, men and ammunition guaranteed us from Sweden, and help has been offered us by the King of Prussia. The Prince himself is positive of the scheme's succeeding, and if all goes well, as it must—as it must—the English government will soon hear of a fine hurly-burly, and German Geordie be sent packing. And this time"—suddenly Aeneas smacked his fist down on the table so that the glasses rattled—"this time we must and shall succeed." We will sail shortly. I will not give you the date. Do not speak a word of this to anyone, and never, never commit anything to writing." Then he said more quietly, "We have suffered enough. No nation has ever suffered as we have done. We have endured the most diabolical and inhuman cruelties after Culloden, we have had our land taken from us, our homes destroyed, even our tartan is forbidden us. Some of us still skulk in the hills, others have been transported to the West Indies, many have ended on the block and gallows. But we are still here, we will always be here. The English cannot trample us underfoot, they cannot forever deprive us of our own country. The moors are still there, the hills, the lochs. And we will see them again. I promise you. We will see them again."

They burst out cheering and stamping their feet. Then one of them began to sing, in a voice thickened by wine, but it rang out clear and true, and they all joined in, raising their voices so that it seemed as if the very pictures might fall from the walls.

It was a romantic, sentimental song. It was not entirely appropriate to the occasion. But the words jerked at the tear ducts as they were meant to do:

> Bonnie Charlie's now awa',
> Safely o'er the friendly main.
> Many a heart will break in twa,
> Should he ne'er come back again.

Coll sang too, only in the middle of the chorus his voice stopped and his eyes moved sideways. He could not have begun to explain why, and his brain was fuddled with all the drink he had taken, but it seemed to him that it was all wrong, the emotion, the rejoicing, the enthusiasm; it had no basis, as Grizel would have said, in reality. The room, dispassionate, rich, cold, unalterably French, looked down on them, and around the table sat the other men who had scarcely spoken one word: the schoolmasters, the lawyers, the shop owners, the bourgeoisie of Paris who, God knows, had no place in this gathering, yet belonged to the setting as he and his countrymen could never do. Their faces were cold, detached and fanatical, their eyes watched everyone, and they sat there primly, unmoved by all the excitement, as unlikely supporters for the Stuart cause, or indeed any romantic cause, as Coll could imagine. He could not, however much he tried, see these stony-visaged men digging into their pockets to help a young man now notorious for his drinking and whoring. It was impossible to understand how they could sympathize with this ragged collection of ruffians who had been kicked out of their home and were now passionate to return. It did not seem reasonable, and these men looked reasonable, reasonable to an almost frightening degree. He could see them tumbling a king from his throne rather than putting a debauched young man upon it.

He came up to Aeneas to say good-bye, but Aeneas murmured below his breath, "Wait for me, Coll. I'll walk to the end of the Place with you."

They all staggered out into the street. It was not an impressive spectacle. It was difficult to see these men as heroes, though heroes they had perhaps been, and certainly they had given up everything for a cause. Coll realized suddenly that Davy was not there. He was surprised. It was a ploy after Davy's heart, Davy who would charge into any battle, support any cause, provided he could handle his claymore and dirk, Davy who would rejoice at the thought of bloody action, whatever the outcome.

He waited outside for Aeneas who, he saw, was talking to a young man, presumably someone from the household. Presently he came out, and the two men began to walk silently, side by side.

It was two in the morning. It was now bitterly cold with a hint of snow. Tom's coat, though it had looked well enough for the occasion, was not very thick, and Coll huddled into it, his hands dug deep into the pockets. Then he remembered the pear. He pulled it out, with a laugh. He did not explain why he had taken it, and Aeneas, glancing down, shrugged, displayed neither amusement nor astonishment.

"Is this serious?" asked Coll.

"You can ask me such a thing!"

"You are a devious man. I have never understood you. How do we find this precious treasure? There have been a great many looking for it, and some of it has been already discovered. It is now something of a joke."

"I do not," said Aeneas, "find forty thousand louis d'or a joke."

"My wife told me in one of her letters of a fisherman who hooked up something heavy from the loch, and they cried out that he had caught one of the Prince's money bags. It was a fifteen-pound salmon. Perhaps that is the only treasure there."

"Do you believe that?"

"I do not know what to believe," said Coll, "for we lead a life composed entirely of gossip, rumors and hope deferred. It is no matter. I am with you. But I would be interested to know our chances of success, and"—he turned his head to peer into Aeneas's face, marble-cold in the moonlight—"I would like to know more of these men who are apparently prepared to find money for us. They do not look the kind to concern themselves with lost causes."

"The cause is not yet lost," said Aeneas, "and these are good men." There was a perceptible tension in his voice. "You cannot judge people by their looks. And the French are a romantic people."

"Are they?" said Coll. "I would not have thought so. I have always found them intensely practical, with a great reverence for money. Their only streak of romanticism appears from time to time in their poetry, and that is largely concerned with death and the tomb. And these men do not wear so much the faces of visionaries as of fanatics."

He felt Aeneas, whose arm brushed his, jolt beside him as if he had tripped over a loose stone. But his voice was even and pleasant. "I tell you again, we cannot go by faces. Look at our own countrymen tonight."

"I have looked," said Coll rather grimly. "The sight of men vomiting in the gutter is not the most edifying. But I myself am far from sober. As for these fellows, don't you think that once they have set foot on the heather, they will leap away to find their families and then make for the nearest whiskey house? I fancy they'll end up in prison faster than they left it."

"They will find the money first," returned Aeneas. "No man despises forty thousand louis d'or."

"And then?"

There was a pause. Aeneas touched Coll's shoulder. "I turn off here. What happens then? I don't know. Nobody knows. But I hope you are still with us."

"I have already given you my word. But not for you, man. Nor for the Prince. For my wife. Only for my wife."

Aeneas made a gesture, French fashion, moving out his hands. He did not answer, only turned on his heel and disappeared round the corner. And Coll began to make a swift if staggering progress toward Grizel's room.

He went there as if propelled. In outer consciousness he did not entirely realize where he was going. The cold air on top of all the wine he had taken was making him feel very drunk indeed. The street shivered around him, the cobblestones beneath his feet seemed like a rolling sea. And his mind too was like a sea, with Grizel in it and Henny, but mostly Jean whom, it seemed to him now in his fuddled state, he was going to see in a matter of hours.

It was by now past three o'clock. There was no one abroad except for the wretched creatures who huddled in doorways or curled up in the gutter, with rags and paper their only covering. How they could sleep at all was unimaginable, for the snow was beginning to fall in small, thin flakes that dissolved as they touched the ground. It was a grim promise of a hard winter, and a hard winter to men who had little money for firewood was no laughing matter. But Coll did not notice the sleepers any more than the snow. He came up to the building, and only then for one moment did a kind of warning float through his wine-soaked mind, as if something whispered in his ear, "Don't go in, don't, it is unwise."

He shrugged the warning off. He made his way into the hallway, nearly falling over a cat as he did so. The animal spat and squawled at him, diving away into the shadows. There was no sign of Madame Thierry, who would surely be tucked up in her cozy bed.

He stumbled up the stairs, nearly falling several times, and making enough noise to herald in the revolution. No doors opened. The inhabitants here were used to clatter and drunks. If he had fallen headlong over the broken banister, he would have had to lie there till morning.

He managed to arrive on the landing. The drink was roaring within him. He gave Grizel's door a shove and fell headlong into the room, landing at her feet as she leaped out of bed, huddling on her dressing gown as she did so. She had certainly heard the noise of his ascent, and must have guessed who it was.

She whispered, "For God's sake, Coll!" then, on a choked, startled laugh, "Man, you're fou!"

"And why, pray, should I not be?" demanded Coll, with the colossal dignity of the hopelessly drunk. He was now in a huddle on the floor. He tried to get up, fell down again, then clutched at Grizel's outstretched hand, and managed more or less to right himself. He was aware of his own drunkenness; a small portion of his mind still functioned soberly. But he could not control either his speech or his legs. He glowered fiercely in Grizel's direction. He could not see her very well in the half-light; the only illumination was a small candle flickering by Henny's cradle. He sensed that under the astonishment there was something like fear. Tom Ryder had not been an abstemious man, and there must have been many an occasion when Grizel had to put him to bed, but she must be startled to have Coll here at this hour in the morning, so unsteady that even now he had to cling to the chair to keep himself upright.

He began, "I want to talk to you—" but she at once interrupted in an outraged whisper, "If you waken Henny, I'll kill you. It took me two hours to get her to sleep."

At once he lowered his voice dramatically, yet somehow it still echoed through the room. Grizel sighed despairingly and made no further attempt to quieten him, though his next remark could hardly have been what she expected.

"I would like," said Coll in a trumpet whisper, "to go to bed with you."

She replied immediately and with considerable spirit, "Then you can just get that idea straight out of your sottish head. You are as drunk as a lord. If you were sober, you'd never dare say such a thing to me. Tomorrow I shall insist on an apology. The idea of it! To come in such a state to my room, and at this hour of the night too. You think you want to go to bed with me, do you? Well, you can just want. I'm not one of your whores. If you want a woman so badly, go out and find one. I'm not here just for your drunken pleasure. You should be ashamed of yourself, speaking to me in such a way."

Coll heard all this well enough, but as the drink in some strange way had heightened his perceptions as well as twisting his tongue and his legs, he was aware that these indignant words held something else beneath them. Grizel was by no means so outraged as she chose to pretend, and indeed, Tom Ryder's widow could hardly be a complete innocent.

He said thickly and coaxingly, "Ah, Grizel, you're a beautiful girl—'

"I am not," said Grizel. The deep voice roughened. "I am as plain as a pikestaff, and well you know it. You will leave this instant, Coll Macdonell, and go straight back to your own room. I hope you have a terrible headache in the morning. I hope you are so ill you want to die. And you'll not get any sympathy from me, I can promise you that."

"If you don't want me," he said, "I'll go." But he made not the slightest attempt to move.

"I do not want you," said Grizel, "so please go."

But a nervous laughter surged beneath her words, and Coll, hearing it, began to laugh himself, only checking his mirth as she sprang forward to seize his wrist in an angry grasp.

"Henny!" she said, almost in a hiss. "Are you out of your mind?"

But it was a mistake to have touched him, for at once his arms were round her waist, and he was trying to kiss her as she turned her head violently from side to side.

"Oh," she said, "you stink of wine, you're disgusting. To come here in such a state and imagine that for one minute I could endure a creature like you touching me. . . . You make me sick. How dare you insult me like this?"

Then her mouth was quiet beneath his, and the hand on his wrist moved up his arm. For a moment she lay heavily against him. He heard her sobbing breath. She muttered something he could hardly hear, but he thought it was "I'm so lonely."

He said urgently, "Let's go to bed."

She pushed at him, and he was unsteady enough to lose his balance and hurtle back against the door. The noise was too much. Henny awoke and at once burst into a thin, penetrating wail. Grizel, running over to the cradle, snapped over her shoulder, "Now look what you've done. Will you please do as I ask and go. Please. Haven't you done enough mischief already? My poor pettie, poor, poor. . . . We'll send this horrid man away, and then you can sleep in peace, poppet, without nasty drunks frightening you in the middle of the night."

"If I go," said Coll, who was beginning to sober up, "I shall fall over the banister and break my neck."

"You can break your back for all I care," said Grizel, but there was no longer any conviction in her voice, and the face revealed in the candlelight was young, soft and uncertain.

"Give me the bairn. I'll put her to sleep again."

"You'll drop her. You're too drunk—"

"I'm drunk enough," said Coll, "but I'll not drop her." And with this, supporting himself against the mantelpiece, he took Henny up in his arms, and began to sing to her softly:

> There was a wee bit mousikie
> That lived in Gilberaty-O!

And Henny's crying at once stopped, and presently the purple-veined lids drooped slowly down, and the little parcel in his arms collapsed against him, while he gently lowered her back into the cradle.

Grizel whispered, "It's not fair." There was a tenderness in her voice, a hint of laughter again. "And you so drunk— She should be screaming at the very smell of you."

"Tom was not a sober man," said Coll.

"No," said Grizel. "No, he was not. But you are not Tom, Coll, and Tom has been dead a bare six months, he is still my husband, and I will never love a man so much again, never."

He came up to her. She did not move away. He said, "I'm lonely too."

She made a derisive noise. "Oh," she said, "so you are lonely, poor Coll. Your bed is cold and you want a woman in it. Why do you not say so? Why do you make it so sentimental? But you're like all men, they are all softies when they want something. When they've had it, that's a very different matter."

"Why don't you stop talking?" said Coll. If not sober, he had at least regained his balance, and now he tried to push Grizel down on the bed.

She said, "No! Certainly not. Coll— You'll get a box on the ears in a minute—"

"I don't mind," said Coll, much as he might have spoken to Henny. "I wouldn't mind at all." Then he said urgently, "I have to talk to you. There is such news—" He broke off. The warning sounded again. "I can't tell you, except the one thing perhaps, but there is hope again for us, for you too, for all of us. That is why I came."

"That is why you came," repeated Grizel, then as if her legs gave beneath her, sank down suddenly on the bed. When Coll flung himself down beside her, she made no further protest, only her eyes, enormous in the thin face, gazed at him in a kind of fear, longing and sorrow.

He said in a whisper, as if he had remembered the baby,

"Oh, let me." Then the words burst from him in a torrent, like the drink he had taken. "It is not natural, the life we lead. You say you are lonely. We are both lonely. I half-live here. I look after you. You must admit that. I am not trying to force you, but we could almost be husband and wife, except—"

"Except," said Grizel in a cool, small voice, "we are not. And you have a wife already, Coll. Your Jean. Do you think she would forgive this?"

He was still drunk enough to speak without thinking. He retorted, "She'll never know," and at this Grizel astonished him by speaking in the saddest voice he had ever heard from her, saying, "You should not have said that. I know it's said now, but you should not. I don't know about your Jean, but it is you who will never forgive. You'll never forgive me, Coll, I know that. I think you must go away. I can't take any more."

She lay back on the pillows now, and Coll, leaning over her, choosing to ignore what she had just said, announced triumphantly, "I've brought a present for you." And he turned to fumble in the pocket of the coat he had thrown onto the floor, only to produce a disgusting, sodden, pulped pear, which made him exclaim in distaste as he let the mess drop to the floor.

He said, "I'm sorry."

Then he saw she was weeping. In his fuddled state he thought it was because of the pear. He said, "I'll buy you another. I'll buy you a dozen. I'll buy you anything you like."

She did not answer; only when he folded his arms about her, she pulled him down to her, and this time did not turn her face aside.

But he was too drunk. He had forgotten what it was like to be so drunk. Normally he was an abstemious man; only at hogmanay and at weddings did he overindulge himself, and then Jean, like a good wife, had looked at him resignedly and put him to bed.

He said at last, sobriety crawling in too late, "I can't—" Then in a fury, "I'm sorry. I've made a pig of myself. I'm so ashamed—"

She said in an exhausted voice, "It don't matter, Coll. Perhaps it's all for the best."

He sat up, scowling down at her as if it were her fault. The wine still held him physically, but it was as if his mind were ice-clear. He said as if he wanted to hurt her, "I'll be seeing Jean again. I'll be seeing her soon. I can't tell you any more, but now you'll see why I am so drunk. This is news I never thought to hear. I believe it's sent me a little out of my mind." And in the same breath, "Where are my clothes?"

"They are on the chair," said Grizel. "I have pressed them for you." She did not move. She lay there, looking up at the ceiling.

He began to dress in his own clothes again. He made a sorry mess of it, buttoning everything up wrong, and nearly falling as he stepped into his breeches. But he dressed in a wild haste, as if frantic to be gone, swearing as the shirt refused to slip over his head, stamping his way into his shoes. The baby slept; perhaps she knew the noise meant her no harm. Grizel still lay motionless and silent.

He could not endure her silence, or his own conscience; the combination of the two made him so angry that he could have killed her. He said, as if he were delivering a blow, "I'm sorry. This should not have happened." Then, "You should never have let it happen."

She only said, "No."

"I must have been crazed in my wits," said Coll. But he could not like the sound of his own words, any more than he liked the sight of Grizel lying there. He took a step toward her, then thought better of it. He said, "With all this happening, I'm afraid I'm going to be very busy. I'm sure you'll understand that I may not be able to come round so often."

"I suppose you will not," said Grizel.

"There'll be so much to do. I cannot tell you about it. You must not even ask me."

She said nothing.

"Of course, if you need anything—"

"I'll not need anything."

"I'll be sending the money. Do you have enough to go on with?"

Then she sat up in bed. The unfastened hair streaked witch-like over her face. She demanded in a ringing voice, "Are you offering to pay me, Coll?"

He was shocked. "You know perfectly well I did not mean that!" Then he cried out in shame and fury, "I think you have a most vulgar mind."

"Perhaps I have," said Grizel calmly. She seemed to have recovered herself. She was fastening her shift and reaching for the dressing gown, then she began to pin up her hair again. She presented a strange spectacle, oddly compounded of innocence and domesticity.

It touched Coll very much, but did not prevent him from continuing in the same harsh voice. "I am naturally," he said, "prepared to help in any way I can. You need never hesitate to ask. Only as long as you understand that with this— Well. Of course I cannot speak of it. For your own sake, as well as mine. It's not that I don't trust you, but I did give my word—"

"I suggest," said Grizel, in her most exasperatingly matter-of-fact manner, "that you remain sober until whatever this is, is over. You make a poor intriguer, Coll. Anyone with half a mind would have the whole story out of you by now. It is as well for you that I am not given to havering. You have not fastened your left shoe."

"That is quite im-immaterial," said Coll haughtily. The dawn light was coming through the window. His face was wild and pale, his mind a gale of confusion. His main desire was to put as much distance between himself and Grizel as possible, yet he could not bear to leave her in such a fashion. He said in a different voice, "Are you sure you'll not be wanting anything? The bairn—I could always send anything, by a messenger. Perhaps by Davy. I would not want you to be in any need."

She replied calmly, "Thank you, Coll. I shall be all right. You have no need to worry." She raised her eyes to his. She said in a strange, withdrawn voice, "Then I'll not be seeing you again?"

He thought she was going to make a scene. He backed away. He said quickly, "Oh, that's nonsense. You don't imagine I'll not be calling around. It's only that time is short, there are affairs to tie up, and besides, it would be dangerous for you to become too involved. But I'll be seeing you often. In fact, I hope to come round tomorrow. It's just that—"

"I understand very well," said Grizel. She rose from the bed, then began to rearrange it, shaking the pillow and tucking in the sheets. He noticed again that she was a tall girl. Perhaps she seemed so because she was so thin.

"Then I'll be going," said Coll. Now he was almost sober, but the room still wavered around him so that he felt sick; there was within him a great cold and desolation.

"Good-bye, Coll," said Grizel.

He came up to kiss her good-bye, but she turned away at that moment to fold her counterpane, so that he was left looking foolish, his head tilted for the embrace. She did not seem to notice. She moved back to the mantelpiece.

He said awkwardly, "Don't forget to let me know if there is anything you need. You can always reach me through Jean-Pierre. You know where the Club is. A small note—"

"You have still not fastened that buckle," said Grizel. "You might fall over it. The stairway is dangerous."

He looked at her angrily, hopelessly. For a second, as she stood there, he saw transposed over the thin, motionless body, the girl and baby who had waved him good luck, not so many hours ago. He could not endure it. He had never hated himself so much. He turned without a word and opened the door. She heard him rushing down the stairs, making as much noise as when he came up; he must be taking three or four steps at a time.

Grizel turned back to the cradle. She began to cry, as if her heart would break. But this only lasted for a minute, and by the time the outburst was done, Coll was in the courtyard making desperately for home.

He spent all the day in his room. He felt very ill, which was not surprising. He knew that he would not go back to Grizel, and he knew that she knew this too. This was too serious. This committed him, this was betrayal. But he could not rid his mind of her, and the thought of Henny made him so desolate that he almost broke his resolution and rushed back.

He spent almost all the time cursing his stupidity and folly. Her words came back to him clearly. There is no harm in it, she had said, until the fantasy is broken. She had understood with far more perception than himself, but would she also understand his appalling behavior? He could barely understand himself, only knew that he could not go back.

He saw now with a frightening clarity the absurdity of their life together. What sort of imbecile had he been to believe this could possibly continue? A ready-made baby . . . those were her words too. And a ready-made wife who was not a wife, but who had given him so much of what he needed. A fantasy . . . and then a few bottles of wine, a couple of brandies, and the fantasy was gone, together with a friendship, his honor and his duty to Jean.

She would be all right, of course. He told himself so repeatedly. Of course she would be all right. The rent was paid. Aeneas would continue to send her Tom's money. And Henny . . . he could hardly bear to think of Henny, but managed to force himself to do so. The baby was stronger now; with warmth and sufficient food she would survive the winter, and after that be as healthy as any other child. Perhaps Tully could be persuaded to keep an eye on her, after all.

Grizel would be all right. She was a sensible girl. It was a pity that for a while neither he nor she had behaved sensibly, but she would understand that with the prospect of seeing Jean again, it would not be wise for either of them to risk involvement. If anything went wrong, she would certainly let him know. It was all a pity, it was his own fault, he had no right to have behaved so, but in a fashion the drink had proved his guardian angel. No harm had been done, and Grizel, being as she was, would accept the whole episode as the kind of thing to be expected from men who had overindulged themselves.

Grizel would be all right.

But the chill phrase was not enough, and Coll called himself a bastard, was savagely ashamed of his behavior—and did nothing whatsoever about it. When he had at last slept off the effects of his drunkenness, he went for the first time for a long while to spend the day at the Club.

It seemed strange to step once more into that bare, vast room. He saw that the noose still swung from the window. He had forgotten how cold and desolate the place could be; his brief meeting with Aeneas had taken up his mind so that he had hardly noticed his surroundings. He had after all been spending all his spare time with Grizel. Her room was, God knows, no palace, but she had a way of making the place cozy, there was a fire, there was food prepared for him, and she would be sitting there, rocking the cradle with her foot. He could see her now, sewing for Henny, making clothes out of Tom's old shirts, dresses of her own, anything she could lay her nimble hands on. The sight had always warmed him as the memory of it chilled him now, turned the desolation and loss and shame within him into a cold, hard stone.

He wondered how much she would miss him. He told himself that he did not really miss her, it had only been a kind of self-indulgence, almost a sentimentality, but of course this was not true; he missed her dreadfully. It was only the thought of Jean that restrained him from bolting back to her.

This thought was so strong, so bewildering that it did not enter his head that his weekly letter had not yet arrived. He only resolved to write to her instantly, sitting on one of the barrels, as he used to do in the old days. But when he settled himself there, he found that his pen produced nothing but little drawings, while his mind revolved constantly round the picture of their first meeting, how it would occur, what it would possibly be like.

And the heather smell was in his nostrils again, the sound of the lapping water in his ears.

He would be home. Home. Home.

He supposed he would have to creep up to the house, like an intruder. It would be lunatic to do otherwise. He was an attainted man, forbidden to return, condemned to perpetual banishment. But the glory of striding in at the main doorway, calling out, "Jean!" and then the children's names, was so absorbing that he briefly believed he would risk the gallows for the sheer delight of it. But this of course was absurd. He would be reduced to sneaking into his own home, by way of the farm buildings at the back, arriving in the kitchen like any beggar with his bowl.

What would happen then he could not imagine. He struggled to picture Jean's face, imagine the words she would speak, but all that came to him was a kind of mist, with the outline of her features, the night-dark of her hair. She was never the fainting kind, she surely would not faint, but what would she feel, what would she think, to see once again the husband she must in her heart believe was gone forever?

And Grizel . . . he could send her all the money she wanted. Clothes for Henny, and for herself, anything and everything. Jean would surely long to help this girl so much worse off than herself; she at least had a husband and a home, while Grizel had nothing but a sickly infant who might not survive.

Amy and Donald. He had not seen them for nearly three years. They might well not recognize him, Donald certainly would not, and—shocking thought—he might not recognize them. Children at that age changed so quickly—

Coll bowed his head on his hands, letting the paper drop to the floor, and was so immersed in his thoughts that Davy's voice almost shot him off the barrel.

"Are you greeting, you poor fellow?" demanded Davy. "A grown man like you, too. But I've the very cure for you. Look at this! If you'll dry your eyes, I'll give you a snifter, and that'll send the tears back to their dungeon."

"No!" said Coll, raising his head and pushing the proffered

bottle of wine away. His eyes were dry. "No, thank you. I made a pig of myself yesterday. I find today that the very thought of wine brings me near to vomiting. Take it away, Davy. Drink it yourself. Maybe later on—but not now. Now I am as sober as any judge. There's no sobriety like that of a man who's been drunk the day before."

Davy grinned at him, sat himself down on another barrel, and took a swig of the wine. His bright eyes skimmed over Coll's sallow, shadowed face. "You were none of you what I'd call sober," he said. "But you looked very bonnie in your fine duds, even if your feet were walking sideways. What was it all about? It was a fine, grand house, and I saw that my lord Aeneas was the master of ceremonies."

Coll stared at him, his face suddenly blank. "And what were you doing there?" he demanded.

"Oh," said Davy, twiddling the bottle round, "I was just passing the time of day."

"At two o'clock in the morning?"

"Ay. It's as good a time as any other. I was just taking a wee dunder, as you might say. I was very surprised, very surprised indeed, to see my old friend Coll, full of wine and good food, walking down the Place des Vosges." He pronounced the name as it was written. "He's come up in the world, I thought, him and his fancy suit and all. Where did you get the duds from?"

"They were Tom Ryder's."

"Ah. Mrs. Grizel again. And how is she, the poor lass?"

"She's well enough," replied Coll stonily.

Davy eyed him, his gaze malicious and observant. He said at last, "And what was it you were doing there?"

"I was dining."

"Why was I not invited?"

"I have no idea," said Coll.

"Oh, I daresay grand folk like that would have no time for a common Highlander. Tully wasn't there either, was he?"

"Tully," said Coll, not liking this interrogation at all, "is in no state these days to dine anywhere."

"Oh, I don't know," said Davy. "I saw him— When was it now? Yesterday. Yes, that's right. Yesterday. He was asking for you."

"Was he?"

"He was drunk, of course, but then he always is. When a man is always drunk, it's as good as being sober. We had a fine wee crack together, and drank some brandy. Good stuff too. He is an educated man, Tully. It's a pleasure to talk with him. He is not the one to talk of women and bawdry like so many others."

This came well from Davy, who seldom talked anything else, and Coll broke into a smile, despite his apprehensions.

"But," went on Davy who, as Coll remembered, was as persistent as a terrier after a rat, "what was the reason for this grand dinner?"

Coll was thinking unhappily about Grizel's remarks on his talents as an intriguer. It was true that he was not much use at this kind of thing. He had lied in his time, as all men lie, but he was a poor liar all the same, and as a child had developed the habit of staring frenziedly into his interlocutor's eyes, so that it was plain from the very beginning that he was making everything up. Even now he did the same, unless he checked himself. In addition his mind was still confused by yesterday's drinking, the unhappy events of last night and his own exhaustion.

He struggled to think of some realistic reason for this extraordinary gathering in the Place des Vosges, but could only come out lamely with, "Aeneas, I believe, had some money left him. He wanted to celebrate. Why not?"

He knew as the words left his mouth that Donald could have done better. Davy, needless to say, was not impressed, and more unfortunately his curiosity was now fully aroused. He repeated derisively, "So he wanted to celebrate. But how generous of him."

"Oh, for Christ's sake, man, you worry at everything like a bone."

"I have an inquiring mind," said Davy, his voice soft, "and I must confess it interests me that my lord has become so generous as to invite a multitude to a dinner that must have cost him a small fortune. It interests me too that I was not invited, or Tully, or Mrs. Grizel. Just you, Coll. Now, why you? You are not such great friends."

Coll exclaimed angrily, "This is really none of your business"—then saw that he could have said nothing that would intrigue Davy more.

"It is a strange world," said Davy, raising his gray eyes to the ceiling, so that he looked like a preacher about to deliver a sermon on damnation. "So many pots a-boiling. They say our *comte d'espoir*—is that not what they call the bonnie laddie?"

"I have no idea," said Coll, "and with all due deference, Davy, I am in the process of writing to my wife. So if you don't mind—" He set the paper on the barrel again, and began determinedly to scrawl upon it; he was writing gibberish, but Davy could not see that from where he was.

Davy went on, paying this no attention, "They say he may be leaving us."

"What are you talking about now?" asked Coll in exasperation. "You tattle like any lady's maid."

"Oh, that is what they say. They say—now, there's a fine

Greek phrase for you, let me get it right to show you what an educated man I am—they say he is becoming persona non grata in France, is our wee prince, what with his spending the king's money like water, all at the expense of the Frogs, too. I don't know. I don't even know what it means. What does it mean, Coll?"

"It means," said Coll, "he is simply not wanted."

"And what will they do with the poor laddie? They cannot send him back to Scotland, for his head would roll from one end of the Highlands to the other."

Coll flinched at these words, and Davy saw it. His eyes narrowed. However, Coll managed to say calmly enough, "I think you're making all this up. Why should they throw Charles out of France? Where do you get this remarkable information from?"

"I have good hearing," said Davy, adding with his wicked smile, "I am no fine gentleman, and I go to places that decent, well-bred folk like you would not care to see. Why, only yesterday I lombarded the last of my things, two shoe buckles they were, of fine silver, and with the money rattling in my pocket, I went to the fair at Saint-Germain. They had a strange, rare animal there, Coll, that I have never seen the like. A rhinoceros they called it, if I have got the name rightly round my tongue. A monstrous great beast, brought in by a Dutch skipper, it was in a cage on four wheels, drawn by six horses. They say it eats fifty pounds of hay a day, fifteen pounds of bread and downs fifteen buckets of water."

Davy paused impressively, and Coll, only too aware that he was being encircled, laid his letter down with a sigh, and tried to keep his speaking countenance as impassive as possible.

"They can't keep the poor beastie." Davy sighed, shaking his head. "They'll be slaughtering it soon, and feeding it to the cats and dogs. I wonder what rhinoceros meat tastes like. I'd not fancy it myself, but then I have a queasy belly. Oh, but it was a rare sight, with all the people staring, and music playing. I'll confess that French music has much the same effect on me as scraping with the point of a knife upon a dish. But then—"

"Davy," said Coll, losing all patience, "what the devil has all this to do with anything? I've never seen a rhinoceros, and from your description, doubt I'll ever want to do so. Why are you telling me all this nonsense? And what has a rhinoceros got to do with the Prince? He's put on weight, but he is not as stout as all that."

"He eats a great deal," said Davy almost wistfully. "And of course there's his lady friend, the De Talmond lassie. I daresay she eats a great deal too. And there's the coaches and the velvet waistcoats and the gold brocade. It must cost a lot of money, Coll, and what does anyone get out of it? Oh, they'll have to get rid of him, whether they like it or no. I hear they are trying to persuade him to join his daddy in Rome, and that fine brother who is a member of the true church at last. But he's an obstinate man, Charlie, a sair obstinate man."

"Are you telling me," said Coll, "that they plan to assassinate him?"

"Oh, no," said Davy, shocked. "What an idea! They'd never dare create such a scandal. But there are other ways."

"I cannot imagine how you hear about such things."

"I hear about a great many things. There are informers all around. It is interesting that my lord has chosen such a time for his grand dinner. But he is like me in that, he hears of things too."

"You always call him my lord. Is he a lord?"

"Oh, how would I know?"

"A poor, common Highlander like you," said Coll in derision, and at this Davy made him a monkey grimace, and jumped to his feet, saying, "I think I'll have a wee word with Tully."

Coll remembered that Dr. Tullideph in his nonalcoholic days never spoke to Davy at all. It was odd that the two of them had apparently become such cronies; he could not imagine two more unlikely friends. Presumably the bottle was the bond.

Davy, now at the door, said suddenly, "Do you ever hope to go home again?"

The treacherous color swept up Coll's face, and Davy must have seen it, despite the poor light. But he managed to riposte with reasonable calm, "Do you?"

"No," said Davy flatly.

At this Coll, astonished, exclaimed, "How can you be so sure? Is there no hope left in you?" Then he said, as they all said from time to time, "This cannot go on. Governments change. They cannot punish us forever. One day there will be an amnesty, and we will all troop home, old, sad, shabby creatures, maybe, but at least we will end our lives on Scottish soil. You know that. It is reasonable, after all."

"I'll never see Scotland again," said Davy, and he spoke in so strange a voice, like the sounding of the pipes, that Coll felt cold inside himself, for this was not canny, this was not the wild rogue he knew.

He said at last, as Davy continued to stand there, staring ahead, "If you did go home—and I believe you will—what would you do?"

And it struck him again how little they knew of each other, despite their being more in each other's company than most families. He found that he had no idea of Davy's life. He could not see the little man settling down to any kind of domestic existence. He would perhaps indulge in what he would call "fair trading" and the world smuggling; he was so sure of this that he added, "What do you smuggle, Davy? Is it brandy or silks or spices or what?"

Davy turned upon him a grand, dramatic, outraged face, though the eyes gleamed with amusement. "What are you accusing me of now, Coll? I'll be sharpening your throat in an instant, if you do not take care."

"Oh," said Coll pacifically, "I was only jesting. I daresay you're a fine, respectable man at home, a pillar of the kirk. I would like to see you on the Sabbath day, Davy, with your prayer book under your arm. I have no doubt they call you the present-day John Knox. The very thought of it makes me shiver. But of course you're Popish, I'd forgot."

Davy shot him a look, swung round, then was gone.

It was only then that Coll remembered that he was far too interested in that dinner in the Place des Vosges, and that certainly he would be turning his dirk-sharp mind to the matter, to find out everything he could. Perhaps it was not important. Davy was a rogue, and he hated Aeneas, but he too had been caught up in the skirl of pipes and the groans of dying men at Culloden; he was unlikely to betray his own countrymen. Perhap Aeneas should be warned. But the two men were such enemies that Coll decided against it. The odds were that Davy would find out nothing, or drown the memory of this conversation in copious drafts of brandy with Tully.

Chapter 9

NOVEMBER shivered icily into December, and Coll spent the time in a kind of limbo, mostly lying around in his uncomfortable room, sleeping the time away, eating hardly at all, drinking a great deal of wine.

He did not always write to Jean. He could not bring himself to do so. The only words he could have written were, "Dear, I am coming home. Dear, I shall be seeing you again. Dear, I shall be with you and the bairns. And, Dear, how I love you, oh, God, how I want you." There was nothing else to say. What was there? The idle events of the day, the gossip, the scandal, the unusually cold weather, the continual *tracasseries* —all the Jacobites loved this word—of their small, isolated world. More and more this world grew unreal for him. As he walked the streets, to do his meager shopping, to breathe an air less foul than that of his room, he scarcely saw his surroundings. The heather was eroding like the waves of the sea, the tawny buildings faded into the outline of the hills, the voices around him became not the quick, angry voices of the French, but the soft, lilting accents of his own people.

He did not go back to the wineshop, except occasionally when he had no money at all. His funds were very low, his pension was overdue, but he had no appetite, and as for firewood, he used this meagerly for cooking, and otherwise wrapped himself round in coats and blankets. When the cold was unendurable, he went into some small bistro for a hot coffee.

He did not by any manner of means push Grizel out of his mind. Once he walked to the building where she lived, left some money carefully wrapped up, with Madame Thierry, who took it surlily and with suspicion, then skulked in the courtyard, peering up at her window, as if he were a thief. There was no light there, not even the flicker of a candle flame, but then it was late, and she was doubtless in bed. He half-hoped to see her shadow at the window though, if he had, he would have turned and run like a hare. But at least she had a roof over her head, her rent was paid, and the money he had left—almost all his month's allowance—would provide food and warmth for the baby. At the thought of Henny, poor ugly little Henny, his heart turned over, but he still did not go up the stairs, only walked quickly away, and wondered as he did so, if he had ever in his life felt such an unmitigated bastard.

He tried to salve his smarting conscience by telling himself that once he knew the date of the sailing, he would call on Grizel to say good-bye, to make sure she was all right. Jean could surely not object to that.

And his conscience continued to prick him; this did no good at all.

As he left, he was certain that he saw Paulette lurking in the shadows. This jolted him, for though she had once seemed to him a harmless enough creature, there was now something about her that he found ugly and evil. He came after her, but perhaps he was mistaken; when he turned the corner, there was no one there.

And presently he forgot about both her and Grizel, even Henny, as he lay on the bed in his cold room. He lounged there, muffled up in almost everything he had, and tried to calm himself, for the excitement was welling up in him again, so that he did not know how to endure it. He told himself repeatedly that this was dangerous and absurd, there were a hundred plots and intrigues surging around him, all of which came to nothing. But it was no use, and at last, seeing that he must do something or else go out of his mind, he decided for lack of anything better to pay a call on Dr. Tullideph.

The doctor was in and so, a little to Coll's discomfiture, was Davy. He thought again, as he looked at them, what an unlikely couple of conspirators they were. Both were drunk, but each in his own way. The doctor must by now be pickled like a herring, and Coll could see plainly enough why Davy called the permanent drunk sober. It was as if brandy ran in his veins, not blood, and as if his body had adapted itself to so strange an assimilation. He did not sway or stagger. His speech was almost unnaturally distinct, and his face was no longer glumpy, as Davy had always described it. But it seemed to Coll as if he were no longer a living man, as if he were one of the undead who dwelt in graveyards, only kept alive not so much by blood as by alcohol. The toothless mouth was set in a permanent grin that was not pleasing, the skin was smooth and very red, while the body, once so plump and sturdy, was now completely emaciated, as if Tully never ate anything at all.

As for Davy, he was simply belligerent. In this he resembled so many of his countrymen; the drink within became a permanent battle cry, a kind of vinous Cruachan. It was as well that Dr. Tullideph was as impossible to fight as a child's toy. If Davy had squared up to him, he would simply have continued to smile and reached for the bottle. If Davy had hit him, he would have fallen over and picked the bottle up again. Coll found it impossible to see them as friends, for they could not have a word to exchange, but certainly they were allied against him; he saw at once that they regarded him as the intruder.

Davy, as might have been expected, made no attempt to hide his feelings. He demanded, "And what do you want?" while Tully continued to smile.

Coll was a little taken aback by such blatant antagonism. They were after all friends of a kind, if only because they were united by a common misfortune. He said warily, "Oh, I just came by to see how you were." Then, as they went on staring at him, "Are you not going to offer me a drink?"

Davy snapped, "You can buy your own," but Tully was more civil in his grinning way, and immediately offered Coll the nearest bottle—the floor was littered with them, full and empty—but without a glass.

Coll, after consideration, did not take it. It now seemed to him that at least one of them should remain sober. He said, a trifle uneasily, "Well, Tully, and how goes the world with you?"

"The world goes," returned Dr. Tullideph, "as it always goes. I am only relieved that I am now outside it."

"Are you?" said Coll. "How can you be? You live in it, you are part of it."

"No longer," said Dr. Tullideph with satisfaction. Certainly drink had turned him into the deadest bore. He had never been what one could call a lively man, but at least he used not to talk in such portentous platitudes. "I have abandoned the world," said the doctor, speaking very pleasantly, and wearing the smile as if it were painted on his face, "for I consider that we are all self-seeking, cruel and destructive beings, except perhaps briefly to those we wish to impress. It does not please me, yet it is interesting to witness the complete egotism and brutality that hem us about. There is at least one thing." And he made an amiable gesture at Coll, as if somehow he were the host at a party and wished to draw him in. "I am no longer hurt or astonished. Though in this case, perhaps a little—"

"Oh, haud your wheesht, man," snapped Davy quickly, then to Coll, "What are you doing here? Can you not see we are having a personal conversation? What kind of gentleman are you to intrude in such a fashion? We are private, Tully and I. We have things to discuss. We do not require your company."

"I am much obliged to you," said Coll, both taken aback and irritated, for he was not accustomed to being dismissed in such a summary fashion. Then his curiosity got the better of him. "What the devil is the matter with the pair of you? Is this some intrigue? Are you planning to put the Duke of York on the throne? You look positively pregnant. Can you not at least give me some idea of what all this is about?"

The doctor at once put his finger to his nose in a roguish fashion, but Davy, who was plainly in a raging temper, said in a cold, thin voice, "You'll know soon enough. Go and dandle Mrs. Grizel's bairn. Go and play daddy. Leave us be. We're better off without you."

"You are remarkably uncivil," said Coll, then saw that if he stayed there would be a major brawl, for Davy was white with a fermenting fury, and looked as he must have looked in the old days before he dirked his enemy. "Oh, very well," he said, "I'll leave you to it. You're an ill-mannered couple of drunken devils, I must say. But I daresay you'll soon cut each other's throats."

He turned back toward the door. But he had to glance back once over his shoulder, for really, he could not understand this at all. Davy was standing there, hunched into himself, but Dr. Tullideph waved him good-bye, then at once fell into one of his strange dwams, his mouth a little open, his eyes staring. The lack of teeth was distressingly plain. Coll saw again how dreadfully thin he had grown, and wondered if, in such a mood, the drumming and the screaming still sounded faintly in the doctor's ears, piercing through the barrier of alcohol.

But the doctor only continued to wave, then said, "You should drink more. You would be happier."

"Will you stop your blethering," exclaimed Davy, and Coll, remarking his disturbance, thought that the secret they plainly shared must be something very ugly indeed. Davy was always a devious man, in and out of all kinds of illicit byways; he talked mainly of his conquests, but Coll knew, as they all knew, that he had a finger in many pies, and some of them ill-smelling. It might have been fair trading at home, but here it was honest-to-God smuggling, with perhaps the odd knifing slung in, chatting in thieves' kitchens, even a murder in a dark alleyway. What in heaven's name he had run his head into now, Coll had no idea, but it was clearly something he was not allowed to know, and he wished privately that he could have a few minutes alone with Tully, who would not require much persuasion to blab it all out.

He shrugged, and turned the door handle.

Davy said in a different voice, "There was a note left for you at the Club."

"May I have it then?" said Coll, extending his hand.

"I've lost it."

Coll was not particularly upset. He could not think it was anything of much matter. Aeneas would certainly not write to him so carelessly, and he could not think of anyone else who would do so. He was about to ask Davy what was in it, for the little man certainly did not suffer from the kind of scruples that would prevent him from opening other people's letters, then remembered that he could hardly read. He merely said crossly, "That was damned careless of you. Why don't you look for it? It might be something important."

"I tell you, I've lost it," said Davy, suddenly angry.

It struck Coll at this point that the note might be from Grizel. The very thought of it filled him with embarrassed shame. He wanted to pursue the matter, then the thought of Davy's derision stopped the very words on his lips. He made an impatient gesture, turned on his heel and went away without another word.

He might have come back, had he not on the stairway met the proprietor. The man, who certainly was unusually civil and friendly, pressed him once again to take a glass of wine with him in his office, and this drove all thoughts of Grizel out of Coll's reluctant mind.

He asked, "And how is the doctor? He don't look well to me. I've never seen a man grow so thin."

"He eats nothing. My wife's a good-hearted girl, and sometimes we send him up some dinner. But I don't think he so much as looks at it, much less touches it. He lives on brandy. He's not long for this world."

Coll believed in his heart that Dr. Tullideph would not be sorry to hear this, but nonetheless the words jolted him; it was never pleasant to have death at one's elbow.

He said uneasily, "Is there nothing to be done? It is not as if he lacks money. Sometimes I think he has more than all of us put together. I know he is a doctor, but physicians seldom look after themselves. Do you not know some medical man who could help him?"

"He'd not see him. And it wouldn't make any difference. When they take to the drink like that, they feel no desire for food at all. It would probably make him ill. And brandy's the worst of all. Oh, he'll kill himself, and it won't be so far away neither. I had a cousin who went the same way. He was a big fellow, nearly six foot, and when he passed away, he weighed no more than a child. It was dreadful to see him. He was just a skeleton. It's turning bitter cold, and one day he'll go out and catch himself a chill, and that will be the end of him. Who is that friend of his?"

"What? Oh, Davy. He's another of us. He's been kicked out of his own country like myself. Why do you ask?"

The proprietor looked down his nose, and fiddled with some papers that lay before him. He said in a distant voice, "I think you'd be wise to keep an eye on him."

"I am not a nursemaid," said Coll, smiling. "I've better things to do with my time. He's not a child, after all. What makes you say that?"

"He's meddling in things that don't concern him."

"Oh, Davy's been a meddler since he was weaned. I shouldn't worry about him. He can look after himself."

"I think," said the man, suddenly very ominous, "he's one of those revolutionaries."

"I can't believe that," said Coll. "He is a meddler, yes, but the human condition don't interest him except when it concerns himself. Davy would consort with marquises and beggars, with equal enthusiasm, provided he gets something out of it for himself. I swear he joined our Rising simply because he likes a brawl and thought there might be pickings on the way. Anyway there is no revolution, for all Paris mutters so much about it."

"There will be, mark my words."

"Do you really think so?"

"I can't understand it, of course. Some people have nothing better to do than grumble. I don't hold with this kind of thing. The good Lord has set us all in our appointed places, and it's not right to go on so about equality and liberty and all that kind of nonsense. I don't believe in it at all."

Coll reflected that a man with a prosperous little greengrocery might well be content to leave things as they were. But he only said, "What makes you call Davy a revolutionary?"

The proprietor looked embarrassed. "I've seen him—" He added in a flutter, "Not that I'm spying on him, of course. I believe in minding my own business. But I get around, you'll understand, with my deliveries and so on, believe in doing these things myself; boys nowadays are so unreliable. I saw him at one of the houses in the Place des Vosges. Lurking outside the kitchens, he was. I wouldn't have noticed particularly, except that next day he turned up here, and he and the doctor got together all confidential-like, as if they were planning the revolution single-handed."

"The Place des Vosges?" repeated Coll sharply.

"That's right. There's a real nest of them there. We all know that. That's where they hold their meetings. Oh, I daresay it don't mean nothing, but when my fine gentleman turns up here, I begin to ask myself what he's up to. And he's got a real cutthroat air to him, wouldn't trust him an inch myself, never mind his pinching some apples from me when he thought I wasn't looking. I always keep an eye on him now, I can tell you. Nobody does me twice."

Coll, assimilating all this with some surprise, said, "Oh, I don't suppose it means anything. Davy is just inquisitive. I expect he just wanted to know what was going on."

Then they talked of other things, and presently Coll left, with a kilo of fruit that the generous little man insisted on his taking, free of charge.

Coll might have reflected more on all this, had his mind not been so full of other things. He certainly wondered what Davy was doing in the Place des Vosges, but the explanation was surely a simple one: He was not only wildly curious but also resentful that he had been left out of the dinner party. He did not take the business of revolutionaries too seriously. Paris was full of such tales nowadays; plotters were hidden behind every door.

He did not trouble about the lost note either; indeed, he forgot all about it. There were two things that concerned him far more. One was a message from Aeneas, pinned to the pillow on his bed, asking him to come back to the house in the Place des Vosges on December 10. The other was that there was no letter from Jean.

Her letters had been growing more and more infrequent, but this was the first time she had not written for so long. There was often a gap of ten or twelve days, but now it was a whole month, though he had sent her a variety of brief, scattered notes, each with its little sprig of herbs, filled more with love than news, as he could not tell her the one thing uppermost in his mind, and there seemed nothing else to say. She did not answer. He could not quite believe it. Every morning he came down to see his landlady, to inquire if there was a letter for him, and the answer was always no, spoken at first without interest, then with a sympathy that irked him, for it was plain she felt that he was deserted.

He told himself that the letters must have been opened or lost, and filled in the waiting time by writing again. He did not go near Dr. Tullideph, he forgot about Davy and his strange wanderings, he did not think of Grizel at all.

"My Dear," he began, then in an unexpected way the words poured forth from him, words that he did not mean to say, words extraordinary from a man married for over fifteen years.

"My Dear, do you remember when we first met? We so nearly did not meet at all. It was a dinner party, a dreadful ordeal for a young man of nineteen, who scarce knew which was the right fork, who had no conversation, and whose cravat was choking the very guts out of him. And they were tonish men, and our host was an advocate, and there was too much to drink for me, for they insisted on giving me meridians of brandy and water, which may be fine for loosing the laird's tongue, but poor for a brat of a boy with no manners. You were there, my life, only for a while, what with the brandy and a sticky sweet which made my teeth lair in it so that I believed they would come out, I did not see you. Then I spilled my drink. I was always big and clumsy. And you saw it and you laughed. I was so angry with you! The bitch, I thought, laughing at me, and then my host told a foolish story about a shopkeeper who was asked for some necklaces, which he misunderstood as 'naked lassies,' and who retorted severely that he don't deal in such commodities. And you laughed again, and I saw you properly, with your black hair, your beautiful eyes, and a dress that seemed to me very daring, me being a country boy and not used to such a sight of the female bosom. I fell in love with you, headlong through the soup and the fish and the sticky sweet; it bubbled up through the brandy so that I was both dead-sober and mad-drunk, drunk with love and you and your dark hair. Oh, Jeanie, I never thought of myself as a marrying man, and after that I could think of nothing else...."

Then, "Dear Life, Dearest Heart, swear by the unsheathed sword that you still love me, for I do believe I cannot live without you. It may be time before we meet again. It may not. Nobody knows. It don't matter. There were difficulties when we first met, there are difficulties now, and there will be difficulties to the end of the world. But we will survive them, Dear Body, we must survive them, and one day I'll be home again, to dance with my gay girl with her fine black eyes and soft hair."

And Coll set down his pen, not knowing if he dared send this letter, yet after all it gave nothing away, though Jean might possibly read between the lines. But it was not the fear of the letter being intercepted that made him turn his face into the pillow; it was a fierce bonfire of joy which, until he had written these words, he had not fully realized—joy blazing within him at the thought of going home and seeing her and the children again.

The next day he set off once more for the Place des Vosges, only this time he was not dressed in what Davy called his fine duds; he wore his own shabby clothes. There was a hole in the elbow that he had tried to tack together, several amateur darns in his stockings, and the shirt though clean was poorly pressed, for he had been too excited to give his mind to it.

It was still very cold, though fine. There was for the moment no more snow. It was midday, but Coll had not eaten. In his present state of mind he could not endure even the thought of food. Grizel had cooked meals for him and made him eat, but now he dined mostly on black bread and sausage, washing this down with wine, seldom bothering to heat anything. Perhaps it was hunger that made him a little lightheaded, or perhaps it was the realization that this was the first step on his journey home.

Only strangely he did not feel happy. He should have been singing, walking with a dancing step. But instead he was cold with apprehension, and the cold was not due to the bitter little wind that sniped at him through his threadbare clothes. It was as if, instead of seeing his home with Jean running to meet him, he beheld a covey of redcoats with fixed bayonets, and the slipknot noose hanging from a gallows tree. For that moment he could almost have turned and run, so vivid was the dream. But of course he did not, only walked on more determinedly and, with some idea perhaps of making an oblation to the gods, presented a couple of sous to an old woman by the roadside, which he could not afford, for he was almost destitute.

This time there was no party of men with forbidding faces. He came up the magnificent staircase and was shown into a small anteroom, where Aeneas was waiting for him, writing busily at the table.

There was little in it except a portrait of someone Coll did not know; there were heavy red curtains across the window so that the light was dim, and a small filled bookcase in the corner. The room wore an air of business. Perhaps in the last century my lord did his accounts here, reckoned up how many peasants for the chopping, how many pretty brides for the raping, how many seditious types to hang from the gallows. I am become a revolutionary, thought Coll, mocking himself, for the Rising had been his one excursion into power politics; he had never otherwise concerned himself with such things at all.

Aeneas requested him to sit in the one other chair, then continued for a while with his writing. Coll might once have been angry at being treated like some suppliant lackey, but the cold still lodged within him, and a deep exhaustion; he really must make an effort to do more cooking. He was even grateful for the hiatus. Indeed, he was so apprehensive as to the outcome of this interview that he would hardly have minded if Aeneas had continued writing forever.

He fell into a kind of dream, thinking mostly of Jean, then raised his eyes to see that Aeneas was watching him. He came instantly to his senses, and perceived with something of a shock that Aeneas, always so calm and cool, was intensely disturbed. The handsome, aristocratic face was white, and there was sweat out on the forehead. Some great excitement was churning itself inside him, and his breath was coming fast. Coll could see his chest heaving up and down.

He said at last, "Well, Aeneas? Is this the day? Is this the time to learn how and when I go home?"

"Yes," said Aeneas.

"And what about the others?"

"They will all be told separately. It is less dangerous that way. We cannot afford to take the smallest risk. We never know how many spies there are among us, and if each person believes he alone has the knowledge, he is more likely to keep it to himself."

"Where do we sail from? And when?"

"You are a very forthright man, Coll," said Aeneas with a smile. But the sweat still glistened on his forehead, and his eyes moved sideways from Coll's now intent gaze.

The warnings flickered on and off in Coll's mind. In an unaccountable way he knew that this was not right, this was very wrong indeed. But he only said, "I am a man desperate to be home. How near is all this?"

"Tomorrow."

"Tomorrow! You do not give us much time."

"Do you need time to prepare for going home?"

"Perhaps not," said Coll, "but there is one thing." The words seemed forced out of him, for he had not to the best of his knowledge had the least intention of speaking them. "I would like to be certain that Mrs. Grizel and her child are provided for."

"Mrs. Grizel!" Aeneas looked for a second as disconcerted as Coll had ever seen him. "What in God's name makes you think of her at such a time?"

"I have spent a great deal of time in her company," returned Coll, adding with savagery, "as your spies have certainly informed you. I daresay you will have put another aspect on the matter, and it would not be worth my while to assure you your suspicions are unjustified."

His own self-righteous words jarred on him, and there was a pause before he continued.

He went on, "I owe her something, and the child too. She has been very good to me. I would not want to go away and leave her starving. Once I am in Scotland—" He stumbled over the words, repeating almost in bewilderment, "Once I am in Scotland, it may be a long time before I am in any position to help her. But you can see to this, and you must, for charity's sake if nothing else. She is on her own, the bairn is sickly, there is no one to protect her. I should like to have your word on this."

"Are you by any chance telling me," said Aeneas in his other voice, the cold, disdainful voice Coll was accustomed to, "that unless I give you such a word, you will refuse to go?"

"I did not say that!"

"But you implied it. Is this the great love for your wife and your country that you would sacrifice everything for this young woman who is surely capable of looking after herself? I have already helped her. I cannot take her on as a permanent burden. She is young and healthy, she must have friends. I have done a great deal for her, far more than anyone could possibly expect. I do not understand you at all, Coll. You may have an interest in this girl; you may, for all I care, have conducted a liaison with her." He looked into Coll's furious face, and smiled. "Don't be such a damned fool, man. I am talking of the Cause, and you have to talk of women. Forget Mrs. Grizel. If you must think of women, think of your wife, for in a week's time you will be seeing her again."

A voice spoke from behind the curtain, a voice a little muffled by reason of the folds of red velvet, but nonetheless recognizable enough.

"If you believe that," said Davy, making a rather involved entrance through the curtains, "you'll believe anything and everything."

He swung round on Aeneas, who had risen slowly to his feet. "You bastard," he said. "You damned liar. You son of a whore." And he laid his hand flat on the table, the blade of his dirk between his fingers. "You'll listen to me now," he said, "before I cut your throat for you. There's a witness too. I'm not the only one. Come out, friend. What ails you?"

And with this he lugged out a dazed and reluctant Dr. Tullideph, who stood there, hands hanging down, his toothless mouth agape, as unwilling and bewildered a conspirator as Coll had ever seen.

It was a small room. It now seemed filled with men. They had all belonged to the Club. Coll remembered this with bewilderment. Davy, his eyes snapping with hate, watched Aeneas, who neither spoke nor moved. Neither seemed aware of Coll, who tried to step between the two men but was instantly pushed aside.

He managed to say, however, "What the devil is all this about, Davy? Are you playing Polonius? How long have you been concealed behind the arras, and what on earth is Tully doing here?"

Davy turned his head toward him. He moved it swiftly and spitefully like a snake about to strike. Coll, still astounded by all this melodrama, had to see that it was for this kind of situation that wee Davy had been born. Coll's allusions to Polonius must have meant nothing to him at all, but he should certainly have been an actor; he would have roared the boards away and deafened the audience with his histrionics. Or perhaps he should have lived two centuries back. He could have played the hired bravo and conducted his intrigues in every Florentine gutter. No wonder he had taken to smuggling; his native moors would never have provided enough excitement.

But now he was convulsed with anger, and the anger seemed to be genuine, though certainly he was enjoying himself. The words hissed between his teeth as he spat out his story.

"I'll tell you, Coll," he said. "I'll tell you, and Tully here will back me up. Will you not, boy?" And he repeated, his voice rising, "Will you not?"

But poor Tully was not made for such a drama. God knows how he had ever been dragged into it. Perhaps by now he cared so little what happened to him that he had simply followed Davy, nodded to his tirades and swigged at the bottle while doing so. He stood there, the clothes hanging on his emaciated frame, while his hopeless, drink-sodden eyes moved from one face to the other. When at last he spoke, he said, "I want a drink."

But no one offered him the drink, and at once he began to sulk like a chidden child. The toothless mouth drooped down and tears gathered in his eyes. He turned his hopeless face on Coll as the only possible ally, but Coll's mind was far elsewhere, so there Tully stood, an alcoholic baby deprived of his bottle, his body already shrieking for its sustenance.

Coll said fiercely, "Never mind Tully. I want to know what all this is about." He rounded on Aeneas. "You know, don't you? You've tricked me. You've tricked us all. Why? What is all this?"

But Aeneas did not answer. He simply stood there, his hands square against his pockets, and fixed his eyes on Davy. He did not seem to notice the dirk. And now he was in full possession of himself again. The brow no longer glittered damply, the breathing was steady, and his lips twitched into a faint, scornful smile.

"I'll tell you," said Davy, who took a deep breath and then, as it were, exploded. The high Highland voice soared up, shrill with venom and satisfaction. "I have been doing a wee bittie of observing," he said. "I have been following this fine gentleman. Oh, it was just curiosity at first, I admit it. I have always been a curious man. I wanted to know why my lord here, my bastard lord, this son of a bitch, held so fine a dinner, and him so mean with the money he'd let his own mother starve. It's a long story. I'll not deave you with all the details, but I have good hearing and sharp eyes, and presently I made a great friend of a fellow who works for you, my lord, a kind of a lackey as one might say."

He paused, and for a second Aeneas' face flickered.

"You'll know the one," said Davy. "He is quite a friend of yours, is he not? For all he's just a low-class laddie. No doubt you will now want to stew him in the next bowl of soup, but that's your affair, not mine, and he'd not be much loss. We grew friendly, very friendly indeed, and presently I was allowed to come into the kitchens and eat some of your fine food, my lord."

Aeneas seemed unmoved by most of this, even the implied accusation, but perhaps the iteration of "my lord" was getting on his nerves, for his brows met, and the hand lying against his pocket twitched.

Davy saw this and grinned. He said again, "My lord!" He was not at any time a subtle man. He turned once more to Coll. "I moved up from the kitchens. I am, as you will have remarked, a smallish man. Oh, I have done some lurking in the heather in my time, and it's gey and easy to hide oneself in a grand house like this, with all its fine curtains." He tweaked at the material behind him. "There are big cupboards too and plenty of furniture. Your little friend told me all kinds of things. He talks like a woman, but of course that is to be expected. There's very interesting company you keep, my lord, apart from little laddies like that one. There are whores among it, strange creatures with their knitting, just like my nammy at home, and a great many gentlemen who might find themselves in the Bastille if the chance arose to flush them out. And now I'll tell you, Coll. I'll tell you what I learned." The dirk flickered in his hand, as he moved his fingers to grasp it more firmly. "You are planning to go home, are you not? Oh, it is true enough. You will be going home. You and many others."

Davy paused, but Coll said nothing, neither did Aeneas. For

Coll it was a moment of complete disaster, even though he still had no idea what Davy was going to say. Yet the disaster had lain in his belly for so long a time that his immediate reaction was neither of anger nor despair; it was simply the bitter resignation of a man beaten near to death who sees one more blow descending and no longer cares.

He saw now with the utmost clarity that the whole scheme for going home was absurd. He should have known it from the first. The fate that had picked him up like a weed from the garden and hurled him onto the midden was not to retrieve him from that midden and plant him again in his own plot. It was a fantasy, a child's dream; only when one lived so strange and disoriented a life any dream could become for a brief while reality. The anger would come, the rage of disappointment and frustration, but now he only stood there, and his thoughts such as they were concentrated first on the pathetic indecency of the poor drunk who was already plucking at himself in desperation as if he would milk brandy from his garments, and secondly on Aeneas himself, who made no attempt to check Davy, only eyed him, waiting with a dangerous resignation.

The danger indeed blazed from him, but Davy, so quick on the draw, did not seem to notice. He was too concerned with the drama of his own tale. His hand still held the dirk, but his eyes were on Coll; the recklessness consumed him like a flame.

"Ah," he said, ejecting the word with a great sigh of satisfaction, "but you'll be ettling to hear the whole truth of it. Well, now . . . you will go to Scotland, and there you will be back in your own homeland, with the heather beneath your feet. And the money, the beautiful French money, swimming round in Loch Arkaig. Does that not make you feel happy? Are you not pleased, Coll, to think that my lord here is so generous, to trouble himself over a poor common fellow like yourself, to unite you with your wife at your own hearth, in your own but and ben?"

Coll had grown white round the mouth, but he still said nothing.

Davy went on, "So it's all true. Up to a point, man, up to a point. You'll get the money, you and your friends. If you do not, you are fools, for I swear there'll be a signpost put up to direct you. My lord here is not one to spoil his cooking by lack of a little attention. Even the salmon will doubtless show you the right spots by leaping over them. And not an English soldier in sight. Not a redcoat. Just the loch and the glen and the hills behind, no one to disturb you and all that beautiful gold to be taken away. You will lug it out. You will lay it on the heather. Oh, you'll be so proud, the first men to succeed where so many have tried. But then my lord has a little plan in mind. There will suddenly appear one redcoat, two, three, a dozen, a hundred. You see, my lord has already informed the English, so they will be waiting for you. And that will be the end of you, Coll. And of your friends. What a consolation it will be, to know that you can die on your native soil. They'll take you, tie your hands behind you, and off to prison you'll go, and then a fine wee trial, and—oh, I don't know, a shot, a rope or a knife in your back. You'll not see your wife again, or maybe she'll be there to watch your hanging, with the bairns at her side. You'll not see Mrs. Grizel again either, though they say she is no longer in her room and has no money to feed herself or the babe. My lord is not interested in people unless they are useful to him, and Mrs. Grizel for a while was useful. She kept you quiet, Coll; one knew where you were. But you have not asked me the reason for all this."

"You have not so far," said Coll, his voice shaking out of control, "given me the chance."

"Then I'll tell you. It's very interesting. My lord here is a little on the English side, says his litany for King George no doubt, but that is by no means his main interest. My lord is a very versatile man. He is working here for a revolution. Did you ever hear speak of a revolution, Coll? When it comes, it will be partly my lord's doing. The fine gentlemen you met at his dinner are all planning to destroy the king and the nobility, but for that they need money. So what could be better than the fine French gold in Loch Arkaig? After all, it is easy. You pick a handful of poor, sentimental Scottish gentlemen with no prospects and no money, you hold before them a tasty carrot, a promise of going home and seeing their wives and bairns. You lead them to the loch with no one to disturb them, because the English know all about it and will let them through. You make them do all the work, then you wipe them out, for they do not matter, and you take the money back to France. At least I myself am not so sure if that money goes back, for the English like money as well as the next, and they're as good liars as my lord here. But that is something we will not know. And that," said Davy, his voice changing, "is what I learned. I understand the French very well, though I do not speak it. That is what I learned. Is it not, Tully?"

But Dr. Tullideph only stood there, his eyes hollow for lack of drink, his mind only concerned with one thing, the thing that was denied him, that these cruel people would not give him.

"Is this true, Aeneas?" asked Coll, his voice small and cold.

"Perfectly," said Aeneas, with the utmost calm. "There are a few incorrect details, but in the main that is how it is."

"You don't even attempt to deny it! You would send us all to our deaths for—for God knows what. What kind of a man are you?"

"That is none of your concern," replied Aeneas, his eyes not on Coll but on Davy.

"It will be everyone's concern," said Davy in a snarl. "You'll end in prison, my lord, chained to the wall. Or maybe broke on the wheel—I'd go a long way to see that. Oh, I was never one to cry out for the Prince, and Coll here, his clan was a traitor to the Cause. They'd not fight at Culloden, they lost the battle for us, but he is a man, he is a Scot, he don't deserve to be sent to his death like a dog. And there was one other thing I learned too, my lord. Tomorrow, so they say, the Prince must leave Paris."

At this Aeneas for the first time did show emotion. The knuckles of the hand over his pocket whitened.

"They don't want him here any longer, the poor laddie," said Davy softly, turning his eyes up to the ceiling. "There's some kind of treaty or other, I've forgot—I never had much mind for things like that—but it's called, I believe, Aix-la-Chapelle, and it says that the countries concerned do not want any Stuarts on their land. So poor Charlie has to go, and tomorrow he'll be arrested at the Opéra and no doubt have his throat cut. These Frogs are grand at cutting throats. But," said Davy with sudden savagery, "it's not only Charlie's throat that'll be cut, and my dirk has been waiting for a long, long time—Sodomite!"

The last word came out in a shout and, almost before it was uttered, Aeneas moved his fingers and shot Davy through the chest with the pistol that had, through all this, lain in his pocket.

Coll sprang forward, but it was too late. Davy's love of drama had overcome his common sense. Perhaps he had felt safe with Coll there, perhaps he believed Aeneas would never dare attack him in a house where there were servants within call, people walking outside. Or perhaps, as was most likely, he had been too overcome with the glory of the situation to see things in proportion. Davy in the heather must have been a kittle customer, but Davy in this grand house was out of his element, and had forgotten his natural caution. Coll did not even have time to catch him as he fell.

He made a small choking noise, then jackknifed as if hit in the belly. He fell on his face and lay still.

He was a small man and in death he looked nothing. The blood spread under him. Coll, shaking and ashen-faced, put an arm beneath him and turned him over. He was already quite dead. His face, the sharp, cunning face, so alive, so full of movement, had in that instant collapsed on itself, the mouth gaping, the eyes astare.

Coll knelt there, Davy's head on his arm. He looked up at Aeneas who appeared completely unmoved, and who had sat down at his table again. He whispered, hardly able to force the words out for his hate, horror and revulsion, "Why did you do that?"

"Do you imagine I would swing for him? He threatened me. I do not accept threats from anyone."

"You killed him because he called you a sodomite!"

"It don't matter, one way or another." Aeneas shot him an indifferent glance, then pulled his papers toward him.

"You'd best murder me too," said Coll fiercely. "Do you imagine I'll let you get away with this?"

"You have no choice," said Aeneas. Then suddenly Dr. Tullideph, whom they had all forgotten, and who had been watching this uncomprehendingly, began to scream.

It was a dreadful noise, shrill and wild and mad.

"Oh, oh, oh!" wailed Dr. Tullideph, rocking himself to and fro, then in a terrible shriek, "Ah, stop, stop, stop! I cannot stand it anymore. For Christ's sake, stop, you're killing me." Then, "Why can't they leave me alone? Why is there so much wickedness in the world? All I want is to be left in peace."

And with this he was out of the room, banging from side to side like a moth in the candle flame. They heard him going down the stairs, a crash as if he fell, then the bang of the front door.

Coll said slowly, "I could kill you."

Then Aeneas smiled. He looked up at Coll from where he was sitting; his foot swung idly over his crossed knee. He seemed entirely at ease, and did not so much as glance at the body crumpled on the floor.

"You'd not dare," he said, "and I'll tell you for why. I'll tell you a lot of things, Coll. Do you imagine I am any more afraid of you than I was of him?" He briefly touched the body with his toe. "I shot him because he deserved it. He insulted me. He was never the least danger to me. Who would listen to a mean little rogue like that? Or to you. I am an established citizen here. I have friends who are highly placed and influential; they would speak for me. And you? What in God's name are you all? You are lonely, lost and damned. A thief here and a lecher, a drunk there who is as good as dead, and as for you, you're a poor, miserable creature with neither home, wife, nor money, wandering about with nothing to do, a cheap sentimentalist who seizes on any chance to get back to Scotland, which you'll never see again. You are the ideal dupe, Coll. You was always the most suited to my purpose. You'll not tell a soul about this. Who'd listen to a cheap-jack like you? And you know full well you dare not attract attention. You are a foreigner here, dependent on charity. The French government would only be too glad to be rid of you. If you open your mouth and start making trouble, do you know what will happen to you?"

"It might be worth it, whatever does happen."

"Oh, you say that. You know very well you don't mean it. They'd ship you back home, and there you'd hang, as you should have hung long ago. This carrion here will disappear, and no one—no one—will even know he is gone. Of course it was all a story. You may as well know that now. Only a fool would have believed it in the first place, even with a grand dinner thrown in. It don't matter now. It seemed a fair enough idea at the time, to get my dupes to work for me. Oh, yes. I work for the English government, among other things. Why not? They are not so anxious to see you all again, but they would not mind hanging you. You are potential troublemakers. They were perfectly willing to let us have the money for the privilege of finishing you for good and all. Well, this idiot has blown it all sky-high. This meddler— It makes no difference. You will go on living, if you call it living, away from everything that means anything to you, in a country that despises you, with no future. I think myself you'd be better off dead. I have no patience with any of you. I cannot abide romantic idiots who are prepared to give up everything for the loutish son of a Polish madwoman and a Scottish nincompoop, and what they call a Cause—a cause doomed before it started. You could say that the Stuarts have never been off the throne, and the Rising you are all so proud of was completely unimportant from the very beginning. You have forfeited your future for nothing. For a silly dream."

"That is surely better," said Coll, breathing hard, "than pledging it for a traitor's fee."

"No! Do you really believe that? Oh, your head is in the air like all Scots. Do you not know by now that the day of dreams is done? Clans rising in the heather, raising the standard, following the bonnie lad who had not even the sense to know his friends, who reviled the one man who might have brought him victory—such bloody nonsense! Look where your dreams have led you. Do you still dream? If you do, it must be because there is nothing else to occupy your mind."

"At least," said Coll, "I can warn the Prince."

"Yes," said Aeneas, "you can warn the Prince. You have my full permission to do so. I will even help you. He leaves for the Opéra tomorrow evening. When he arrives there he will be arrested. Tell him. Stand in his path and shout it in his ear. He'll pay no attention. He is pigheaded and stupid like all the Stuarts, and as obstinate as the devil. He has always known better than everyone else. He will smile at you, pat you on your loyal head, thank you cordially for having fought for him. Then he will continue on his way, and all will go according to plan. There is nothing you can do to stop it. Do you think you'd leave this room alive if I believed there were?"

Coll could endure it no longer. He lunged at Aeneas with his fists, only to be brought up short by the pistol pointing at his head.

"Do you wish to accompany your friend?" asked Aeneas pleasantly. "Why not? I'll put a term to your existence, if that is what you wish. It makes no difference to me. There will be two bodies instead of one, and I have those who will easily and quietly dispose of them. There will after all be no one to mourn, for no one will know or care. You should think of that, friend. No one will care."

No one will care.

Coll stood there, staring stupidly at the pistol. The anger and despair convulsed him like a fever. He said at last in a rough, choked voice, "Who the devil are you? You betray your own people, you rob, you murder. Who are you?"

"Oh," said Aeneas, laying the pistol on the table but not releasing his grip, "sometimes they call me Monsieur Sansterre, sometimes Mr. Lackland. Sometimes they call me uglier names. The blood of Bruce runs in my veins, but so it does for most Scots; our Robert must have been a very generous man. It don't matter. I am as I am. At least I do better than you. I have a decent roof over my head, good food and presentable clothes." His eyes moved derisively over Coll's shabby suit. "You call me traitor. What is that but a word?"

"And sodomite!"

"Another word. We are all entitled to live in the best way we can. I would not change places with you. You'll go crawling back to your hole, you'll eat your soup and black bread. That will go on till the day you die. If that's being a hero, I am only thankful that I am no such thing."

"I think you are the most evil man I have ever met," said Coll.

"You are beginning to bore me," said Aeneas, rising to his feet. "You'd best say good-bye to this little gutter rat friend of yours. There's no one to tell of his death, but I give you permission to see if there are any papers on him. I doubt there are. He is like you. Nobody gives a damn whether he is alive or dead. He'll be thrown into his grave tonight, and that's the end of him."

"I suppose," said Coll, dropping to his knees by Davy's body, "that Paulette is one of your spies."

"Oh, yes. I had to keep an eye on you. I knew you were ideal for my purpose, being weak and gullible, but I like to know where people are and what they are doing. She is useful to me. One has unfortunately to use these contemptible creatures."

"And all this for a revolution. What in God's name does a revolution mean to you? It would be full of these contemptible creatures, as you call them."

"It means nothing," said Aeneas. "Why should it? It means nothing but a little power, a little money. That's all. I do not know when it will come. Perhaps not for some time yet. But it will come, and in the meantime there are pickings to be won. It don't matter to me if a king is on the throne or a dictator. All I want is to be beside whoever it is. Besides, it amuses me. I lead an entertaining life. I shall continue to do so."

"It's you who may end up on the gallows," said Coll.

"Do you know," said Aeneas, "I very much doubt it. People like me seldom do. It's idiots like yourself who run their heads into a noose. But I've had enough of your moralizing. Look through this fellow's pockets and go. I trust you enjoy meeting your Prince tomorrow. I don't suppose you have ever talked to him personally. They say he has the common touch, but that was when he skulked in the heather, and then he had no choice. I daresay you will find him agreeable enough. Words cost nothing, and that is all he gives to his faithful followers, so he can afford to be generous."

Coll did not answer this. He went through Davy's pockets, to find almost nothing but a few coins, a paper with an address scrawled on it by someone else, then at last in the innermost pocket a note so stained with blood as to be almost illegible. But he could still read his own name, and he recognized the handwriting. This must be the note Davy believed he had lost. It was from Grizel. He pushed it into his own pocket, then rose to his feet.

"I do not suppose we will ever meet again," said Aeneas.

"I pray to God not," said Coll.

At the door he looked down at Davy's body. It seemed extraordinarily small. He said in a voice that was bewildered, almost inaudible, "How could you kill him like that? You act as if it means nothing to you, nothing at all. But he was a man like yourself, a Scot, a fellow countryman. And you murder him for nothing. You said he could do you no harm, and you simply shoot him down as if he were vermin."

"That is all he was," said Aeneas.

Coll stood for a moment staring at him. He had begun writing again, his handsome head bent low over the paper. He was in his way a magnificent-looking man, and the hand that held the pen was white and elegant. To Coll it was as if a cold light encircled him.

He said, "I believe, Aeneas, you must be the loneliest of all of us."

For one second Aeneas raised his head. In that second his face changed, grew ugly, menacing and old. Then he continued with his writing. He did not so much as look up as Coll closed the door.

Chapter 10

THERE WAS at last the letter from Jean waiting on the table in Coll's room.

He did not open it immediately. He was too depleted to do so. He felt as drained of blood as poor Davy, lying there on the floor, perhaps already bundled into a pauper's grave. Davy had said, "I'll never see Scotland again." Now he would end, like Tom Ryder, away from his own land, never to return. The thought of Tom made Coll remember Grizel's note, but he could not summon up the energy to read it; he could only manage to drag himself to his bed and fling himself down upon it.

The note stiff with dried blood, Davy's blood, remained in his pocket. Jean's letter, unopened, lay across his chest where he had dropped it. Once the mere sight of her handwriting would have quickened Coll's heart; he would not have been able to wait a moment before tearing it open. But now he gazed down at it listlessly, as if somehow he sensed that this was one further stage in the ill fate that dogged him.

His landlady had said as he came in, "There's a letter waiting for you." And she beamed at him, for she was a kindly woman, and she liked this large, red-haired creature who after all caused her no trouble, who was always willing to help her lift heavy things, and fetch and carry.

He raised his head without a smile. He looked so white that she thought he must be ill.

"Are you all right?" she asked him, and he turned on her so desperate a look that she was quite alarmed. She said, "Is there anything wrong, monsieur?" and at that he smiled, a dreadful smile as it seemed to her, saying, "Oh, no, it is simply the end of the world."

Oh, well, men were always so dramatic. But she shook her head as she went into the kitchen. She was on the verge of offering to bring him some supper, but natural caution and common sense prevented her. After all, if one started that kind of thing, one had to go on. He was a nice enough fellow, if a little erratic with his rent, but she had other things to do than feed him. But she hoped it was not bad news, and once she came out to listen in case he needed help.

There was dead silence from the room above. Coll still lay on his bed, and watched his dream disappearing like smoke rings. *The day of dreams is done.* It scarcely mattered after all what Jean had to say to him. He would not see her again. Jean was the dream, with Donald and Amy, and the loch and the heather, the hills and the trees. Jean was away in another world, his beautiful, dark-haired girl; the dark hair would whiten, the beauty would disintegrate, the children would grow into people whom he would never know. The dream was gone forever, and now it seemed to him as if it had never existed, as if it had had no reality, even in the past.

He dragged himself to his feet and heated up some of the morning's leftover coffee on his little stove. It was hot and bitter, it nearly choked him as he swallowed it down.

Then he opened the letter.

"You must try to forgive me, Coll. I cannot continue like this. I have tried and tried to believe we shall see each other again. You know as I know that we never shall. I could never come to France, even if there was a home for me and the children. This is my home. I must stay here, and try to make a life for myself as best as I can. I shall not write again, and I must entreat you not to write to me. Let us forget each other. It is nearly three years since we last met, it is a long time, and since then the whole world has changed. And there are the children, Coll. It is bad for them to be without a father, especially Amy who is growing up so fast, and Donald too, who needs a man's care. The other children make fun of them, tell them their father is a traitor who fought against his own people. Amy often comes home in tears, and asks me if this is true, and now I have nothing left to say, I do not know how to comfort her. I know you love the children very much. It is chiefly for them that I ask you to leave us alone, for there is nothing more you can do for us, except harm, and I know you would never want that. Do not answer this. There is nothing left to say between us. I am very sorry. I cannot help it. I did warn you, but you would not listen. I think you will be very angry with me, but I hope that later, when you have reflected, you will understand. I am a normal woman, I am still quite young, and there is someone here who wants to look after us. I have thought this over for so long, it is not a hasty decision.

But now I have made up my mind. I am not capable of spending the rest of my life in a wifehood that is a widowhood, yet leaves me quite alone. I wish you everything that is good. I was very happy with you. Try not to think too badly of me. Coll, please forgive me. Please."

And then just her name. "Jean."

Jean.

Coll did not emerge from his room until the late afternoon of the next day. The landlady came out to have a look at him. She thought he looked strange, and he walked as if he suffered from the vertigo, holding onto the walls, but he seemed more cheerful. He wished her good-day, and commented on the fine smell of cooking coming from her kitchen.

She forgot her sensible principles. She suggested that he come in for a bite to eat. "There's plenty," she said. "When I cook for three, there's always enough for four. I can't help it. It's just my way."

But he refused, very civilly. He said he was not hungry, besides he had a business appointment. He told her that he had to be at the Opéra, which surprised her a little, this being a fashionable and expensive district. And off he went, leaving her to shrug her shoulders and think as always that men were odd creatures.

Aeneas had said that the dream was over, but Coll felt as if he were still walking in a dream, and scarcely noticed the dizziness that overcame him from time to time. He was light-headed with exhaustion and lack of food. He could not have touched a morsel of anything and was unaware of hunger; his weakness did not trouble him.

He came up to the Opéra. It was not of course the first time he had seen it. In the first weeks when he had walked all over Paris he had passed it a number of times. But naturally he had never been inside. It struck him now in this strange state of his, which was shock though he did not trouble to analyze it, that it was odd that he should live in this big city so full of theaters and beautiful *objets d'art*, yet never have the means to profit by them. But now he was not interested in the performance, only in the fact that the Opéra was guarded by the military. The duc de Biron, who was colonel of the Guards, was pacing to and fro before it, and there were sentries at the doors and corridors.

Aeneas had not exaggerated. But then Aeneas was not in the habit of exaggerating.

Coll turned and made his way to the Rue St. Honoré, where the prince's carriage was bound to pass. It was very cold again, and he was inadequately clothed, but the burning obsession within him kept him warm, and he propped himself up against the nearest wall, waiting for the sound of rolling wheels.

There were many people in the street. They were all better dressed than Coll, and some of them looked at him with a kind of suspicious surprise that this large, pale, shabby man should be standing there as if waiting for some appointment.

Coll noticed none of them, not even when they knocked against him. He did not even think again of Jean's letter. Too much had happened, he could no longer take it in.

Last night he had drunk himself to sleep, or done his best to do so, but in the end the wine no longer helped him. His limbs were clogged, the room spun round him, but his mind remained shockingly clear. At first he thought of her with raging anger. "Bitch!" he shouted at the revolving walls. "Slut! Whore!" He longed passionately to get his hands round her throat. He could almost feel the fragile flesh and bone beneath his fingers, as he pressed the life out of her; he could see her face as the head fell backward and broken, the staring eyes, the ugly, protruding tongue of the strangled. He heard her cries for mercy, he thought of himself striking and kicking her, banging her head against the floor, smashing his hands down on her dead, hideously transformed face.

Then, as the drink took hold of him, the self-pity followed, and he cried, the tears pouring down his cheeks, the gulping sobs coming from his throat. "Jean, Jean!" he bellowed to the walls. "Oh, Jean, my dear, my darling—" Then the cold calm descended on him. He stopped weeping and railing, he no longer dwelt on her murder. He grew cunning, with the sad slyness of the hopelessly drunk. He waved a finger at her. "Na!" he said. "And who is he, the son of a bitch? Who is he, the whoring devil who's stolen you from me?" And he struggled to think who it could possibly be, but now the drink was shooting through his head, and every face that swam into his mind was instantly blotted out by another, so that there was nothing but face upon face, and half of them he could not put a name to, and half were people who had nothing to do with her at all. Aeneas was there, damn his soul, and wee Davy, and poor, sottish Tully, already dead, who would never look at a woman again. And others, a myriad others, some of them ghosts, people around his home, men who had died on the battlefield.

Then the drink smote him like a stone, and he fell backward into a thick, whirling, feverish sleep, to wake in the morning to an appalling, thumping head, a nausea that made him think he was dying, and an icy misery such as he had never known in his life.

It took him a long time to recover enough to get up. He managed it at last, deluged his pumping head with cold water, then tore Jean's letter into tiny pieces. It was childish, it did nothing for him, yet in some ways it was a satisfaction; if the dream were gone, let all traces of it be destroyed.

And now, still ill and dazed, yet determined to stop the Prince's carriage, he waited in the Rue St. Honoré.

The Prince was late. Perhaps princes were always late, it was their privilege. It was not until half past five that the carriage, with its royal coat of arms, trundled into view. Coll could see the Prince in it, accompanied by three gentlemen of his household. He leaped into the roadway, waving his hands. At first he believed the carriage would knock him down and pass over him, but he saw the Prince saying something to one of his companions, and then it stopped, the horses within an inch of him, and the door opened.

Coll looked up into the Prince's face. He had never before seen Charles at close quarters, never spoken personally to him. He had seen him from a distance on the battlefield, once in the flight from Culloden had almost brushed against him. But now the face bending toward him was within touch of his hand.

For a second he stared silently at this man whom he did not know, with whom he had never exchanged a word, yet who had in a sense taken him from his native land, turned him into a penniless exile, broken his marriage and savaged his life. He stared without hate, almost with bewilderment, at a handsome man, a little gross now, a little stout, a little blurred by drink and sexual excess, yet still fine-looking, with a high, broad brow, a shapely nose, chestnut-hued hair golden at the tips, and dark-brown eyes. They said his eyes were blue, but this was not so; they were as dark as the eyes of the "Black Bird," his father, and his great-great-great-grandmother, Mary Stuart. There was an air of distinction to him, an arrogance too, yet the mouth was a little petulant, and for a moment, when the eager smile flickered, a great air of debauched weariness, as of a man who had sunk below the level of hope, who had once achieved the golden heights, then fallen away, never to see them again.

And Charles— He saw a youngish man, prematurely aged, with red hair, and a face pallid with eating always the wrong food and seldom enough of it, a face that should have had the Highland air blowing upon it, which had now grown accustomed to the stench and stews of Paris. He saw the hands shaky with drink, the shabby, darned clothes, the down-at-heel shoes, the uncared-for look of a man not accustomed to dealing with himself. He had seen hundreds like him, and they always came to him cap in hand: We fought at your side at Culloden, sir. We rose to your standard at Glenfinnan, sir. We have been kicked out of our own country for your Cause. We are poor, we are starving, we have no roof over our head, nowhere to go and nothing to do. Help us, Highness, a little money, Highness, perhaps a place in your equipage, Highness—

My poor, good fellow, I am so grateful to you, but unfortunately, what with my mistresses and my velvet suits and my fine carriages, I have not a penny to spare. I am as impoverished as yourself. You will always however have my warmest gratitude. I will never forget what you have done for me.

"Your Highness," began Coll, but Charles swiftly interrupted him, waving aside his companions who would have urged the carriage on again.

"I think I know you," he said. "Was it not at Culloden? Yes, I believe it was. During the retreat. If only Lord George—but never mind that now, it is past history. I remember that you behaved with the utmost gallantry. Your face comes instantly to my mind—"

"Your Highness, I beg of you—"

"How this brings back the old days! Were you with me at Perth? Why, yes, I thought so. There is nothing wrong with my memory, not where my dear friends are concerned. Do you remember—" He broke off, to laugh in a boyish way. "Do you remember how the baillie there wore a large peruke while I was bareheaded? One of my Highlanders, a rough fellow with a heart of gold, as they all have, snatched the peruke off and set it on my head, saying—I mind the exact words, for they so amused me—saying, 'It was a shame to see ta like o' her, clarty thing, wearing sic a braw hap when ta very prince hersel' had naething on ava'.'" And here he laughed again merrily, while his companions, who had doubtless heard this before, gave wan smiles.

It was a fair imitation of the Highland accent, but this was not what Coll was here for; he was frantic for time and so far had scarcely been allowed to speak one word. He began again desperately, "Your Highness, if you would listen to me—"

But Charles was away again. "You were not of course with me on my wanderings. No. I would have remembered. By that time you would be safe here as I was to be shortly. What is your name?"

"My name is Coll Macdonell, sir, and—"

"Ah, you are attached to Clan Macdonald. My oldest friends. Two of the seven men of Glenmoriston were Macdonalds. Those were grand days, terrible perhaps, but grand too. One grew to know one's friends; one felt somehow part of the Highlands. You would scarce believe it, friends, but I lived on biscuits and hill water. I remember how Captain Malcolm warned me against drinking it, told me it was dangerous when I was sweating and would provoke a fever, but I told him it would never hurt me in the least. If you drink a cold thing when you are warm, only remember to piss after drinking, and it will do you no harm at all. And it never did, it never did."

Coll said almost in a shout, "Your Highness, you are going to the Opéra—"

"Ah, the Opéra," said Charles. "Faith, I go because it is expected of me, but it has never seemed to me true drama. I infinitely prefer the theater. Can anything be more unnatural for a man to sing three or four minutes to his valet to give him his gloves, and the valet to quaver out as many minutes in saying he will bring them?"

He laughed again, the brown eyes moving warily across Coll's face. Then, as if he expected he might be asked for money, he cut across Coll's words, saying in a harsher voice, "I must go. I cannot keep my friends waiting. But it has pleased me to see you. I am always glad to see my old friends, and you must know that as long as I have a bit of bread I am always ready to share it."

And with this he moved back and suddenly slammed the door. The carriage swept instantly along, leaving Coll standing there, not knowing whether to weep, laugh or swear, for not only had he had no opportunity to utter his warning, but he had had no chance to say anything at all. Then he knew that he must see the drama out. He took to his heels, running at full speed, taking a shortcut through the side streets that would bring him to the Opéra before Charles and his friends.

He was there one minute before. He saw that the theater was indeed surrounded by troops. He watched in a kind of weary acceptance as the carriage steps were let down for the Prince to descend. Instantly the officer in charge gave a signal, and Charles was seized by his arms and legs, to be carried through a narrow passage into the Court of the Palais Royal.

Coll silently followed a small crowd of Parisians, to hear the officer say, "*Prince, je vous arrête au nom du roi.*"

Coll could not see Charles' face, which was turned away from him, but he heard him say in a dull, angry voice, "The manner is a little unceremonious."

Then his sword and pocket pistols were taken from him and, in spite of his loud, furious protests, he was bound with what appeared to be silk ribbon, and carried into the Palais.

Coll walked away. He saw now that all the neighboring streets were held by police, and the troops stretched along the road to Vincennes, where presumably the Prince was to be taken. He was filled with anger and sorrow, not because he had much feeling for this young man who had destroyed his country, but because it was humiliating to see such humiliation, and because this was the end of the story, not only for Charles, but for himself.

Three years ago a standard had been raised, and now the beautiful boy was tied up like a parcel, to be thrown out of France, as he had been thrown out of Scotland, to end his days like Coll himself, in exile.

The dreams were done indeed.

It was only as he walked morosely back to his room that Coll remembered Grizel's note. He drew it out of his pocket, grimacing as he handled it, for it was black with Davy's blood. He opened it. He found it hard to decipher, it was so stained, but at last he was able to make it out.

Grizel wrote, "I would not trouble you for myself, but the baby is very ill, and I do not know what will become of us. There is no more money being paid, and we have to move and I have nowhere to go. If you can spare the time, will you come to me? It is for Henny, not for myself."

And then her signature, firm and rounded as might be expected; Grizel, however desperate, would never entirely lose her strength.

Coll did not so much as hesitate. He went straight with the utmost speed to the building where she lodged, ran up the stairs and banged on the door. It was opened to him by a young man he had never seen before.

Coll said, breathing in exhausted gasps, "There was a young lady lived here. A Madame Ryder—"

The young man shrugged. He had been here for ten days. He knew nothing of a Madame Ryder. When he moved in, there was no sign of any previous occupation, and, no, he had no idea where she was to be found.

There was no sign of Madame Thierry either, though after knocking repeatedly on the locked door, Coll was certain he heard movements inside. He called her name. He shouted at her to open up. But it was no use, and he came out furiously into the courtyard, wondering what the devil he was to do now; the only person likely to know Grizel's new address was Aeneas, and he suspected that he would not even be admitted again into that house in the Place des Vosges.

When he saw Paulette he was so away in his own despairing thoughts that he almost passed her. She was standing there, her knitting in her hands, exactly as he remembered her: dowdy, middle-aged, impassive, wearing as always her intense respectability with the most disreputable air imaginable.

She saw him just before he saw her. Her eyes moved sideways, then with surprising speed she made for the street. But he was before her. The fact that she wished to avoid him convinced him that she had the information he needed. He leaped across her path, and seized her arm.

"Where is she?" he demanded fiercely. "Where is she?"

"I don't know what you're talking about," said Paulette.
"You bloody lying whore. Of course you know. You've been spying on us ever since I met you. You were engaged as a spy. I suppose you are another of these would-be revolutionaries. I want to know where Grizel Ryder is. You tell me, or I'll throttle the life out of you."

Then she came for him with her knitting needles, and she came straight for his eyes. He was so taken aback by the unexpected onslaught that she nearly succeeded. It was the last thing he had foreseen, and besides, she was a woman so that for a moment he merely dodged her, making no attempt to defend himself. But the next instant he came to his senses, seeing that this was a matter of sheer survival. He fought her as ferociously as she him. Her violence was extraordinary, especially as throughout her face remained expressionless, while she savagely jabbed the needles at him, as if she would gouge out his very eyeballs.

It would have been easier to stop a wildcat. She fought like a demon. She aimed her knee between his legs, kicked his ankles, butted him with her head, and those damned needles were only an inch away; once they scratched his cheek, and once ripped the corner of his mouth. He held her wrists away as well as he could, then completely losing his temper, what with fright, amazement and exhaustion, swung his fist back and smashed it into her face twice, then with his other hand struck her in the chest so that she lost her balance and fell onto the cobbles.

She lay there motionless. She had not uttered one word, nor did she now. Only the eyes remained open, watching him, black with malice and spite, while her mouth mumbled at him as he had seen it once before. The knitting needles had rolled away from her.

"Tell me Grizel's address," he said, and his face, scratched and bleeding, was hard as a stone.

She did not answer, only continued to mumble with this strange, slavering motion of her jaws. It was like a wild beast, a wolf.

Coll crouched beside her, and set his hands about her throat. He felt as if he were touching something unclean. There was neither compunction nor pity in him. "The address," he said again, "or I'll kill you. I mean it. I think you know I do. The address!"

For the first time she made a faint sound, a kind of moaning whimper, then, as Coll dug his thumbs remorselessly in, she gave a gasp and made a feeble gesture with her hand.

He slightly loosened his grip. "Well?" he said. "What is it?"

She told him in a hoarse, choking voice. If looks could have leveled him, he would be lying dead beside her. He had never seen such intensity of hate in a human gaze; the opaque eyes were alive with it as if snakes were swarming within. He released her. She fell back against the cobbles again. Her strength was demolished, for she was after all a woman, but the look that followed him was the look of one who would gladly have seen him tortured slowly to death.

He was never to see her again, but he was to remember that look to the end of his days.

He went instantly to Grizel's room. It was not far from where he lived himself. Their paths must almost have crossed many times. He could not understand how it was that he had not met her. He walked almost automatically, but so fast that he was nearly running. The horror of the brawl with Paulette was still with him, the violence of it sickened him almost to the point of physical nausea. The blood trickled unnoticed down his cheek. But there was another horror in his heart, the realization that he had abandoned this girl, left her and Henny without so much as asking for her, even calling to see how she was.

The room this time was on the ground floor, and the building was a small house, not a tenement. It was evil and black and old, it stank of decay and dirt, but the room itself was polished and clean, and Grizel sat by the window, sewing by the light of the oil cruisie that he remembered. There was no fire. It was intensely cold.

She lifted her head as he came in. She half-moved to rise to her feet, then did not but laid the sewing down on a small table beside her.

He said, "Grizel." He could not say anything more, the words stuck in his throat.

She did not answer immediately. She was even thinner than he remembered, but her hair was pinned up neatly, the apron she wore was clean. She made a little motion with her head. Then, as her eyes took in his wild appearance, she exclaimed, her voice rising, "What has happened? Have you had some accident?"

Coll realized at this point how deplorable he must look. Not only was his face marked and bloody, but Paulette had wrenched out a tuft of his hair, his clothes were torn, and his hands filthy with dirt and bruises and blood. But he did not answer this, only muttered through the guilt and remorse that were tearing at him, "I'm sorry."

Then, his eyes moving round the room, he realized what was missing, what instinctively he had been expecting.

He whispered, "Henny."

"She's dead, Coll." Grizel's rough voice was steady, but her eyes moved away. "I do not believe she ever had much chance. I suppose I deceived myself, one always does, but in my heart— Perhaps if we had been home, and there had been warmth and proper clothes and good food—I don't know. I doubt it would have made much difference in the end. She was so weak and small, she never put on weight, she could scarcely take her milk. And winter came, and I had to leave my room, and the money stopped. I wrote to you—"

"I have only just had the note."

"I thought that must have happened. I didn't believe you would not come." She sighed. "They threw me out. Madame Thierry was so delighted. She always hated me, and when Aeneas stopped paying my rent, she couldn't get rid of me quick enough. If the sisters at the convent hadn't found me this room, I don't know what I would have done. But the move was bad for my poor wee Henny, and I had no money to buy kindling for a fire. She caught some kind of cold. She didn't last for more than a day. There was nothing I could do for her, any more than for Tom. I don't think anyone could have helped, not even a doctor." She must have seen Coll's appalled face. She said quickly, "Don't reproach yourself. It is not your fault. It would have happened whether you were there or not. What could you have done? She just didn't have the strength to live. It was a miracle really that she lasted so long. And—and it was very peaceful. She just went out like a little flame. Perhaps it was as well."

Coll could not speak. The fact that even now Grizel thought of his feelings, that she wished to comfort and reassure him, was almost worse than anything. The shameful tears were bursting from his eyes, tears for Henny, tears for Grizel, tears of horror at himself. He stood there, unable even to move, and Grizel's next words made him turn violently away so that his back was to her.

"You are in a dreadful state," she said quite censoriously. "You must have your face bathed. You are covered in blood."

He cried out in a shout, "No! Leave me alone," but she only said, "Ah, don't be so silly, Coll. I simply cannot imagine what you have been doing with yourself. Do you think you can walk around looking like that? You'll frighten the entire neighborhood. Why, your breeks are half off you, your shirt is ripped to the waist, you're simply not decent. What good do you imagine it will do me for you to look such a disgrace? As for your hair . . . it looks as if a bit has been pulled out." Then in a different voice she said, "Oh, my God, what has happened to you? What on earth have you been doing?"

He did not answer this. He said in a choked voice, his back still turned toward her, "I don't know what to say for myself. I am so ashamed. You pretend to believe me, and I deserve it that you cannot, but it's God's truth. I have only just had your note. Davy picked it up at the Club and forgot—" He broke off. He could not tell her yet about Davy. She had more than enough on her plate, poor lass, without murder being thrown in. He went on, "I would have come at once if I'd known. You must believe that, however badly you think of me. But it makes no difference, I can see that. After all, I simply walked out on you, and for no reason except something that was entirely my fault. I had no right—"

"Oh," said Grizel crossly, "such havers! Such havers. But then that's men all over. You had no right! What does that matter now? I know how it was. I warned you it would happen, but of course you never listened. It was the drink. It's always the same. It was like that with Tom, too."

"It didn't give me the right to stay away," he said, then, almost in astonishment at himself, "It wasn't human." He turned now and came toward her, holding out his hands. "Will you forgive me, Grizel? Can you forgive me? I know I don't deserve it, but you are all I have left now. If you don't forgive me, I don't know what I shall do."

"What is all this now?" she said. "Why do you say such silly things? This is your conscience speaking, Coll. It is making you say nonsense. Of course I'm not all you have left. You have a wife, have you not?"

"No. Not any longer."

"What do you mean? Oh, she's not dead—"

"She is very much alive, but I have no wife," said Coll. He had recovered his self-control, and spoke more calmly. "She has just written to me. She says she can wait no longer for me. There is another man. She says it is not right for the children to live so, with a father who is discredited, and who is never there. I can understand it in a way."

Grizel, apart from a brief grimace of disbelief, said nothing, but he had, even in his distress, to notice that the look on her face was remarkably lacking in understanding; the very mention of Jean's name seemed to tighten her features.

He gave her a bitter smile. "You would never understand that, would you? But then you have never liked Jean, and one never understands people one dislikes. I don't think there are so many women like you. You'd wait for your man till the end of the world, wouldn't you?"

She still said nothing, so he went on, "Be fair to her. If I can, so surely can you. She is still quite a young woman, and she's very beautiful." His face contorted for a moment, then he said, "I wasn't so reasonable last night. Last night I wanted to kill her. I think I wanted to kill the whole bloody universe. It's strange, Grizel, but everything seems to happen at once; there are times when the whole world caves in on you. It's been like that these past two days. I wouldn't have believed it possible am even wondering what can happen next. Well, that is that. It's over and done with. I have no wife, and I believe I may never get home again, never. I can even think of it quite calmly."

He looked at her. She was pouring water from a jug into a basin, then soaking a cloth in it. He said, "You see, I cannot stop thinking of myself. I daresay that's what made me so fine a dupe—but never mind that. You've not been treated so kindly either, girl, have you? And here you are, listening to my troubles. I think perhaps it's time I listened to yours."

She was by him now, the wet cloth in her hand. She pulled his head toward her by a lock of the tangled hair. Then she must have noticed the bald patch, for she exclaimed, "But it's true! A bit has been pulled out by the roots. Oh, my God, who did that to you? Who could possibly do such a thing?"

"A woman," said Coll on a sigh, then instinctively shuddered. "If you can call her that. But, yes, she is a woman. She at least fulfills a woman's functions. I don't think that is a story I had better tell you. You cannot have many illusions about me, and I don't wish to take the few remaining ones away."

"You talk too much," said Grizel, then began to sponge his face. When he winced, she said gently, "My poor Coll. You really are in the wars, are you not?"

He said in a rough, angry voice, "Are you trying to shame me even more? How dare you pity me? What is there in me to pity?"

"I think," said Grizel, "you should stop being so sorry for yourself," and at this he gave it up, surrendering to her ministrations in silence. Only he looked down once at the bloodstained basin in a kind of resignation; he had been in the wars right enough, and Paulette must have marked him for life.

Only when she had finished, and was emptying the basin, he looked around him and said, "I just cannot believe that Henny is gone."

"You loved her very much, didn't you?"

"She made me remember how much one can love." And he closed his eyes, as if hearing again that thin cry, the rare cooing sounds, and the echo of a silly song:

> There was a wee bit mousikie
> That lived in Gilberaty-O. . . .

He had sung that to Amy. He had sung that to Donald. He had sung that to Henny. They were all gone from him. One was dead, and the others, for all he could hope ever to see them again, might as well be termed so.

He opened his eyes. He probed gingerly at his sore and smarting face. He could still see those damned needles aimed at his eyes. He saw that Grizel was back in her seat by the window, and had picked up her sewing again.

She said, "Don't touch your face. It's a terrible mess. It looks as if a cat—" She broke off, then said, "The sisters found this work for me. They have been very good, especially as I am not of their religion. It don't bring in much money, but at least it's something. I believe I would have starved without it." She gave him her ironic smile. "You do not ask what I am doing. I am making shifts for fine ladies. Is it not pretty material? It will not keep them very warm, but then fine ladies perhaps need no warming. I do not mind. It gives me something to do, and I was never one to sit with idle hands."

He looked at her very carefully, but without speaking. It seemed to him then that Grizel, sewing away in a light that must be very bad for her eyes, represented the only hope and sanity that he had seen for the past three years. Jean had told him that he had sacrificed his life for a dream and a dram. Grizel would have little time for dreams, or drams either; whatever she held within her was real, not fantasy. A tall girl, painfully thin, her face white and shadowed by grief, there was a truth in her that Aeneas would never know, nor Davy, nor poor, sottish Tully, nor perhaps himself. The vain hopes, the illusions with which he had barricaded himself from loneliness, fell away from him as if they had never been; he saw her as home and security, longed to hold her, gather her in to himself.

He came over slowly to her side, then knelt beside her. His face was still damp with water. As she laid her sewing down with hands that suddenly shook, and turned her head toward him, he said as he had said at their first meeting, "My poor lass. My poor dear lass."

And his two hands reached out for hers, so that they lay clasped in her lap.

They both were silent, staring ahead, seeing dimly a receding dream of lochs and hills and glens and braes, while the cruisie flame flickered and the dark lay about them.

Grizel said with a deep sigh, "We are a long way from home."

She turned her gaze on Coll. They stared at each other with intent, unsmiling faces, and remained motionless, enclasped, in silence.